TATTOOED ANGELS TRILOGY

DEATH

Tattooed Angels Trilogy

DEATH

Valerie Willis

4 Horsemen
Publications, Inc.

4 Horsemen Publications, Inc.
1497 Main St. Suite 169
Dunedin, FL 34698
4horsemenpublications.com
info@4horsemenpublications.com

Cover by Valerie Willis
Typesetting by Autumn Skye
Edited by Heather Teele

Library of Congress Control Number: 2022948710

Paperback ISBN-13: 978-1-64450-074-3
Hardcover ISBN-13: 978-1-64450-588-5
Audiobook ISBN-13: 978-1-64450-587-8
Ebook ISBN-13: 978-1-64450-073-6

DEDICATION

I want to thank all my friends and family who encouraged me to finish this story and the books following close behind! (And that goes out to my Ruths, Chris, Diana, and my Shadow Legion Gang too!)

More importantly, a special thank you to my loving husband Justin for putting up with those nights I refused to come to bed.

Thank you to Shannon for being my constant cheerleader and fellow artist at heart, plus reading right behind me as I finished edits! God Bless you for that!

To all of you out there still making your path, never give up.

ACKNOWLEDGMENTS

Thank you to my amazing support team both local and afar! From Alpha and Beta readers, to my small collection of volunteer editors to the Writer's Atelier gang and Racquel Henry to Writers of Central Florida and Thereabouts.

I cannot forget family and friends who cheered me on!

You are all so amazing!

A special thanks to Joel, Kim, Karen, Ryan, Trudy, Carlee, Troy, Richard, Margaret, and the many other eyes who help in my efforts to edit and polish this piece!

TABLE OF CONTENTS

TRIGGER WARNING

This story contains themes of genocide, suicide, verbal and physical abuse, bullying, violence, and murder, which may cause a reader distress. Read with caution, and please understand this is a fictionalized world but some of the events are very realistic in nature. This is a trilogy about overcoming the tribulations of the past, present, and future as you uncover who you are and who you wish to be. This particular book features some very scary, real historical disasters, fictionally retold to capture the despair and fear that may have transpired.

I

BLACK HONEY

Present Day

Bursting into a full run, Talib left the car far behind. Stepping up and over car after car was proving too slow. Sprinting to the right, he took an inhuman leap to the top of the nearest building; centuries of physical conditioning and the advantage of immortality allowed him to do the impossible. He ran with urgency toward the power source, leaping effortlessly from roof to roof, drawing closer with amazing speed.

Landing onto the apartment building, he skidded to a stop, spraying pea gravel across the rooftop. Panting, he caught his breath, quelling the stinging in his lungs. He looked toward the back of a black trench coat flapping in the wind. The man with black hair stood unflinching at Talib's arrival. His chest ached from the frightening sensation urging him to flee.

The element of Death, Talib's thoughts whispered, goosebumps forming across his skin.

His mind flashed a lifetime's worth of glimpses reflecting those same broad shoulders. He had seen this man before on more than one occasion. The full scale of those memories and where they came from were beyond Talib, far out of his reach. A nostalgic chaos of emotions inside his soul told him he had found the source of his brother's sins, but it was a threat he had lost memory of somewhere during his lifetime. This was the man in black which plagued the deepest reaches of his own mind and the nightmares the current Hotan suffered.

"Stop!" The determination in Talib's voice was startling even to him; standing tall, he was prepared to do anything necessary to stop the element of Death. "He is not who you think he is!"

"Who are you?" Standing motionless, the deep, calm voice mused, "No one has ever found me, let alone been brave enough to speak to me in that tone."

"I am Talib. I was the brother of Hotan." As his lips hit the last word, there was a change in the man's power. *Did his power falter, flinch even?*

"Brother of Hotan?" The man shifted to peer over his shoulder, revealing the dark pools of black which glowered back at Talib. "My, my, you definitely must be. No one carries the genetic coding for silver hair in today's time. I guess I can call you uncle."

"Uncle?" It all made perfect sense; the puzzle pieces were falling together. *I have been so blind. He is my brother's son. He wanted Liora back, but instead, he got this.* "I am so sorry. My brother, your father, is gone. I cannot undo what crimes have been committed to you, but please understand, this boy is not who you think he is. The person within this building is someone who looks like him and holds his powers, but Hotan's soul is gone. The boy knows nothing of my brother's wrong doings. If you wish, we could finish that business here between the two of us."

"Then a look-alike will suffice." Sneering, he turned around to face him, his wild smile sending chills across Talib's entire being. "And will you attempt to stop me?"

"Yes." His body tensed. Talib would have to use the small revolver tucked in his back holster where the handle of the gun urged for him to shoot. "You have no right to take innocent lives. So many were killed by your hand and had nothing to do with your endeavors to kill my brother. It must end; I will not allow this slaughter to continue further."

"Sorry, I guess I have a nasty habit of losing my temper." A step forward was followed by a nonchalant shrug. "Do you even realize who or what you are facing, Uncle?"

"I do not care what or who you are." He pulled the gun as black flames leapt off the man's skin in response, crawling outward like snakes. "I will stop you here. I am his protector, and I owe that child my life for what my brother has done to him."

"So be it, Uncle. Know that Iapetos, harbinger of Death itself, was the one who ended your life. Reborn from the cold womb of the dead and rejected by his own father." The black irises became glassy as he continued his growling speech. Another step closer sent Talib's heart racing. "I won't be satisfied until I have sucked the life from the soul that once was my father's. I will devour it; it will be mine."

"It pains me to know such evil was created by my own flesh and blood." As his fear mounted, he took an involuntary step backward. The man's power resonated through him like bony fingers of ice scratching at his soul. An eerie calm washed over him.

BANG! He squeezed the trigger.

The kickback from the revolver shook his arm and left his ears ringing, but his aim was impeccable. Gunpowder stung at his nostrils as he sighed. He landed the shot front and center—a single hole in Iapetos's forehead. His head fell back, still wearing the maddening grin. Laughter erupted from Iapetos, stirring from his chest and spilling from his mouth in an uproar. Tilting his head forward, Iapetos stared him in the eyes again. Opening his mouth, he let the lead roll off his tongue and bounce between his feet.

Talib responded by emptying the revolver into the demon before him. There were no more chances for negotiations or patience to entertain mind games. He hit the heart and neck, anywhere deemed vital to assure a kill shot, praying it would do damage or at least slow him down. The laughter grew hysterical as Talib realized the small black holes lacked any signs of blood.

How does one kill Death itself? Talib's gut tightened.

His resolution to stop Iapetos stood firm. Talib threw the empty gun to the ground in frustration. Fearlessly, he ran toward his opponent. Pulling a hidden dagger from his shirt sleeve, he plunged the silver blade deep into the neck of the soul-eating beast. It was then that he felt something demonic in nature. He had only entertained the harbinger of Death. Before he could withdraw from his dire mistake, a firm hand grasped Talib's neck. Coldness like nothing he had ever felt, snaked its way into his body and soul. His power had no sway here, and he felt his life seeping into Iapetos's fingers.

I have failed again.

Talib could do nothing. The sensation of being flung away from his killer like a wet rag rattled his body. As he hit the ground, the last thing he saw was the rooftop door opening, giving way to Hotan's shocked face. His eyes rolled back, the darkness of death pulling him away from the present, muffling the shouts and numbing the grip of those rushing to his body.

Hotan, run away...

2

NOWHERE KIDS

"Talib!" Hotan made it out of the door first, scrambling onto the rooftop in time to see a pale Talib crash and slide across the gravel toward him. "No! Talib!"

Flipping him over to see ashen skin and hazed eyes, he knew he was dead. Hotan screamed, crazed with sorrow as he pounded Talib's chest. Shaking in choking sobs, he knelt beside him, ignoring the cold and decayed aura approaching him. Laughter rolled from the shadow figure—the same laugh he had heard time and time again in his nightmares—and Hotan hated it. He was tired of it. His thoughts were bitter and angry. *It needs to go away, forever.*

"Hotan! I shall take my revenge." The animosity in the voice gripped his soul, but it wasn't like in his dreams. This time he was stronger. "I want to thank you for my tortured life for all these centuries! Let me send you to a lonely darkness equal to the one you gave me!"

"I hate you!" Looking up, Hotan saw the face so clear for the first time, and his soul crumbled. *It can't be him; this has to be a nightmare. The dark hair, the dark eyes. Why him of all the people in the world? Why does the shadow figure have to be HIM!* "You, why you? Why now!"

"I have searched the world over for you!" The man in black lifted Hotan by the throat, choking off the air from his lungs and breaking his mother's necklace from his neck. Hotan fought as the script he knew too well played out before him. He glared into the face he had spent his entire life loathing, but his voice wouldn't come. "This was the first time you've stayed long enough to see me in quite some time."

"It can't be. Not you." Hotan struggled for air; he could feel his soul being sucked out of him from the touch of Iapetos's hand to his skin. "Why does it have to be you?"

"Huh?" The sunlight was drawn away by the black flames whipping off Iapetos as he picked up the small object that had broken under his grip. "Where did you get this?" Paling, Iapetos's fingers flung open, and he released Hotan.

Landing hard, coughing and gasping, Hotan looked up at him, bewildered. "You should know that already. You remember where—"

"Answer me!" The kick to the ribs sent him rolling over Talib's cold body. "How dare you come near her!"

"She was my mother! You left us behind!" Hotan's cracked rib sent pain searing with each breath as he tried to maintain eye contact with his father. He was identical to the photos taken so long ago. "You left her, pregnant and helpless!"

"Your, your mother?" Fear washed over Iapetos's eyes as the flames faded, and he stood, shocked. Feelings long forgotten made themselves known in his eyes. "But, but *you* are my father. Hotan, you brought me into the world only to cast me out. Ashamed of me! Cold and lonely! Only death kept me company on my first days on this Earth! You are the one I have been tracking over these tormented years."

"I'm not *that* Hotan." Rolling onto his feet, Hotan spit blood between them. His breathing wheezed and whined as pain shot through him. "I am your son. I am the child you thought was impossible. The son you damned to misery, cursed to be alone."

"Why would he do something so cruel? He left me behind … again." Iapetos stabbed his Katana deep into the rooftop, roaring like an animal. All the searching was in vain, and the reality that he was no better than his own father crashed down over him.

"Tell me your name!" Hotan demanded as he healed himself, building up the courage and focus needed to take down his own father—a face he had seen and never given a name, even after asking his mother about him. "I WANT YOUR NAME, YOU BASTARD!"

"Iapetos." The dark eyes stared into him as if the Devil himself had caught sight of his soul. Iapetos huffed, his rage devouring his despair, bringing him back to the objective he was there to complete. "Rightfully one of the Titan Gods. Is that not what we are?"

"We are not gods. We are the cursed ones." Hotan allowed his power to let loose; it boiled out of him as it overfilled him. This was his chance to own the power he'd been given by his grandfather, his incarnate, his birthright. "You have brought enough destruction and agony on this Earth. I have waited a long time to meet you, and now that I know who you are, I'm not afraid."

"Not afraid?" Laughing, Iapetos stretched his arms out, revealing large, decaying wings with sparse clumps of black feathers clinging to what remained. "Oh! You should be afraid! You may be flesh and blood, but I will take that soul. It still smells like him. I can taste it in the air. His soul will be mine! I will not give up so easily!"

"My God…" Saphellia had appeared from thin air. She stood, shaking, before sliding to her knees. Fear overcame her. The image of the Dark Angel reflected in her eyes. "May God have mercy on us."

"I couldn't care less what affairs you had with Hotan. You are dealing with me, your son, not your father."

This is the crime, the sin, and the fear that the old Hotan had hidden from us all. Talib is dead. People have been hurt and killed over the centuries because he hid—no, ran—from his own son whom he brought back to life. It wasn't what he wanted. He wanted to bring Liora back, and all he got was something cold and dead, something that wanted to be with him but was cast aside. Iapetos had cast me aside with the same fear and resentment. He will pay for the innocent lives he has carelessly destroyed while chasing a coward, a broken man. I will show him the man I have become… that he failed to be.

The heated stares between Hotan and Iapetos radiated through all who stood to bear witness. Talib's body lay limp in Saphellia's arms behind Hotan. For the first time, he faced the man who haunted his dreams—his own father. The black eyes glowered at him. Clenching his jaw, Hotan took in one last deep breath before he launched himself into a full stride. They ran for one another, black and blue flames collided forcefully in an explosion of bright light. The two fighters were no longer visible behind the flash.

Hotan failed to realize his father was far stronger than him and stumbled backward; he lacked the muscle and weight to hold up against a larger opponent. His tripped over his own feet and slammed his shoulder onto the rooftop. Hotan froze as years of tortured nightmares locked his mind and bound his muscles. He couldn't move, no matter how desperately he tried. Fear had won.

No, not this! Not like in the dream! I can change this!

Iapetos was quick to leap toward him. Sunlight flashed off the Katana, and Hotan raised his arms. *This is the end.* The air burned, forcing Hotan's eye to open. An explosion of flames bounced off the sword and sent Iapetos sliding back. He now stood in a defensive position, glaring over Hotan. Looking over his shoulder, he saw Kyle. Another ball of fire left his hands, pushing Iapetos further back. It was grotesque seeing the seared flesh it left behind, but the gap between him and Hotan kept the nightmare at bay.

Hotan scrambled to his feet to watch Iapetos's flesh return to normal, a sickening, crawling of the flesh snaking back into place. Again, he ran at Iapetos with renewed confidence. He dodged his father's first swing and aimed to knock him off his feet with a low, swift kick. He misjudged Iapetos's speed, and a hand caught his leg, jerking him closer. In his hand, a ball of black flames raced down on him. Instinctual in motion, Hotan met it with his own blue fireball. Another blinding spark loosened Iapetos's grip, and Hotan back-stepped to Kyle's side, both panting from their failed attempts to do him any damage.

Gunshots rang out.

Jacob unloaded his Desert Eagle into Iapetos's head and chest. Laughter rolled out of him once more; bullets did nothing. It was clear nothing could slow Iapetos as he charged toward Hotan. Kyle pushed out one last fireball before his legs buckled; he was at his limit from using his element. The flames stopped Iapetos's approach. Concentrating, Hotan gripped a handful of pea gravel. *I have to do something, and I need a weapon.* A burst of blue flames erupted and faded into an elegant sword.

Gathering his nerves again with all his friends at his back, Hotan pushed forward yet again. Screaming from frustrated rage, he swung with all his might. Iapetos reached up to catch the blade, but it sliced through his fingers and lodged itself halfway through his skull. Wide-eyed, Hotan stared at the eye it had cleaved in half. He tugged the blade but couldn't dislodge it from his father's skull. In horror, he watched him grip the blade with his other hand, and it fell away to ashes in an instant. The way it crumbled away mimicked his own power. Hotan felt sick.

Stumbling backward, his heel locked on something, and Hotan landed next to Talib's lifeless body. His chest swelled. Soon, he would join the old man who had given up so much. His nightmare played out once more, the taunting unbearable dream working through the motions for a second time in this fight. Even with this power, he was falling back in line with the dream foretelling his death. Black flames restored the missing fingers before scurrying outward from Iapetos's palm and fading to reveal a Katana.

Each step closer was breaking Hotan's mind further. *This is it. This is the part where I die.*

Every crunch of gravel gripped Hotan's soul ever tighter, suffocating all hope.

<*Hotan! I am still here…*> Talib's voice pulled him from his drowning panic.

"No!" Annie slammed her hands against the rooftop, and a massive wall of earth rose in their defense.

Seizing the opportunity, Hotan crawled over to Talib's body. Summoning a fireball into his palm, tears streaking his face, he let his instincts take over. With all the weight of his desperation, he slammed the blue orb into Talib. There was no way of knowing if he was doing the right thing. *Talib is here, I heard him, and I need him more than ever.* He needed the power that only Rebirth could perform to bring him back from death's edge.

"Please, let this work. I need you!" The exertion of power drained the last of Hotan's energy.

A gasp escaped Talib and his body arched from the surge of power thrust through him. Rebirth had given him his life back.

3

IN BETWEEN

A warmth exploded from Talib's chest and shot down his limbs. Looking down, he saw the tentacles of power from the element of Rebirth wrapping themselves around him within his subconscious. He looked up at his brother to see him smiling. He waved, and with it a harsh tug, sent Talib soaring backward. Gasping, the sunlight blinded him. Hotan looked down at him wide-eyed as tears fell. Blood painted one side of Hotan's face where he had fallen or taken a hit. Talib had returned as the battle still raged on.

Elation took hold, and Talib scrambled back to his feet, relieved he wasn't too late. *Not yet!* Much to his surprise, a wall of earth had risen to shield them from Iapetos. He looked to Jacob's tearful, purple eyes as he held a ghostly Annie in his arms. She had only been in control of the powers for a few hours but already showed more control than Cassie ever had. Kyle was unable to stand and had exerted too much power as well. They had all come to his aid, working together to support Hotan in this battle.

Now it is my turn. I know what is wrong, what is missing, and what needs to be given back.

The wall crumbled, and Talib gritted his teeth. Swallowing his doubts, it was time to trust in his recovered memories and experience. His brother had broken the shackles forced onto him so long ago. *I am the true embodiment of Judgment.* Looking over his shoulder, everyone Talib cared about watched the wall fall away with mind-numbing fear. Anger poured out of him at a radical speed.

Their glares broke away from the falling wall to the red glow surrounding Talib; they forgot the fear they felt. There was a sense that he would shield them all with the power he held. Unlike them, he had walked every day on Earth as himself—nothing more or less. *With these wings, I will shield them from the monster my brother created.*

"W-wings…" gasped Saphellia.

As he heard the word, the wings flared wide as if to confirm their existence to her. Red and orange feathers covered the massive appendages like fire. They were large, much more massive than Iapetos's or even the cerulean blue ones his brother brandished. A smile crawled across his face as the gap between the Angel of Death and himself closed. The wall crumbled away, and Iapetos glared at him from the other side. His cold, emotionless stare was nothing like the past versions he recalled. The centuries had destroyed him, but Talib knew this wasn't who Iapetos was—or wanted to be—deep down in his soul. Memories stung at him of the kind-hearted, tortured immortal who had been abandoned. *He deserves a second chance. He deserves the shackles to be removed and memories returned.*

"You," snarled Iapetos. "You're the one I remember flying away, leaving me for dead on Mt. Pelée all those years ago."

Talib sighed. "That is not how it happened. I was forced to leave, and I would have taken you with me if given a choice in the matter."

"I was crippled on the ground!" he roared, raising out his arms. "What sort of threat was I?"

Closing his eyes, he responded, "We were not alone. Your father is to blame for how it all happened. He is also to blame for us not remembering one another."

Iapetos flinched at the idea. Talib's words struck something deep within him and made his rage falter. He felt the emptiness from lost memories, the nostalgia with no name or place. His eyes were searching for the same gaps Talib had recovered. Seizing the opportunity, Talib took to his wings and launched himself at Iapetos. Iapetos leapt back, and Talib's hand missed his throat but gripped his wrist.

"You missed," scoffed Iapetos as he struggled to jerk his wrist free.

"No … I did not." Talib's eyes glowed red, emanating the fiery steam of his power. "Let me remind you of everything my brother has wrongfully taken from you…"

Iapetos fell to his knees as a burning surge filled his entire body. Screaming, he grabbed the side of his head. His eyes rolled back, and he fell to the ground, dangling from where Talib still gripped him. Talib released him and stood over him, waiting to see if any immediate whiplash would strike. The palm of his hand tingled from where he had gripped Iapetos. Looking down, he saw the tiny blue flame absorb back into his hand. His brother had done his part. Now, they had to wait.

You owe it to your son to give back what you stole from him, Brother. What you even stole from this boy who carries your name, your face, and his own power.

"T-Talib!" Hotan came running up behind him, his eyes still fixated on the elegant, long feathers which comprised Talib's wings. "What happened? Did… did I do something to you?"

Laughter erupted from him, and he patted Hotan on the head. "All you did was save me from death."

"Do we all get wings?" Jacob's voice cut in with Annie fast asleep in his arms. "How come you never told me you had wings, old man?"

"I was not aware." Talib looked to his palm where the blue flame had been. "It happens when we resonate with our element. I guess Judgment is a perfect fit for me."

"Is, is he dead?" Hotan stared down at the lifeless face of the father who had haunted his dreams. "What did you do to him?"

"Ah, technically he died." Talib calmed his nerves, and his wings burst into a swirl of power and faded away. "However, since he is the element of Death, he will eventually wake up. When that happens, he will remember the things my brother took from him."

"So, is it true that my dad is Hotan's son?" Hotan's voice was a whisper, as if he wanted to keep it between them. "That somehow he could conceive a child because of something the old Hotan did?"

"Yes…" He gripped Hotan's shoulder, catching his attention. "Do not judge him so swiftly. The mistakes he made were based on confusion from missing memories."

"Missing memories?" Saphellia knelt next to Iapetos, looking him over with great interest. "Good lord, there's no mistaking his relation to you both."

"As my life flashed before me, I discovered that I did not know what was happening before." Swallowing, he willed himself to continue. "Over thousands of years, Hotan used me to erase my own memories and Iapetos's as well. Disasters in Antioch, Hama, London during the plague, and many more resulted from his clashing with the element of *Death* and the turmoil of an unbalanced *Rebirth*. On Mt. Pelée, me, my brother, and Iapetos met, and it was there that Hotan essentially destroyed himself to create a seed for reincarnation, which he left within Iapetos."

"Y-you can't be talking about the 1902 volcano eruption…" Hisota found his voice, breaking himself from his stunned state. "If those two drawing close together caused natural disasters, then that means in 1902…"

Talib locked eyes with Hisota, and everyone shuddered. "Correct. The eruption was their fault, and innocent lives were lost. Natural disasters were a cover for what was happening on more than one occasion."

"It took Iapetos nearly a hundred years…" Hotan's brow folded as he let the information settle. "Then he fell in love with my mother, didn't he?"

"Knowing who he was before his rage and sorrow destroyed him, I can believe that." Iapetos began to show signs of shallow breathing. "Let's get him back to my place. I would like to be there when he wakes to gauge whether he intends to continue his aggression or wants to start his life over."

Gritting his teeth, Hotan walked away as anger stirred within him. "I don't know how I feel about any of this."

Abigail stood by the stairway door. "Hotan…" She reached out to him.

He ignored her, brushing past and leaving out of sight. She followed, but Talib stopped her. "Abigail."

Flinching, she looked to him with tears streaming down her face. "Y-yes."

"You and I need to have a long talk." He locked eyes with her, and she knew he remembered. He remembered how often she had interfered and lured. The old Talib was back. "Out of everyone here, you were the only one who has never been wiped of her memories. You remained by my brother's side without fail through it all."

The heated glares stung at her. She felt as though everyone detested her.

Shaking her head, tears falling, she pleaded, "You don't understand! After Roanoke, when he wiped your memories with no need to do it, I left!"

Turning, she ran down the stairs, and Talib's eyes widened. He reached back through his memories. The last time he recalled her at his side was in 1587. At that point, his actions had gone too far for her to watch his destruction continue.

"Your brother was a monster," breathed Jacob.

"Agreed," he huffed.

"Is she going to be okay?" Saphellia broke the morbid conversation, bringing everyone's focus back to what needed to be addressed first. "Annie gave Hotan just enough time to save Talib, but it may have been too soon."

"She's fine." Sighing, Jacob kissed the top of her head. "It wore her out, but she'll pull out of this. I think she's a much better fit for the element of Earth. Never thought I would see someone so new to this have that much control and power at a time like this."

Smiling, Talib sighed. "I'm relieved to see he is far wiser in his choices than my brother ever was."

"No kidding." Jacob looked down to Iapetos. "But still … this whole situation is twisted; I'm not sure he'll be able to keep it together."

"I am hoping the Iapetos I recall from my past returns when he wakes." Squatting down, Talib checked his pulse. Iapetos was cold and clammy, his heartbeat slow. "It seems he will be down far longer than I was."

"Maybe it'll give us time to sort ourselves out." Saphellia stood up. "Where did you leave the car?"

Talib's face reddened. "In the middle of traffic."

Jacob groaned. "You've got to be kidding me."

"Kyle…" Talib's voice broke Kyle from his shock where he still sat on the rooftop, exhausted. "Are you well enough to move?"

"I, I think so." He wobbled to his feet. "I'm fine. I'll see about following Hotan. You guys have a bigger problem to figure out."

Grabbing Iapetos's arm, Talib slung it over his shoulder and lifted him off the rooftop. Hisota took his other arm. An exhausted silence resonated among them as they brought him down the stairs. Jacob carried Annie close behind them while Saphellia rushed ahead to find the car. They made it to Annie's apartment and laid Iapetos's limp body on the couch. After placing Annie on her bed, Jacob walked out and closed the door behind him.

"What should I be doing?" Hisota rubbed the back of his neck, still fighting the shock of what happened. "This is all so much, so fast, I feel useless…"

Jacob gave him a few hearty pats on the back. "Be yourself."

Hisota's face turned red, and he glared back at him. "You sound like my school counselor."

Laughing, Jacob gave him a more accurate answer. "Right now, you need to be Hotan's friend, no different from before. Don't let yourself feel useless because you didn't use those new-found powers. I didn't use mine because they wouldn't have done much in this case."

Hisota's brow knotted, and he looked at his own hands. "It was frightening, feeling everyone's fear while I was up there. It was overwhelming to have it hit me."

Talib interjected, "I am glad to see you take in that sensation with caution. Your predecessor would have become intoxicated from a wave like that." Hisota grabbed his stomach, the idea of it making him ill. "My thoughts exactly. Regardless, there will come a time when your powers are needed. I do not think altering anyone's sense of fear any more or less today would have done any good."

"Agreed," snorted Jacob before gesturing at Iapetos. "But I can't help but ask if he felt any fear."

"He did…" Hisota's eyes fell to the sleeping body on the couch. "In fact, he's afraid right now. When he realized Hotan was his son, it was the highest sensation of fear during the fight. But now, now he's even more afraid of that."

"That's because my brother is undoing the chains he put into place." Rubbing the side of his jaw, Talib looked down on Iapetos with pity. "Out of all of us, he has suffered the greatest from the mistakes put into motion."

"Wait, your brother is undoing the chains?" Nerves were tightening, and Jacob rubbed his shoulder out of habit. "I thought he died, Tal?"

"Not in the traditional manner that we thought he did," he replied. "The last piece of him is trying to make things right. I pray he can make amends with Iapetos in this limited time he has left."

A car horn blared outside. Nodding to one another, he and Jacob grabbed Iapetos and dragged him to the car where Saphellia waited. Closing the back passenger door, he and Jacob gave one another a hug and hard pat on the back. They knew the tasks ahead of them. He was to see over Iapetos, and Jacob had Annie to care for in the meantime. As for Hotan, they left it to Abigail, Kyle, and Hisota to console him.

<What are you doing inside his head, Brother?> Staring out the window of the car, Talib looked at his reflection, knowing his brother could hear him. *<How are you going about this?>*

<First, I will give back what I have stolen.> The old Hotan's voice in his head was so clear that it made him shudder. *<Then it's his decision whether I will allow him to wake from this.>*

His stomach twisted. <*Now, it is Death's turn to decide what he truly wants his life to be about. It is not your choice. You will allow him to wake, and he will face me.*>

There was silence, but a whisper relented, <*You are right. I will give it all back and leave this world. I will leave my son in your hands, Brother.*>

<*As it should be, alef chet. As it should be.*>

4

HERE'S TO THE HEARTACHE

Hotan slammed into his apartment, blood dripping off his chin. He was drowning in emotions from what had unfolded in a short span. Images of Talib's lifeless body sent his shoulders shuddering. The nightmare that had haunted his dreams for so long had revealed itself; the face he could never see clearly belonged to his father. If the shock from looking into the real-life version of the photos that plagued him weren't enough, the notion that the old Hotan was his grandfather added insult to injury. *This entire mess riding on my shoulders was all created by one man who was too proud to ask for help and too scared to admit he couldn't do it alone. Annie and Hisota are official immortals, and watching them use the powers I bestowed on them in a fight immediately after is heart wrenching. I never intended for them to have to think about using the power to defend themselves or those they care about.*

As he marched into the bathroom, every muscle ached with the tension of regret and anger building at his core. Turning on the water, he leaned on the sink, glaring at himself in the mirror. He felt disdain toward the man who looked identical to himself and had started so much pain for so many people. The crimson streak running down the side of his face was startling in his eyes. *So much blood was spilled before I was born. Even now, I've lost Shellie, condemned two immortals, and cursed two friends. How far will this madness spiral before everything I care about is lost?* Grimacing, he splashed his face, and swirls of blood mixed with the water and disappeared down the drain.

"Hotan?" Abigail's voice was meek and still shaking. "Are you… are you okay?"

Another splash of water relieved him of the last of his sweat and blood. As he glared at his reflection, Abigail's worried face slid into view from the doorway. The life he had worked so hard to make for himself was shattered. Worst of all, the man who he had spent his life blaming for the follies and obstacles he encountered had shown himself, leaving a mangled nest filled with despair, fear, anger, pity, and even a flash of hope. *Can I blame Iapetos, my father, for the sins committed by my own incarnate?* The faucet squeaked off, and water tapped from his face onto the counter. The sound of it *tick-tocked* in his ears like a countdown to something far more dangerous imploding inside him. Abigail's lips were moving, but his mind and heart had swallowed his soul, and he couldn't hear her.

Heated fingertips gripped his shoulder, "Hotan?"

Closing his eyes, he sighed. *Where do I even start?*

"I'm sorry…" Abigail whispered, her eyes falling to the floor. "I wish I could have stopped things sooner with the old Hotan… stopped it all before it became this broken, but all I could ever do is just watch. I didn't realize how far he would go, how long the wakes of this would reach long after he destroyed himself in 1902."

"How could anyone have known?" he asked, huffing and closing his eyes tight. "No one could have known how twisted this would become. The hard part is deciding how I want to feel about it all."

Abigail bit her bottom lip, and a tear trailed down her cheek. He brushed past her and opened his mother's photo album on the table. The pages fell open to the photo of Iapetos and his smiling mother. His emotions gripped his heart tightly. *He hasn't aged at all since the days he spent with her. He was out there this whole time and never once looked back to what he left behind.* Swallowing, he turned back to Abigail who covered her mouth with trembling fingers. Tears raced down her face, and her eyes filled with guilt. Twisting around, Hotan threw his arms around her. Burying his face in her shoulder, he ignored her hair sticking to his wet face.

She started to speak again. "I did—"

Hotan squeezed tighter, silencing her.

"I don't want to end up like they did," he said. His trembling voice sent chills across her. "I won't lose myself to revenge and grief. This stops with me."

"If I had—" Another squeeze of his arms cut her short again.

"Listen, Abigail…" He felt her heartbeat racing from where his ear pressed against her neck. "If I have anything in common with the old version of myself, I already know there was nothing you could have done. He would have tossed you aside if you had. Unlike him though, I crave companionship. I've been a loner from the start, and I am tired of it. I don't intend to be alone like that ever again."

Pulling away, he thumbed a tear off her cheek, and she cupped his hand. "What should I do?"

"Let's go for a ride. I need to clear my head, and hanging around here won't help. I'm tired of hiding. It's been a long fall from grace, and Shellie wouldn't want me to stay here." Grabbing his helmet, a flash of Shellie's face came across his thoughts. "I loved her, you of all people know that, and she loved me, but this is not how she would want me to continue my life."

"I didn't realize Geliah would take matters that far…" She swallowed, hesitant to take a step closer. "It hurts to know one of us could throw a life away like that with no guilt. We may not share in their mortality, but it's such a precious and fleeting quality we miss in our own never-ending lifespans."

"I have to make this new, endless life bearable, worth lasting for eternity. Hotan and Iapetos squandered it. Talib forsook himself for it. This has to change, and somehow, I will bring closure to this." There was a flash of determination behind his green eyes.

He handed the helmet to Abigail, grabbing her wrist and dragging her close behind. Opening the door, he halted, and she slammed into him. Hisota stood, hand raised to knock and eyes wide. Hisota's eyes fell to Abigail's arm hugging the helmet. Smiling, he looked at Hotan with a knowing expression. He could relate to the need to go for a ride, find a safe place, and let his thoughts flow. Hotan tensed, not sure what Hisota would do. Furrowing his brow, he looked at Hisota puzzled.

"Need to go clear your head, right?" Hisota sighed, making the gesture he was free to go. "I'm glad you're not going alone, so just this once, I won't put up a fight."

"Thanks." He tugged Abigail, and they headed down the hallway.

"Just don't get into any trouble!" Hisota shouted, making him pause. "Remember, you dragged me into this bullshit! We'll talk about this later!"

Hotan chuckled and gave a nod. Racing down the stairs, they found themselves on the last stretch of the hall before reaching the exit. The entrance doors opened, and light flooded in as Jacob walked inside. His voice bounced off the walls as he spoke on his cell phone, rubbing his forehead. Hotan hesitated, unsure if he intended to stop them from escaping after what had unfolded on the rooftop. Tension still lingered in the air; every person was still tight-muscled. They had escaped Death himself by a sheer miracle.

"Yeah, I think I might have been the target." Jacob's face scowled at his own words. "Not sure, I was with my girlfriend, Frank. Yeah, yeah, okay, I'll wait for the investigators before I go anywhere. Yes, I am very aware of protocol. I don't need to be reminded that I could lose my job over this, Frank." Jacob's hand lifted, acknowledging them and signaling to stay quiet. "Right, that's the address. I'll be here. Go ahead and send an ambulance or at least a paramedic."

He hung up the phone, and Hotan sighed. "I didn't mean to put your job on the line."

"No worries, it wasn't your fault this happened, Hotan. Talib will help me fix this mess later; it's one of the perks of having the element of Judgment as a best friend." Sliding the cell phone in his pocket, he gave them a half-hearted smile. "Talib took Iapetos with him. I just sent Kyle to the hospital in a taxi. He'll pull through, but he might be down for a while. Not sure what's happening, but your former doppelgänger took the screws to everyone, even his own son."

"That's putting it lightly." Rubbing the back of his neck, Hotan asked his first concern, "Will Iapetos attack again?"

"I don't know." Rubbing his jaw, Jacob's eye caught the helmet in Abigail's arm. "But I think you leaving the premises will make things less complicated. Get going; they'll be here soon."

"Thanks." With no delay, they pushed through the doors and left Jacob to his own obstacles.

"Hotan." He had straddled his motorcycle, but Abigail stood, holding the helmet with a helpless expression on her face. "I don't know how to put this on ... and I've never done this before."

Slumping, he had forgotten Abigail had disconnected herself from the world. Pulling himself back off the bike, he walked up to her and took the helmet. He placed it on her head and set to work snapping the straps and tightening them to fit. Again, he tugged her close behind and straddled the bike. Twisting around, he patted the back padded area, encouraging her to follow him. He kicked out the passenger foot pegs, and with caution, she saddled into place. He grabbed her hands and put them around his abdomen, noting how they trembled.

"Hold on tight." He started the engine, and the roar made her huddle tight against his back. "It's loud, but I think the ride will remind you of flying like a bird … if you've ever done that."

The helmet shifted in acknowledgement, and he smiled. Sirens screamed ever closer, so he edged onto the road and wasted no time opening the throttle, making the engine's hum bounce off the buildings as they raced past. Abigail's hands balled his shirt in fists, and her arms were stiff from the surge of speed that erupted. He leaned to the left, taking the turn, and sped up again as they straightened. She lifted her head away from his back, laughing as they rode. Another lean to the right, and they headed out of town, accelerating to new heights on the stretch of highway. Her fists softened, but her fingers still dug into him, showing her nervousness about the mechanism in which they rode at such speeds.

5

BASEMENT

900 BC Mediterranean Sea

The first memory is a black, icy, wet realm with nothing but a blue beacon of light calling me. I had no name, but it spoke to me from where I slept in the ocean's bottom. Cold. That's the only sensation I knew. The blue light beckoned me, urged me to move. It was this point when I discovered I had legs and arms. Excitement filled me, and I moved frantically, eager to see who called me away from my lonely prison. It was so dark. I tasted the salt in the water that I took in and out of my lungs like air.

I moved like a pale phantom under the waves. The closer I came to the light, the warmer and more alive I became. The blue beacon was bright among the flashes of light which erupted above the waves. Despite the angry currents shoving me this way and that, I swam on. I didn't know exhaustion; I was everlasting, and I yearned to be something more. The storm that raged above and below the water's surface matched my turmoil of emotions. Fish and many creatures hid, frightened by my glowing form in the black abyss. It ripped debris and seaweed from their roots, and sand swirled, threatening to escape the sea and become a sandstorm.

A single thought haunted me as I pushed forward toward the siren's call.

What am I?

Hours upon hours brought light to the water above, trickling down like curtains of blue silk. The storm was gone, but I still saw the blue light through the brightness of day. For the first time, I saw daylight, sunlight, and the colors of fish and coral. I had no name for them but later came to know them as yellow, red, green, and blue. Even pink and purple sea anemones found their way back into my dreams. Some part of me misses being there in my prison of water. It was silent and peaceful—unlike the world that awaited me.

The moon did nothing to lure me away from the blue beacon. My feet and knees scraped sand, and my body was tossed forward with a wave only to be dragged back again. It took all of my being to crawl and swim toward the blue and red auras dancing in my vision. The warmth they gave me as my head broke the surface of the water was thrilling. I took in my first breath of air, choking on the last gulps of the ocean. My fingers dug into the beach, pulling me closer to the two men standing before me. The one made of blue had called to me, and warmth emanated from the man made of red. With my eyes wide, I smiled, my voice not yet found.

My lips made the motion toward the man of blue—*Father.* The aching in my chest from my beating heart baffled me. This was a newfound thumping I hadn't known. Confusion took hold as I saw fear and disgust in my father's eyes.

But you made me, you brought me to life, you beckoned for me to come to you.

The blue aura shattered, and he fell to his knees, shrieking and wailing like nothing I had ever heard. Free of the waves, I sat up as worry and fear took hold of my soul. *Something is wrong.* My stomach tightened and twisted from another new sensation: nausea. Frantically, I tried to call out, but all my throat could produce were raspy, hushed spats of air. Still aflame, the man in the red aura took pity on me. He opened his mouth but had no words for me. I tried again to plead with him to not cast me out. *The blue aura man is my father; I know this at my core, but I still don't understand what I am or what any of this means.*

"I wanted her!" Hotan of the blue aura sobbed, shouting to the sky. "Why give me this stranger… I wanted my Liora!"

"Hotan." Talib of the red aura kneeled next to Hotan, still giving me a look of pity. "Do you not see who this man is?"

This man knows me? Does he know my name?

Hotan struggled to catch his breath. My heart ached for him, and I reached out. A wave rolled past me and slid back into the ocean, taking the last of my hope with it. The dangerous look in his eyes scared me, and his next words burned like embers from a fire.

"No, I do not know this man."

"It has been over twenty-eight years since Liora drowned, pregnant with your child." Talib spoke of something, and Hotan flinched. "You have made it clear to me that you do not know the full consequences of your powers. This outcome is a result of that unpredictability."

"Are you proposing…" Hotan paused. Another angry glance at me and he hissed, "Are you proposing this man is my son?"

My posture straightened as Talib spoke what I could not. *He is my father, and I am his son.*

"Yes." Talib jerked Hotan to his feet. "And if you are the man I pray you are, you will find the compassion to welcome him here."

"I would have to tell the others…" Hotan begged, "They will know what I have done…"

"Yes, but you need to tell them." Talib's grasp tightened as markings crawled across his skin. "You must tell them. They need to hear the sins you have committed and how you intend to set it right."

Am I the sin?

"No." The cold answer slipped through Hotan's lips. "I will cast him out of paradise and make this all disappear."

<No! Please, Father!>

I opened my mouth, but again no words or sound came. Talib screamed, engulfed by flames, and I saw the blue slithers of power dig into his red aura. Father was trying to do something to him. Desperately, I tried to wobble to my feet, but my legs failed, and I fell again. Talib struggled against it, glaring at Hotan who was covered in blue flames and markings. Again, I failed to stand and splashed backward into the water.

Hotan dragged Talib toward me with a look of rage, adding to the fear we exchanged. Talib no longer controlled his own body or element. Hotan reached out and gripped my hair; my scalp was on fire as I looked into his heartless eyes. The greatest fear I had in this short existence was happening. *Father is casting me out. Talib would have accepted me. A stranger has more passion for a monster from the depths of death than my own father. He called me here, only to reject me.*

Unforgivable.

"You will leave here and never be able to return." Blue tendrils of power ripped red power from Talib, and they dug into me like a thousand needles. This was the element of Judgment. "You will not remember this place or who we are. Go, leave here now."

<I cannot forget my maker, but I can't fight the command to leave. When you leave this place, I will find you. With my

own words and power, I will condemn you for this sin. You are unworthy of the title of father.>

As if in a dream, I stood with ease. Painful and unable to resist, I turned to face the ocean as I filled with dread. Power roared through me. This was the element of Death. Wings ripped from my back, black as night against my pale, naked form. Like my mind, these appendages were broken with decaying black feathers. With ease, I took to the air as if it were natural and instinctual to do so. The air was icy, and the distance between Father and I was agonizing.

In my mind, I heard Talib whisper a promise. *<We will find each other somehow, someway.>*

I flew for days as my mind faded in and out of consciousness. I finally woke on a shoreline with the desert sun baking my flesh. A priest of the Greek gods found me and told me my name.

"Where did you come from?" He sat me up, offering me water. "How long have you been here like this?"

I tried to speak, but it failed me; I took the cool, fresh water offered.

"Your wings, they've been broken." The old fingers caressed a feather as the wings fell away to ashes. "Sorcery … by the gods. What are you?"

Everything about me was soured, and I found my voice after another gulp of water. "I am Death."

"Death?" Blinking, he refused to take his canteen from me. "Does this mean you are Titan Iapetos, the harbinger of Death?"

"Iapetos," I repeated; the word felt nice. "I suppose that's a good name for me."

He threw a cape over me. "Come, Iapetos. Your temple is a day's walk. There, we can give you proper sacrifice, clothes, even food if you wish to eat."

As I rose to my feet, I realized this man wished to use me for his own gain. Regardless, I wanted to learn more about my namesake, the Titan called Iapetos.

6

SILENCE & SCARS

"Where are we going?" Abigail yelled over the roar of wind. "I thought you were headed to the church?"

"No, Lilly's." He squinted his eyes from the painful wind as he pushed the bike to speed. "I need a place to test something…"

"Lilly?" she repeated.

Nodding, he tried to recall the way. The wind washing over him and the vibration from the motorcycle were melting away his tension. Abigail hugged him tighter, resting the helmet between his shoulder blades. A swell of anxiety erupted within him, stirring his emotions as his thoughts shifted to Abigail. His mouth ran dry as questions surfaced, and he wrestled with the precious memories of Shellie. He had relented on never loving again, but for those feelings to come back with such renewed vigor over Abigail was painful. She was the new and unknown, even to Talib and Jacob. Though they had kissed, the feelings it surged compared to when he was with Shellie were so different.

His shoulders slumped as he slowed down and leaned into the next turn. *Should it be so easy to fall for someone, even considering what has unfolded? Why do I feel guilty? Wrong even? Shellie, is there a chance you're pushing me toward Abigail? You always felt I needed to know I am loved... or is it that I want to feel loved?*

Hotan's sour thoughts were interrupted by the approaching junkyard at the end of the road. Lilly had the garage door open, and she stood outside smoking a cigarette and drinking a beer. Inside the shop, an old pickup truck from a forgotten era was laid out in pieces, waiting to be reassembled and brought back to life. The bike rolled, bumping across the pitted and worn asphalt until he brought it to a stop in front of her. She didn't flinch or react except for the lifted eyebrow over the female figure who hugged onto him. Flicking the last of her cigarette to the ground, she stomped on it and twisted her foot. A plume of smoke left her pursed lips as she waited for her guests to dismount.

"So, what brings you back here so soon?" Her hands were on her hips, and black smudges painted her face and arms.

"Need a place to test out a theory." He gave her a knowing glance as he helped Abigail off the bike. "Do you need help getting the helmet off?"

Nodding, Abigail lifted her chin to expose the clips. Lilly took a swig from the brown bottle in her hand and watched with intrigue, wondering who the girl could be. From speaking with Jacob and Talib, she was aware that Hotan had locked himself away to grieve Shellie. The helmet lifted, and black locks of hair fell. Big doe-like eyes hit Lilly, and she choked on her beer. It didn't take much imagination to recognize an older version of a child from her past.

Catching her breath, she squeaked out her suspicions, "Abby?"

She blushed at her name and looked to Hotan as if needing approval.

"I helped her grow into a more adult body." Hotan's face flushed, realizing how awkward the fact rolled out on his tongue. "Nothing more than breaking her from being stuck as a child."

"Christ, I didn't think we'd ever see you again." The beer bottle hit the ground and rolled away as Lilly rushed Abigail, wrapping her arms around her. "There hasn't been a day that I haven't wondered what happened to you!"

"I've been here the whole time, just too scared to speak for myself." She was taller than Lilly, but it didn't keep Abigail from burying her face in a familiar shoulder.

"Thank you, Hotan." Tears welled up in Lilly's eyes, and he gave a knowing smile. "I can't believe he could have fixed this so much sooner."

"It wasn't that." He sighed, hanging the helmet on a handlebar of the bike. "Honestly, I think his powers were unstable, fluctuating without warning. Deep down, I know that if he tried, he could have killed her. Seeing how things turned out, he's never handled death well…"

"It doesn't matter." Abigail pulled away, wiping tears from her face. "It's fixed, and I am coming out of hiding. I have no more reason to hide away."

"Good!" Lilly nodded. "Now, what brings you two out here?"

"I'm not sure." Abigail looked over her shoulder at Hotan.

"I need to test something." Looking down at his hand, he summoned a ball of blue flames as if it were no different than taking in a deep breath. "We left the apartment. It's a mess; everything is still a big, confused cluster. Iapetos attacked and—"

"Who? Did what now?" Lilly paled; her eyes locked on the power he summoned with ease. "Iapetos?"

Abigail sighed, glancing away in the weight of her own shame. "Iapetos is the former Hotan's son and this Hotan's father."

Lilly's eyes were wide with shock. Taking a moment to digest the information, she muttered under her breath, "What a mess…"

Hotan clenched his fist, and the flames disbursed and faded from sight. "He had some plan designed to repent for his mistakes, but he did it all alone." Glancing back to the girls, he shared the promise he made to himself. "I don't intend to do anything in secret or alone. That was his mistake; maybe we can say it was his ultimate sin. He tossed precious family to the side, both his son and brother, so whoever he was, I have no interest in following in his footsteps. Be glad I was a failed reincarnation." His words came out bitterly as he marched for the junkyard.

Lilly rubbed her forehead and let him go. Pity painted her face, but she couldn't argue with anything he said. His former incarnation left a wake of despair and destruction which had destroyed countless innocent lives. Abigail started toward the junkyard, but Lilly caught her by the wrist. Shaking her head in disapproval, she nodded toward the shop.

"Let him unwind. He's got a lot of weight on those shoulders. He'll find us when he needs us." Abigail looked longingly in his direction before following Lilly inside.

Hotan walked aimlessly through the towers of broken cars. The deeper he stumbled through the labyrinth of twisted metal and broken glass, the older the cars became. The sun was falling behind the rusted mountains, and a cooler bite blew across his sweat-soaked shirt. With a few unsteady footsteps, his thoughts weighed him down, and he sat at a five-point intersection. He didn't care if the ground was soaked with oil and transmission fluid. His eyes were fixated on his hands, staring at his palms as if they were strangers who may betray him at any moment.

Clenching his fingers and unfolding them again, he wanted to make sure it was still his body. Swallowing, he inhaled deeply, imagining his power, and flames effortlessly filled both hands. With curiosity, he placed a hand down on the dirt beside him and willed it to become a rose. Flames twisted and tightened, pulling the dirt and chunks of glass into the mix. They dissipated, leaving behind a single red rose like he had cut it from the garden himself. Squeezing the stem, he let the thorns bite into him.

"It doesn't feel right," he mumbled.

He willed it to become ash, and the very thought was enough for it to fade to nothing. The speed and lack of flames made him jerk to his feet. Nausea rocked him. Looking at the ash and blood across his right hand, a cold sweat sent shivers up his spine.

It should never be this easy to destroy something. Bringing his hand closer, he marveled over the gruesome ability. *You spent more time taking life than you ever did giving it. I am not you; no one can ever ask me to become you or take your place. I hate this burden, and I have no intention of being your replacement. It's insulting that we share the same name.*

The sky overhead was fading to a lavender hue, and crickets hiding in the debris were chirping. Slow and steady, the gentle metronome matched each breath he took in and back out. He walked to a pillar of flattened, unrecognizable vehicles and placed his palms on one of the few solid panels. He closed his eyes, focusing on the new sensation of instinctual understandings that had invaded him in the last year.

All things are connected, though souls are another matter. The fabric of everything around me is nothing more than clay waiting to be molded. If that's true… if this feeling burning through my core and shouting answers to unknown questions I have yet to ask is real, then this can become a tree.

Inhaling both breath and power, he gave the air back in a slow steady stream. Power pulled up through his legs, invaded his heart and lungs, and flowed outward to his palms before disconnecting. This was far more strenuous to push and wish for, and a pain rattled through his taut muscles. Sweat tickled at his face, dangling for a second before dripping off his chin. Clenching his jaw and squeezing his eyes shut, he demanded the metal give way and become the living flesh of a tree trunk. He took in another deep breath, and the air burned as he consumed it. It was as if he was trying to move a mountain.

"I can do this." Opening his eyes, he looked to his hands.

The air all around glowed from a flaming column of cars. He pressed his palms into the metal, and it softened under them. His lungs stung as if he had run a marathon at full speed, but he shouldered it and willed the promises that whispered in his soul to prove they were indeed real. His eyes focused on the metal which vibrated under his heated glare. Rust transitioned to bark, renewing his vigor and want. Urging another surge of power, his blood burned through him. His joints ached in rebuttal, but none of that mattered. Looking overhead, branches snaked out, covering the stars and blocking out the moon. The heat gave way to a cold sensation, and he knew it had been done.

Falling back to the ground, he stared at his achievement. Dead, forgotten cars had become a monstrous camphor tree. The smell of the blooming flowers confirmed that he had indeed made a tree to take the place of the rot. A breeze ruffled the branches, allowing stars to peek down on him. There were no signs of the blue flames, but the cold sweat across his body made him shiver. Another glance at his right hand showed no signs of blood, ash, or wounds. *This is too much power... power that willfully bends with the imagination.*

Long locks of hair tickled his forehead, and he shifted his head to catch Abigail's concerned expression. Her eyes met his, and he gave a halfhearted grin. Her hands cupped his face, and he waited for her to say something, anything. A warm sensation buzzed from her touch, unknotting his muscles and fading his exhaustion. Sighing, he pulled her hands off his cheeks, flustered by her need to care for him in that manner.

"I could have done that myself," he said, closing his eyes, not wanting to see her reaction. "I am the center to all your powers; I can do anything any of you are capable of and much worse."

She whispered softly, "I know, but…" She shook her hands free of his, grabbed his face, and forced his eyes open. "But he made nothing beautiful with it."

Hotan's forehead folded, realizing only one person knew everything about who came before him. "Never…"

Swallowing, she let go. Sitting close by, she turned her back to him, hugging her knees. "Not once. Never on the island or for himself or for his own son. Worst of all, he turned his own brother to ash to avoid being seen for what he was…"

Her voice trailed, and she sniffled. Hotan pressed for more, "What would you say he was?"

She inhaled deeply and held it for a time before looking to the branches and stars overhead. "A sad, lonely, broken man."

Rolling to his side, he watched her bury her face back into her knees. "Even with you at his side?"

Her shoulders flinched at the question.

"He spent all those centuries the same way I spent this last year." The words left a sour taste in his mouth. "The year I wasted in my own filth … but never-ending."

Abigail squeezed herself tighter. Her silence cut through him like a sharp knife.

"All he did was leave scars." Hotan pushed himself to his feet and walked up to the tree. He leaned his forehead against it and deeply inhaled the smell of camphor. "A wake of death and wounded hearts. What a horrible legacy he left behind. Then there's Iapetos, the being of Death itself. I don't want to know the travesties he's committed to catch his father's attention. Here I am, the prodigal son, expected to follow in their footsteps, but I refuse. The abuse must stop, and life needs to flourish. Even death requires a sense of closure to go on living."

He felt the heat of her arms wrapped around his chest as she gripped his shirt with desperate fists. "Don't you ever wish to be him or Iapetos. We never wanted that for you, Hotan."

The bark pressed at his forehead as he glared down at her trembling hands. His chest swelled as fear and compassion wrestled with one another in his mind and heart. Her face pressed harder into his back, and the sensation surged once more. Closing his eyes, frustration and anger took over as his thoughts pierced him with doubts.

Shellie, it hurts without you even after one year. I find myself surrounded by warm arms, but is it because I miss you that I am so moved by her touch? Am I confusing sympathy with affection? I don't know how I feel anymore without you there as my guiding light. What do I do now? Where do I go from here?

Abigail released him and left him in the silence under the shadow of his creation. Relief and sorrow filled him as she left. Turning, he leaned against the trunk of the tree and slid back to the ground. Punching the dirt between the gnarling roots, everything was breaking apart. Somehow, despite his efforts, the familiar sting of loneliness was creeping out from his core.

7

BAD INTENTIONS

I sensed when my father, Hotan, came back to my world. The island faded; perhaps it never existed, or he grew tired of living there. The other immortals came with him here to the land of death. *Welcome to my realm, an unpleasant place where survival and violence reign supreme.* From the nightmares, I only knew of one—the one I knew as my father and maker. Sensing the auras of power, I discovered that each person controlled a different element. My theory was confirmed when I found Hotan's abandoned journal in a hovel in the wilds of Germany. He wrote about all of them—all except me.

I was smitten with jealousy.

Each of them held an element, but none compared to the lethal impact of my own or Father's abilities. I didn't know how many there were, and I only cared to find one. From darkened corners, hooded robes, and crowded streets, I observed the ones I encountered from afar. My rage, my fight, wasn't with them but for the man who held power over us all. He was more powerful than the creation of metal, more powerful than rallying the spirit of the masses, and more powerful than fire itself.

Death sought Life.

I felt his presence loudly—a blue static haze hidden and distorted in the unknown distance. His face was so similar to my own, and the silver hair shading the grave look in his eyes never left my memory. The ability to sense other mortals was new to me, so I was often thrown off the path when I came too close. Pinpointing my father wasn't easy at first.

Then they all fell silent.

A burst of his power rang out. By the time I found the origin point, it was nothing but ash and sand. My father had committed another sin. To what volume, it was hard to say. The world of immortals fell silent, and a single beacon of power whispered. I assumed he could sense me as well.

Did you dispose of them to avoid me? I thought as I sat there, watching the waves slap against the shore.

He was the light, and I was the darkness, yet our actions seemed quite opposite of what we stood for. Every move he made was ruthless. For me, I acted in desperation or out of pity on some level.

Are we all that remains of the immortals now? Regret filled me. *If I had found the courage to speak to one of them, would they still be here?*

It wasn't until Helike that I discovered I wasn't alone in my search for him. For some strange reason, there were others whom he had chosen to walk the earth freely. Again, I wondered if it was a ploy to ease his own guilt or a way to throw me off his scent. He was calculated in everything he did; my failed attempts of finding him and the few times I had given chase proved that much about him.

The sun rose high in the clear blue sky. Under the weight of desert heat and hot winds, Helike's market moved with the river of bodies. Shouts from merchants competing for customers' attention drowned the sound of the seagulls' cries. The glint of Roman armor and a flash or red was sprinkled among the people. They had taken port in need of supplies for their next invasion and war, like hungry dogs to scraps.

I spun away from the soldiers, and the merchant before me was excited to have eye contact.

"Sir! I have many wares, yes?" He motioned between us to the carpet covered with jewelry and trinkets. "I have many delightful treasures that are sure to please a lady friend, no?"

"I'm looking for Hotan. Is there a man here by that name?" I flashed a handful of gold coins but quickly pulled them away from greedy fingers. "Information first or no deal."

"Sure, sure, there's Hotan here in Helike!" The merchant lurched forward, and I shoved him back. "I gave you the answer, now pay up!"

"You have proof?" I narrowed my eyes; this wasn't my first time dealing with a liar. "Any information other than, 'yes?'"

The merchant frowned.

"Ah, I'll take my business elsewhere then." Ignoring his pleas, I faded from his view in the torrents of bodies filling the street.

For the first time, I felt all three sources of power in the same location.

People bumped into me or stepped around. Walking slowly, I scanned the bopping heads and flashes of faces. Each step moved me closer to one power—a power that radiated red every time I closed my eyes. It was as loud and powerful as mine or Hotan's, but it wasn't his. Closing my eyes and standing still, I sought it out. It had stopped moving. *There!*

Turning, my eyes met the silver glare of a man who looked so much like me—like my father. His eyes widened, and I knew he felt my power. Unnerved, my power crept forward to the surrounding people, providing a wider berth from those who would not dare to touch the embodiment of Death. The silver hair glimmered, and his brow furrowed in confusion.

We took the same stance; neither of us was sure who the other was, but we knew we shared a bloodline.

I took a step forward, aiming to find out. I failed in the past to approach the other immortals, and I wouldn't make that mistake again. His head pivoted; something had pulled the silver-haired man's attention elsewhere. Before he disappeared, there was panic on his face. My steps faltered, and one thought came to mind. *Did he see Hotan?*

I closed my eyes to focus on finding the power. The faint glow of the man I had locked eyes with chased after another power; neither were Hotan's glow. I pushed through the crowd, trying to swallow my power to mask it. *Hotan must be close by.* The burning sensation at my core made it clear that it wouldn't be long before I lost what little control I had of my own power. Any time Life and Death converged, it ended in disaster.

But is it from the clashing of powers or because he is lashing out?

A flash of long silver hair caught my attention as both sources ducked into an alley. My power slipped, surging. Grabbing my chest, I cursed. Sweat poured over me as I came closer; I couldn't hide my presence any longer. *Have I already let it slip into his range?* Taking several steps back, I sighed in relief. The perimeter and distance were so fickle.

I could draw a line in the sand, but to what end? Only to have one of us take a step too close?

My veins were on fire. I was frustrated; losing the ability to control the very thing that cursed my existence added to my ire.

It piled onto my hatred for Hotan. The other immortals were within his range, which meant I had lost my chance to reach out to them. I looked to the sky at the seagulls floating on the wind.

I need to separate them, but at what cost? Should I push forward and lose Hotan?

Dropping my glare, I took in the faces all around. The choices I made could end every life here. Worse, their lives were at risk from the actions Hotan might take to deter me.

Last time we were in a mercenary camp, and I leveled it. They deserved the fate I gave them. I saw the travesties done to the villages before reaching the place where he hid among them. He expects me to level this place just the same, but he's wrong. I'm not him, and these people are innocent.

"Hey, move out of the way, or we'll run you through," barked a soldier with a Roman accent. "Are you deaf? Move or be killed."

Turning, I lifted an eyebrow at the squadron of Roman soldiers. The commander grabbed a spear from one of the front linemen and pressed the point hard into my chest. Popping through the black fabric, it broke skin and drew blood.

"Last time, before I drive this through you," growled the commander from under his helmet. "Move or lie down, dog."

Sighing, I stepped back to remove the spear and turned to walk away. *It does me no good to lose my temper in a crowd this big—*

Pain erupted through me as metal tore through flesh, pushing through my back and emerging from my gut. Clenching my teeth, I stared at the metallic spearhead. Behind me, the Romans cackled. Their slurs and lack of respect for the people here in Helike were loud in my ears. Unlike the gasping locals who pushed away from the scene with fear in their eyes, I understood their language. I couldn't take in air from a punctured lung, and blood dribbled from my lips.

How annoying. Gripping the blood-soaked spear, I pondered what to do next. *I am so close to finding Hotan, but I can't let these assholes get away with this.*

The commander yanked on the spear, but it didn't come loose. I held it firmly as a smirk formed on my lips. *He has done this before, but this time will be his last.* A sandaled foot dug into my back and pulled, but again, he failed to retrieve his spear.

"Why is he still standing?" muttered a soldier.

At least one in the lot has good instincts. The commander kicked the back of my knees, and I allowed myself to fall.

"He's on his knees now, ha!" The commander laughed.

I'll make sure he doesn't regain his pride.

A heel dug hard as he pressed his weight on me, but I didn't budge. The commander's muscled arms contracted as he tried to yank the spear free. "What in the Gods is this?" He let go and marched around to face me.

"What's the matter? Did you lose something?" I asked. His eyes were on my smile; blood still dripped off my chin, filling the ground.

"Don't toy with me!" he snapped.

A left hook landed hard across my jaw, and it caught me by surprise. Another kick sent me rolling; the spear's handle snapped. Now, the entire squadron roared to life, cheering him on, egging him to continue the beating. He unsheathed his sword, and it came down in a flash toward my neck. I lifted my arm, and the blade sliced through my flesh, grinding against bone. He paled. Lowering my arm and his sword, we locked eyes. Black flames pulled forth, turning the sword to ash. He leapt back with eyes wide as I rose to my feet.

The squadron rushed around me with their shields and spear poised in defense formation. All eyes were on us. An otherworldly being in black flames stood before a squadron of Romans—the conquerors. They beat against their shields and stepped forward. The commander shook his head to shed his shock and ready himself for a fight. My power stirred deep within me, and I failed to pull it inward.

This isn't the best place for this. If I'm not careful, I'll get too close to Hotan, and the powers will bring destruction and death. I don't want that on my conscience over some bullheaded soldiers looking for bragging rights for battling the Greek God, Iapetos.

Everyone around us pushed further away, whispering over and over in Greek, *"O profítis tou thanátou échei érthei gia ólous mas."*

The prophet of death has come for us all.

I took a step forward. The line was too close. I glanced over my shoulder, trying to gauge the distance from Hotan's perimeter in fear of triggering a natural disaster. Rattling of armor brought my attention forward. Shields and spear heads slammed into me, lifting me. They had done the unthinkable; dragging me far beyond my limit, the power within me came forward tenfold. Shields burst into ash, and I fell upon them with all my rage.

"You've doomed us all!" Gripping the commander's throat, my heart thumped with the anxiety of what would come. "Your arrogance has brought death upon Helike!"

Squeezing tight, the air stopped. I watched as his skin grayed and floated away on the wind. By the time I turned to face the rest of the troops, they had fled. People were in tears, praying to their gods and begging mercy from me. They had no way of understanding that I had no control. If I could make it all stop, I wouldn't be chasing Hotan for answers.

"RUN!" I roared, making all of them flinch. "If you wish to live to see tomorrow, run and never look back to Helike! This place will be no more!"

Screams rang out as panic started, and they rushed to flee the city. At my feet, pebbles and dirt bounced about. Squatting, I placed my palm against the ground. The shaking was building; an earthquake was his weapon of choice. Horses squealed, birds flew away, and the rats flooded the streets to escape. In a normal quake, they would have been unsettled far more in advance. This unrest was brought to life by the clashing of Death and Rebirth.

"It's too late," I muttered, covering my face. "It's too late to run."

Ba-Boom!

The earth's deafening roar drowned out the cries of Helike's people. All around, buildings collapsed and merchant stalls toppled over. Vertigo took hold as the ground shifted one way, then the next. People fell over, unable to keep themselves upright as the earth under their feet betrayed them.

Perhaps if I make some distance, it will slow down or stop.

Desperately, I ran as fast as my legs could carry me. The further I got from Hotan's power, the slower the quaking grew until I stopped at the city's gate. Here, the ground had ceased shaking, but a harrowing sight awaited me. Columns of fire reached into the sky and the city had sunk, leaving no escape. All around, we were surrounded by a cliff. Covering my mouth, I searched for an answer.

Was the city sitting on a flammable resource this whole time? If we sink too far… the port! I need to see the docks!

Turning, I ran back into the city. Fires had ignited from fallen lanterns and braziers. My run was short lived; too many buildings had collapsed between me and the port. The devastation lay before me: a mangled mess of clay, wood, and bodies. Dust and smoke filled the sky, blocking out the sunlight and darkening the world. *I must tread lightly.* I tried to provide mercy to those I came across, letting them pass before the fires or worse took their life.

I can only offer a painless death. Only immortals will remain here. No one will know why Helike fell.

Minutes grew into hours. I wasn't anywhere close to the docks but found where I'd left off. Nothing recognizable remained. Hotan's power fluttered in and out; like me, he struggled to contain his power to slow the inevitable destruction. A low rumbling crept across the landscape. *Here comes the first aftershock.* Scanning the shifting heaps of broken buildings, I dashed for the only clearing in sight. Dust rose off everything like smoke blowing in the wind. A howl of pure pain stood out, competing with the world of screams and crumbling.

Is someone under that collapsed building? Isn't that where I felt Hotan's presence?

I started my ascension to the top of the rubble. Up ahead, a large chunk shifted and dropped downward; a wailing scream, primal and raw, ripped through me. I froze to assess the scene. Shrieks cut through the air, and the smell of blood filled my nostrils.

Has the man been smashed to death? No, he can't be dead. Being this close, I would have felt it with my element; I know for certain this man isn't dead yet.

Swallowing, I pushed closer to where the screams originated, and I felt the wave of a new element. Pushing forward, I crept closer to the rubble. Below me, an immortal was buried alive. If they were anything like me, it would take much more to kill him. I had been in several situations like this before. Death comes as a release only to find yourself naked on a desert beach with the thirst for water like no other.

"In here! I am in here, under you!"

The cries were desperate and frightened. Whoever it was struggled under where I stood. I knew for certain that it wasn't Hotan. I reached down and pulled up the debris to reveal the blood-covered scene where the immortal waited with his arm missing. Removing the last large chunk allowed the sun to flash down on the dust-laden being.

He squinted up at me confusedly and mouthed the words, *Has Hotan returned?*

We glared at each other. His hair silver and features were too much like his—like mine. I gritted my teeth as anger and frustration filled me. My power reacted, and the man gasped in response. He felt it—the power of Death in this place.

"Who, who are you?" he asked with a raspy voice from all the pain-filled screaming. He was equally curious about the new immortal before him. "Where did you come from?"

"Where's Hotan?" I had no time for questions. *He is the only person with the power to save these people … if I can convince him this time.* "Tell me where that immortal bastard went."

"Gone. The building fell on us…" He held his throbbing arm, and I winced as I looked at the nub. "I was pinned, and well, you can see for yourself what happened."

"You know him then?" *This must be his first time losing a limb. Bandaging it like that is a horrible idea.* Reaching down, I offered him a hand. "I've been looking for him for a very long time."

He was reluctant and asked once more, "Who are you?"

"Iapetos." I motioned again for him to take hold, and he obliged. "I need to ask who you are and how you know him. No one has ever known the man whom I have spent decades looking for. You're the first in over a thousand years."

His eyes filled with shock and pain as they fell upon the horizon where Helike once stood only to be replaced with columns of smoke billowing out of piles of debris. Lives were lost, and those who survived struggled under the destruction. Victims covered in blood and mud stumbled about, sobbing in shock. Based on the decimation we observed as we made our way to the docks, I knew Helike would have no survivors. Not even the city itself would be left standing.

Roman ships lay tilted on their hulls on the muddy sea floor. The water at the docks had been stripped away. Silence filled this place. There were no signs of gulls; they did not come to scavenge the fish which flopped about. My stomach twisted. I had experienced a tsunami before, and I didn't want to endure it again. *The survivors behind us will wish they'd been crushed.*

"Dear God…" Talib held his missing arm as he stood in awe. "And I thought the massacre in my village had been devastating…"

"How do you know Hotan?" I gripped his shoulder, ripping him from the destruction. "You look like him. Are you related to him too?"

"Too?" His daze broke, and his eyes met mine. "I am his older brother, Talib."

"Older brother?" My eyes grew wide. Talib's eyes danced from one side, then the other as if reading invisible lines in the air. I realized I hadn't considered the possibility. "Did you know he had a son?"

"N-no," Talib stammered. He scanned past me to the fallen Helike. "Did… did you do this?"

"Is he here?" I shook him, tightening my grip. "Was he here?"

"Yes, but the building collapsed when I found him." Talib stared off as if lost in thought. "He did not want me to find him. I am certain he left me behind."

"Not even his own brother can get close to him." Talib's face twisted and paled, and I released him.

The pain from growing back a limb for the first time ravaged him. I turned back, marching to where I had found him. Desperate for clues, I searched the rubble and debris.

"There's no way this killed him, but maybe he left his journal again," I mumbled to myself, forgetting that Talib had stayed on my heels the whole way.

"Journal?" Talib questioned, holding his throbbing arm. His fingers dug into his flesh as if he willed himself to endure the pain. "He had it with him when he ran into me and the earthquake hit."

"Damn, that journal is all I have. He puts everything I need to know in that thing. The last time I found it, I learned a little about him and who I am." My frustration peaked. *If only the soldiers hadn't interfered.* "But just maybe…"

It was maddening. I peered over at Talib. *Is he lying to protect him? Are they brothers?* I marched over, gripped his throat, and lifted him off the ground. With only a single arm, he couldn't defend himself. My power boiled forth, and Talib's eyes filled with a new sense of fear. I could see my tattoos and black flames reflected in his eyes. His fingered clawed and tugged at my hand. He was losing strength and fighting to keep his eyes from rolling back in his head.

"Just maybe he will come back to save his brother from me," I snarled. "I'm betting yes."

"But…" Talib gasped, fighting for air and trying to speak. "He left me pinned! I begged for his help and got nothing! Is my missing arm not proof enough?"

"Oh, you were in no real danger before." I grinned. *Do you feel my power gnawing at Judgment, Father?* "But the moment he senses this, he should come. I have no real intention of hurting you, Talib. You're just as much of a victim as I am."

"V-Victim…" The element of Judgment would rise only to sputter under the weight of my own.

I kept my power at bay, but suddenly, it began to wave in and out of Talib's body. *He's coming! He's close!* I glanced around.

Which direction will he launch his first attack? Hotan was never one for small talk, but at this stage of my misery, I wanted revenge for all those lonesome nights, for the loneliness eating my soul, and for this never-ending life. Not even the mortals accepted me without some want for selfish desire. I was the black, ugly, broken thing born from sinful wishes.

Something hot and wet hit my hand. I turned back to Talib's tear-stricken face. The fear in his eyes was gone—only pity remained.

I whispered, "Why? Why are you crying?"

"I feel sorry for what my brother has done to you." My grip loosened, allowing his feet to touch the ground. "He wanted your mother so badly that he blindly tossed aside what he was given—his son."

For once, I was offered empathy, and I let him go. "I just want answers. Why would he bring me to life only to cast me out?"

"Because he was a heartbroken fool." Talib winced as another wave of pain hit his arm. Gripping the remaining part, he fought the urge to curl into a ball. "I pray this will not pain me for eternity."

"Is this the first time you've lost a limb?" I stared at the bloody bandages on the nub. "You seem to be in shock from it."

"I have never been injured this badly before." Talib tensed, and his face paled. "I take it you have?"

"More times than I would like to admit." I leaned closer, reaching for the injury, but Talib jerked away. "Trust me, it's better to leave the bandage off."

"Why?" Talib furrowed his brow, hissing as I tenderly unwrapped his stump. "I would think it would get infected or cause alarm."

I reached the last wrap, and the final tug sent Talib reeling with pain. Nodding, I encouraged for him to look down. He gaped at how the flesh had grown back and merged with the wrapping. His eyes shot upward to mine in terror. Flesh and bandage had become one, explaining the pain he had been feeling. He locked eyes with me, knowing what was coming. With a taut face and strong glare, I ripped the flesh-infused bandage free. Nerves had fused with the bandage, and Talib fell to his knees, screaming. I gripped his arm; my work was far from done. *<I'm so sorry. I made this mistake long ago.>* Another rip of his flesh brought tears streaming down his face; I hadn't been able to remove all of it in the first go. Agony rattled through him like a thousand scorpion stings.

"That's why you leave off the bandages. It's painful enough when it returns; bandages fused with flesh slow the process and add to the agony of it all." I released him, and he fell to his side panting and shivering as the pain pulsed through him. "Next time, keep it clear of obstructions."

"IAPETOS!" Hotan's angry voice made me turn on my heels. "Back away from him. He has nothing to do with us." Blue flames erupted around him.

"I am sorry for what he may do," Talib said, trying to make his words loud and clear. "If we meet again—"

"Chances are we won't remember." I knew from his stare, his stance, and his voice that Hotan was beyond angry. He glared down at Talib with the same expression of disdain.

<We are both in for it. How could you! This man is your brother, and you left him here!>

Fists tight, I allowed my black flames to grow. I turned to my newfound uncle and gave him my advice, "He likes to toy with memories, locking them away. He's right; this is our fight, not yours. You have nothing to do with this."

"Locking memories away?" Sweat trickled down his temple. "Why?"

<I think you know why.> My voice reached into Talib's mind as I approached Hotan. *<I am confident I will fail here, and we will not recall my destruction of Helike.>*

<You did this?> Talib's elbow was back, but a gruesome, tangled mix of flesh and bone hung where the rest of his arm should have followed. *<Was it necessary to take so many innocent lives?>*

The earth trembled under my feet. Dust wafted up in the breeze. Another wave of fleeing birds screeched overhead; they headed inland, away from the dull roar coming from the sea. The growling shook the air itself, and I knew a tsunami was coming. My body tensed with each passing second as the sound and vibrations escalated.

Hotan launched himself forward, and I matched him. He had hoped the incoming wave would be enough to distract me. Black and blue flames collided; the clashing of Life and Death sent bolts of electrical energy all around us with a thundering boom. The pressure of it blew outward and slammed into Talib who could barely hold his ground against it.

I leapt back to reassess the first connection. The strength between us was matched. Rushing forward, I launched a full assault. Each step crushed the debris underfoot, leaving a trail of black flames. Hotan blocked the first blow and countered with his own. I took it, waiting for the opening that would follow. Hotan crouched and slammed a fist into my side, setting my ribs ablaze. I swung my knee upward and locked with his chin; I heard his teeth clamp together. He stumbled back, snorting at me.

Again, we ran at one another. I caught his arm and blocked the next. With haste, I surged my power over his. Death had pushed back the blue flames of Life. It snaked across Hotan's neck, but my greed got the better of me and he broke free, making distance between us.

I almost had him. He's afraid of my power; I can use that.

I scoffed and launched my next attack. Each connection left behind black flames meant to gnaw at him. For the first time, I noticed Hotan wince. The monster revealed he felt pain like any other creature on this Earth. It only ebbed my desire to lash out, making each strike more vicious than the last. My flesh sizzled under the blue flames left behind by Hotan. He returned the method, but unlike him, I had died far too many times. *Pain has no place in battle—only focus and drive.* The entire world shook and roared as rubble collapsed around us.

Ba-Boom!

A loud cannon rang out. The ground tilted, but we didn't stop our fury of kicks and punches. Screams mangled with the cacophony of destruction, and pillars of fire burned just beyond the city walls. *This is the result of Life fighting with Death. This is the curse of being at odds with one another.* Hell would devour Helike. The ground dropped again as if the foundation was being ripped away.

Ba-Boom!

Another drop. The fight halted; we both knew this was the worst one to date. Breaking from my hatred, I scanned the area for Talib. He was here, but he was in danger and still healing. Hotan made a dash for him, and my heart leapt to my throat. *How dare you aim to kill him!* With a roar of effort, I launched a wall of black flames. Talib looked on in confusion with his hand raised to greet his brother. Blue flames smashed against the black wall, and Hotan fell back, exhausted.

I ran for Talib. *He doesn't realize the danger he is in and what his brother intends. I have to get him out!* Wings burst from my back. Talib was putting the pieces together, realizing the blue flames were meant for him. His eyes locked onto my wings in amazement. The world was falling apart, and the wall I made was waning. *We must get away!*

"Time's up; we must leave. NOW!" I gripped his good arm, and with a graceful leap, whooshed my wings once to pull us into the air. "I do not wish to experience drowning again."

Stunned, Talib stared down to the ground as we ascended. With each flap of my wings, we gained distance from Hotan. He glared from where he stood in his glowing blue flames. The pillars of fire surrounding the city were dying off, but a mountain of water came from the sea. There would be no mercy from the acts of nature coming for what little was left of Helike. No one would ever walk its streets again.

"You need to figure out your powers, Talib," I said as I tried to get us above the crest of the tsunami. "You could have flown away on your own, or has Hotan kept that secret to himself?"

There was a pause and a look of confusion. "Why?" Talib stammered as the wave rolled under them, and we watched ten massive Spartan ships fly into pieces like boats made of grass. "Why did you save me?"

"I…" My grip tightened. *How can I tell him that his brother has murdered him over and over again to avoid revealing the truth? How do I tell this man who in the fog of my mind has…* "I think you once tried to save me."

Thud!

Hotan flew in from a blind spot. The impact jolted me, and I lost my grip on Talib. My heart stopped. I shoved the blue-winged fiend from me, but he gripped my foot and tossed me further away from Talib. The sight of the water and debris boiling under him added to my anxiety. I lunged, black flames raging. Blue ones smashed into me, and lightning arced across the sky. I regained balance too late, and as I looked to Talib, water consumed him.

"How could you!" I flew forward, aiming for Hotan's throat. "He is your brother!"

Hotan dodged my attack and launched a ball of blue flames into my face. "Why do you care?"

My flesh healed, and I caught his emotionless face. "Do you not have any sense of family?"

"You have none," he snapped. "You can't have mine; he's all I have."

"You're a selfish child!" Flames were building in both hands. "You'd rather break a toy than share it with others. He's not a possession. He's a person—a person who loves his brother and has shown me empathy like no other being on this godforsaken earth has ever done!"

I directed my power at him with all my rage. *He deserves to be burnt alive, stripped from the Earth for the sake of others. Family isn't something you own. It isn't a thing you can break when it is convenient for you. It's something to cherish, to understand there will be times you don't agree but not to be greedy to this level.* The black flames fell away, and Hotan rushed forward. He wrapped his hands tightly around my throat. *I give up. At least this time, Talib and I will have our memories.*

"How dare you tell me what is right and wrong," he hissed with a wild look in his eyes as my limbs faded to ash. "You are nothing! You are a mistake I made! You could never understand what it means to have family and lose what I have lost!"

I was almost gone, but I smiled. "You know nothing but your own greed." And I fell to the wind, free of his grip.

8

SWALLOW THE KNIFE

"What are we going to do with him?" Saphellia asked uneasily as she glanced over her shoulder. "Are you sure you want him here?"

"He has nowhere else," Talib said bluntly with a look of empathy on his face. "I pray that I broke Hotan's spell. Life flashed before me on the verge of death. If this works the same for him, it should shake loose the memories of the time we spent together."

"Spent together?" Fear filled her eyes at the thought. "What do you mean?"

Talib's eyes broke away and looked to the pale face of Iapetos in the hospital bed. For years, it was Saphellia's resting place; later, it became Hotan's when he overexerted his power. Now, a broken man, tortured by his own father, lay in this peaceful sanctuary. The wake of emotions rattled both Saphellia and Talib, but their options were limited. After the harsh silence, he motioned for her to follow him out of the room. She turned, giving one last concerned look at the dangerous man in a coma. Talib gripped her shoulder, breaking her from her thoughts and giving a stern expression that she knew well.

They settled at the kitchen table. He wondered, *How can I share what I discovered only a few hours ago on that rooftop while half dead?* Swallowing, he had to decide which of the events and information was most pressing. Geliah had rocked their world, and a year later, someone far more dangerous shattered the security they thought had been earned. He opened his mouth but closed it. *Reassurance means nothing at this rate,* he thought. Shaking his head, he tried again. *Stick to the point…*

"He is without a doubt my brother's child," Talib said solemnly. Saphellia stiffened, unsure about what he would say next. "And I can confirm that he is indeed *our* Hotan's father."

"But…" she started to interject, but he raised his hand to silence her.

"I remember the day it happened, but I cannot explain how my brother made it possible. It took his life; perhaps that is why they look so much alike. The idea he could have a child unlike the rest of us…" His words drifted, but he regained his composure and shifted to his main concern. "The Iapetos we saw today is not the man I knew and taught."

"Taught?" Her mouth went dry, uncertain of the words falling into the open space between them. "I thought you didn't know him, but now you're telling me you spent enough time to teach him things? That *you* were this monster's tutor?"

"I know, but I had no idea how many times I had interacted with him. So much lost time and memories were hidden away by my brother." Talib rubbed his forehead as he fought back the sickening sensation building at his core. "He manipulated me. All this time, I fretted my mind was falling apart. I thought the missing chunks in my memory were a result of traversing time and living for so long, but…"

"Hotan took your memories?" Her face tightened, and she paused as her eyes fell to the hallway. "Then does that mean his were taken from him as well? Is that what's been happening?"

"Yes, but his was to a far more dangerous level." Talib leaned back in his chair, his eyes searching the air for the thoughts and words he needed. "I imagine being the embodiment of Death would allow fragments to come back, but which memories returned would decide how far into madness Iapetos would find himself. Did he remember sincere moments like the ones we created, or was it memories of the thousands of deaths he suffered at the hand of his father? Or worse, like that horrendous day when Hotan cast him back out to the sea. In the decades we traveled together, he was a gentle soul searching for answers about the man who haunted his dreams. Hotan erased us both of that time, and horrible events unfolded which resulted in Mt. Pelée's eruption."

"I see." Saphellia stared at her tapping fingers at the table. "Does this mean he will remember everything for the first time, like you?"

"Yes." Talib stumbled on the realization. "This is a discovery of many firsts, I suppose."

"And how do you see his mind, his temperament, being when he wakes up?" Her fingers paused, and they locked eyes. "What action will you take if he continues on a warpath after his own son?"

"I do not know." Talib slammed his hands on the table as his frustration bloomed into physical reaction. "But Hell will freeze over before I ask that boy to put his own father down. I have had enough of this vicious cycle my brother has created."

Saphellia swallowed, and a shudder rocked her shoulders. "There has to be another way than putting the kid through any more death."

"Pray he wakes up the man I know he can be." Talib's chair squealed as he stood. "For now, I will sit and watch. I will be the wall and guardian you all entrusted me to be so long ago."

"Wait." She reached across the table, but his back was to her. "I have one more question for you, my dear husband. I need to know…" her voice trailed, lingering in the air of the unspoken question.

Closing his eyes, Talib answered, "We have not walked on the same path as mankind for a long time. I think we are something closer to angels, possibly fallen angels. Living and walking the Earth has allowed me to grow stronger and accept that I am Judgment in soul, body, and mind. It is up to each of us to come to terms with our immortality; we are both cursed and blessed. We represent the cycles of life, nature in all forms, and, most importantly, the knowledge mankind has inherited through their sins, for better or worse. We are tattooed angels; we are the chosen few."

"Why us?"

His shoulders slumped, and after a long silence, he replied, "If I knew, I would not be so desperate to chase my brother's steps back to some inkling of a moment when it all happened." He started down the hall. "I imagine it was God's way of blessing the last of the tribe of Levi when the others broke their promise to God. That or the Devil has a cruel sense of humor."

Birds chirped as sunlight poured between the branches. The center of the junkyard was disrupted by the new playground the camphor tree provided for cardinals, finches, and even a woodpecker. Hotan slowly opened his eyes and blinked. His back ached; the dirt and roots had proven an unsatisfactory sleeping surface. He rolled into a sitting position after refusing to leave the creation he had willed into being. Part of him feared facing Lilly; the other half was afraid it was a lucid dream. He rubbed his pounding head. His mouth was dry and his stomach grumbled; he felt human for a change.

Has it really been a year since I felt hungry or thirsty like this?

"Exerting power seems to have forced your body to want to live again, I see." Lilly's voice startled him. She leaned on the tree trunk just out of Hotan's view. "Here, at least hydrate. Enjoy this want for food and drink while it's there."

She tossed a bottle of water at him, but he didn't complete the catch, and it dropped to his lap. "Uh, thanks. I don't understand it completely though."

"Which?" Lilly pulled herself off the tree and came into view. She stared high above them, watching the wind rock the boughs. "The powers or the body?"

"Both," he snorted as he cracked open the water bottle and took two long guzzles. "The power flows far too easy for destruction, but it feels like I am pushing a mountain in the other direction to create life. As for my body, I feel like I'm human again, but for how long?"

"Until you recover your energy." She gave him a side glance. "It happens occasionally. Where you feel like someone pushed play just long enough to feel the dry thirst for water and the grumbling of an empty stomach. Whether you eat or not, it freezes up again within a day. We often get the shivers and sleep for days. You seem to have found a way around that."

"Not willingly." He stared at the bottle in his hand as shame washed over him. "Sorry about the tree."

"Sorry?" she asked, laughing. "I like it. Sometimes you need a little garden and whatnot to reconnect to nature. Is this what you came to figure out?"

"Not quite." Another rush of cool water pushed the headache down to a low drumming. "What scares me is I can turn the tree to ash with no effort at all. It's … wrong."

Lilly turned, placing a hand on the trunk. "Why on earth would you want to do that?"

"I don't." Grunting, he brought himself back to his feet. "But *he* was better at taking life away than creating it."

Lilly's cheeks tensed. Silence came over them—a mutual understanding of what he implied.

Satisfied the talk had ended, Hotan started back the way he had come in. "I'm going to crash on your couch."

As he marched his way out, he finished the last swig of the water. Smashing the frail plastic container between his palms, he focused the power within him to bring life again. Abigail waited at the gate; her face was painted with confusion and worry. He paused, waiting for her eyes to drop to his clasped hands. He opened his palms to reveal a single white rose blossom. Her forehead creased, and her fingers dipped into his hands to retrieve the fragrant treasure.

"What is this for?" She brought it to her nose, indulging in the smell as a smile grew on her face. "It's so pretty and smells amazing!"

"A sign of hope." He brushed past her, his face reddening at his own unwarranted words and actions. *Why do I feel more complete after seeing her smile? It hurts all at once. There's a hole where Shellie used to be in my life, and I secretly want Abigail to fill some of that space… to dull that pain ever slightly.*

He made it to the small living quarters that Lilly called home. He flopped down on the couch and closed his eyes, wanting sleep to take him away from the stress. Flashes of blue and black flames colliding snapped his eyes back open. A surge of anger rolled in his chest. The man from his nightmares, the picture that haunted the photo album, and the title of Father belonged to one entity. Biting his tongue, Hotan searched his feelings for some inkling as to how he could settle the facts in his own mind and heart.

I can't condemn someone who was tortured by his own father, can I? Doesn't this vicious cycle of father versus son need to end at some point? I don't want to become the new wave of destruction like the man I am reincarnated after. That's not me; that's not a life I want to live. I've accepted that I'll never be able to achieve the dreams I set, but that doesn't mean I can't live my life the way I choose.

"I can't believe that monster is someone Mom loved." The words tumbled out from his lips with resentment. "Why would he abandon the only positive thing he ever had?"

<*Are you okay?*> Talib's voice crept into his head—a weak echo within his own.

Sighing, Hotan closed his eyes, forcing himself to respond. <*I don't know. I feel lost.*>

<*You are not alone.*> The words came with resistance. <*He has not woken yet.*>

Another ache swelled in Hotan's chest. <*I don't know if I want him to wake up.*>

The silence spoke volumes. Talib had a greater weight on him than anyone else.

<*But we need answers, right?*> Hotan asked carefully, tip-toeing his words, unsure if he should further share his thoughts on the matter. <*We need to know what the former Hotan has done—*>

<*I know what he has done,*> Talib interjected. <*Memories were stolen, and the past holds no solution or direction for the future. It is up to us to decide what to do. We do not have to forget, we do not even have to forgive, but we must learn to live with our mistakes.*>

Hotan needed reassurance. <*What if he wakes and still…*>

<*I will not allow it,*> Talib responded sternly. <*For now, stay there with Lilly until we know.*>

<*R-right.*> Hotan didn't want to be home, not yet.

Rolling onto his side, he tried once more to force himself to sleep. A blanket flopped across him, and he flinched. He looked over his shoulder to see Lilly nodding as she went back out the door. He settled in; the warmth it brought made him drowsy and heavy. Finally, he drifted off, making it past the flashes of black flames that haunted him.

9

YOU'RE NOT ALONE

79 AD Pompeii

It took over four hundred years to track my father down in Pompeii. He was tracking someone, and I could only assume it was Talib. I had to stop him before he reached him and erased the memories. Fear and anxiety bit at me. *Has he already erased his memories?*

"Sir." The courtesan tugged on my robe, her amber eyes grabbing my full attention. "I didn't catch what you asked."

"Sorry." I placed a heap of coins in her palm, and she batted her eyes. "Where would you like me to perform? The…"

I raised my hand. "I need information. Consider this payment for your time."

Her eyes widened as she recounted, "Ask anything of me."

"A man, silver hair with a face like mine and eyes like emeralds." I pulled back my black hood. "Is he here? Have you seen a person like him?"

"Y-yes." She paled, shoving the coins in her satchel. "In fact, he paid me three days ago asking about a man like him. You have a strange family, sir."

Relief washed over me. "I thought so. Any idea where he headed?"

Her hands clung to her purse, heavy with coins. "Between all three of you, I can leave. You should too; the mountain is looking angrier."

"Tell me what you know." I noticed Mt. Vesuvius throwing smoke and the ground shaking since my arrival. This was the price of Life and Death coming too close once more. "I need to know where they are. It's urgent."

Her eyes searched my own. "The first man, the one with silver eyes, he went to Herculaneum."

"Talib. You had a chance encounter with him?" I furrowed my brow.

She nodded. "He asked me to tell the second man with green eyes that he was headed to Stabiae. Strangely, he grew angry with me when I told him this lie." The courtesan shuddered, but she smirked. "Being in my line of work, when you have a client who can read lies, you learn ways around it."

I smiled, admiring her tenacity to follow through on the job Talib had handed her. "Then where did you send him?"

She shrugged. "I told him he headed toward Oplontis. It was a half-truth."

"He would come close and pass it. Thank you." A rumble filled the sky, and the pillar of smoke grew. "Now, we both need fast horses. I'm buying." I offered my arm, and she accepted, pressing her breast against my arm. "It's a shame we had to meet under sour terms. I would have loved to hear you moan."

"Ah, and I would have loved to hear you scream." Winking, she pulled me through the busy streets.

All throughout Pompeii, people were conflicted about what to do. Some attempted to carry on with their business. Many courtesans, merchants, and nobleman were determined to make one more bit of coin or trade before the incoming ash fell upon the city. I could tell by the unsettling neighing that we had made it to the stables. One man fought to calm the largest horse while several smaller horses and mules fussed in a corral.

"I need two horses," I barked loudly, unsure of who to toss my coin at to resolve this matter.

The man holding the rope tied it to the fence and shouted for the boy to entice him with treats to calm the beast. "Two, you say? Do you have any idea the amount of coin for one?"

I unlatched the heavy bag at my waist. "This should be beyond what you need for two."

He took it and was stunned by the weight. "Surely, you must be joking?"

"I need saddles and tack. And I need them now."

He spun and went to work. Without hesitation, he barked at servants. The courtesan on my side pulled on my arm. She motioned that I come closer. Her lips and hot breath tickled at my ear, and I could smell the perfume—a warm scent, a blend of rose, cypress, and lilies—emanating from her. It was a popular selection from the perfume house in Pompeii, and many traveled or sent servants to purchase bottles. She was a well-paid courtesan before I, or even Hotan and Talib, filled her pockets.

She whispered, "May you live to see another day, my Angel of Death."

I pulled away, shaken by her words. I opened my mouth to ask and found her lips sealed to mine. Her tongue played with my own, pulling me deeper into her kiss before she broke free. It was then that I saw the fear in her eyes as they reflected the glowing rockets of red from Mt. Vesuvius. I turned around, knowing Hotan must still be in Oplontis. Time was running out. This was a disaster I hadn't experienced, and I didn't care to add it to my list anytime soon.

"Your horses. Be quick. I don't imagine it'll be long before the ash falls." The horse merchant shoved the reigns in my hand and turned to the stable boy. "We're done. Hang the cloth around the corrals. We must protect the animals!"

As I slung myself up on the horse, the courtesan had ridden close and glared in my eyes one last time. "I heard stories about a man like you. Iapetos, the bringer of death. My family talks of Helike and the black angel who brings disaster where he walks."

"I never told you my name." I pulled my hood up, feeling uneasy about the girl I had hired.

"Gods never do." She heeled the horse and took off.

I rode in the opposite direction. My thoughts spun wild with each gallop and huff of the horse. *Had her family been on the outskirts of Helike when it fell? Merchants would have still been traveling the roads or setting up along the main route and watched the destruction. My jaw tightened. Of course, they would have watched the fight and seen the black-winged thing above the mountain of sea folding over their city. This is what the Greeks labeled me: Iapetos.*

The volcano shook the earth and sputtered in the corner of my right eye. It would peak as Hotan and I came closer and the powers of Death and Life competed for balance. I was desperate. I still remembered Helike and didn't want that. I had to protect this chance for something more. For the first time, I could have answers to the drowning number of questions that ate me alive every waking minute on Earth. Oplontis was in the distance as I came over the hill, but one thing stood between me and the city: Hotan.

Letting the horse slow, I approached where he waited. His eyes glowed with a maddening fury. Mt. Vesuvius growled with his rage, filling the air and agitating the horse under me. After calming my horse, I dismounted. Reaching under, I cut away the straps and reigns and slapped it on the rump. It took off, jumping from me and frantically heading for the ocean. Turning back, I pulled my gladius. Hand-to-hand combat was dangerous, though I didn't know how far I would manage with a weapon either.

"Do you intend to stop me?" Hotan hissed, unmoved by the weapon I held.

"What do you think I am here to stop?" A harsh southeast wind blew across us, pulling off my hood. "You look at me as if I've done something wrong, but the blame is with you."

Hotan narrowed his eyes. "None of them can know you exist, especially my brother."

"Ah, I figured that was the case." I nodded, tightening my grip. "Since Helike, I figured you would hunt Talib down. Why can't you let him decide what he thinks of me? Or are you afraid he may take my side when he discovers what you've done?"

"You know nothing!" Blue flames covered his body, and he marched forward. "How dare you hunt me down like an animal!"

Pulling forth my own power, I covered my gladius with black flames. "ME? You're chasing down your own brother to hide your son from him!"

A ball of blue flames barreled toward me, and I parried with the gladius. It proved effective against his attempt to turn me to ash. I had a chance with a weapon. He never carried one; he couldn't be bothered to blend in or pretend to be human even for a moment. I had watched and followed him for so long. *Here I stand, surviving in the changing tides of decades and centuries, but he has never changed. No, that isn't right. He is changing by becoming full of rage and self-loathing, which he projects onto me. When those green eyes look at me, he sees himself and everything he hates about himself. It was never about me, was it, Hotan?*

I rushed forward, swinging down and across. A flame-covered arm deflected my strike. I backstepped and thrust forward. He dodged, reaching out, but I blocked with my own shield of flames. I couldn't risk him touching me. It never went well once he got his hands on me. Stifling to the side, I swung low. He spun around, but I stayed out of reach. The tip of the blade slid across his thigh. Black flames fought the blue, allowing blood to dribble across the dirt before the wound quickly closed.

Leaping back, I huffed. "Do you hate me, or do you hate what I remind you of when you look inside yourself?"

He stood straight, irritated that I had landed a strike and drawn blood. "What sort of question is that?"

"A perfectly good one." I rolled back both shoulders and cracked my neck. "Tell me, what have I ever done to deserve this life you've given me?"

"Nothing," he hissed, scowling. "You don't deserve that life."

"You mean, I wasn't what you wanted." I drew a deep breath, holding it a moment to remain calm. "Stop blaming me because your life didn't go your way. We can't all have what we want."

"Aargh!" Hotan ran at me, rage engulfing him.

I clenched my jaw, refusing to back down. Mt. Vesuvius had blown. Fiery rocks rained down on us, and a wicked heat shot down from the mountain side. The eruption became more violent with each step Hotan took, but he couldn't see it in the blind rage I had pulled from him. I knew Hotan wouldn't reach me in time. I closed my eyes and dropped my gladius as burning ash engulfed us. It was far swifter than my death at the stake or the crushing of a tsunami and far less painful than dying by my father's hand yet again.

109 AD Scotia

Thirty years had passed. I followed in the footsteps of the Roman Ninth Legion. Well over four thousand trained soldiers had conquered and won merit. Their campaigns ranged from Africa to Germania to Spain, and now, they had traversed Britannia and aimed for Scotia. We were in uncharted territory—one I hadn't set foot on until now. I stowed away on a supply shipment, and they would spare no horses for me to follow them. On foot, I was close and saw their campfire smoke towering above the trees in the distance.

Their sudden success and trajectory caught my attention after I woke on the desert beach. Two sets of prints, one following the other, were found in the sand. Talib and Hotan had also perished under the last disaster, and I wondered, *Does Hotan still hunt him?* I followed, gaining supplies, digging out my hidden stashes, and paying in gold to get close. This time, the radius had shrunken even further; I could get closer to Hotan, much like in Helike. Back in Oplontis, our powers clashed well before I reached Pompeii, and even with him miles away, it tore the volcano apart.

I could feel his power, but I felt death in the place it sat. A harrowing feeling filled me as I walked a beaten path so many soldiers had marched the day before. The downtrodden path took a turn through trees where they found a clearing or made one to build a camp. As I broke through the other side of the thickets, I froze, horrified by the scene before me.

Soldiers lay dead in heaps. Four thousand strong had all collapsed to the ground. Their silver armor glinted in the sunlight, and their red capes flapped on the breeze. One man stood at the center of this bloody massacre; another knelt under his hand. Bobbing and weaving through the bodies, I approached with caution. Before long, I recognized the two men. Hotan grasped Talib by the back of his neck. I slowed my gait, cautious to step over the fallen men. Talib's eyes were rolled back in his head, but I could sense he was still alive. I turned to Hotan, and he met my gaze.

"I've been waiting for you." His tone jolted me to a stop; he was acting different from before. "I asked."

"Asked?" I held my breath, uneasy with the situation. "Asked who? About what?"

"What he thought about you." His face crumpled with a look of despair. "You said I should let him decide for himself."

I opened my mouth but was unsure how to respond. *Had my words reached him in Oplontis?* "What answer did he have for you?"

"He said, 'He's your child and if you will not have him, then give him to me.'" His tone of despair soured into a renewed bitterness. "It went on like that. He didn't judge me for abandoning you but instead wanted to do what I should have done. To take up my mistakes and right them for me. It's always been like this. Talib has blamed himself for all my mistakes and sins. I can do no wrong in his eyes."

"Maybe he sees what I see." The words left me before I could reign them in, and my heart leapt to my throat.

"I thought you saw a father who not only banished and abandoned his only son but destroyed the world around him to keep it that way." His jaw twitched, eyes hinting of the madness I had seen countless times before. "What do you see?"

Swallowing, I answered, "A broken man who no longer knows how to live or even be human anymore."

He frowned and dropped his eyes to Talib. "Perhaps you are both right."

"Did you erase his memories?" I needed to know the details of the situation since Hotan was acting out of character.

"I had to," he said quietly. I moved forward to keep the wind from silencing the words. "I left some memories of you, but I had to erase this moment."

"Why leave memories of me? Why erase this moment?" Stepping over another body, I stopped just shy of where he stood. "I don't understand what you're trying to do this time?"

"I can no longer hate you for what I hate within myself." Tears fell; my words had reached him in Oplontis. "But my brother may not forgive me for what I have done here by using him and his power."

I flinched, looking to the thousands of bodies which filled the clearing. "No, you couldn't have." My mouth ran dry as I surveyed the scene. Not one fallen body showed signs of Hotan's power; there were no hints of any part of them turning to ash. "How could you do that to him?"

"There could be no witnesses here. This will be a memory he shall never recover." Talib's eyes were still rolled back, and he screamed under Hotan's grip. "He can never remember how I made him take these innocent lives with his power. I... I know he would never forgive me, not for this sin."

"Stop!" I rushed forward, but Talib burst into ash and was gone. "You're fucking out of your mind!"

Tears streamed down his face. "I want to fix this, to start over and try harder."

I grimaced, no longer caring if I lost this battle. "You can't write life out! It's unpredictable, and you will find yourself wrecked, disappointed, and miserable. You can plan every facet, but we were never meant to follow a clear chosen path!"

"I deserve happiness!" he shrieked like a child throwing a tantrum.

"And I don't?" I motioned to the surrounding bodies. "Your brother and these men didn't deserve happiness either? You've gone from rage to greed. How can a monster like you deserve to gain power like this?"

"I NEVER WANTED THE POWER!" There was a wild look in his eyes. "It has taken everything from me, all that I knew and loved. I want this curse to end." Hotan dropped to his knees, held his head, and sobbed. "I couldn't save any of them."

"Save who?" I spoke softly. It was the most he had ever talked to me without threatening my life.

"Liora, the village, my father." He gave a mournful cry. "I couldn't save them crossing the desert, crossing the sea. I couldn't save them from being enslaved or slaughtered by Salah and his army. I am unworthy to hold this power."

"Then give it to someone else." He froze, and I furrowed my brow. "We both know you have that ability. You can't hide it from me; I feel it within my own."

"You are right." He rolled back on his heels, staring up at the sky in wonder. "Why have I held onto this for so long?"

I was stunned as I watched his mind unravel in ways I hadn't imagined possible. "Who would you pass this curse onto?"

He paled as he filled with dread. "I don't know."

"Give it to me." It was a dangerous gamble; I had no way of knowing what it would do. *I have been broken, but unlike him, I've crawled out of the depths of Hell repeatedly to live my life.* "I'll carry the burden of Life and Death."

"No, that's not fair." He inhaled deeply and released it. "I must search for someone worthy, someone stronger than myself, someone you can willingly accept. I have ruined us. There's no going back."

"You would rather impose this on a mortal?" Sighing, I squatted to be eye level with him. "I don't think that will work either, Hotan."

"Ah, how did you get to be so wise?" He dropped his stare, and for the first time, he smiled at me. "I wish I'd taken you in that day. Your words are so much like hers; perhaps Talib was right when he said I was given what I needed most in this life."

"Don't ask me to forgive and forget." I gave him a dangerous look. "That is something I can never do. I want to see you learn from your mistakes."

Sighing, his shoulders slumped. "I pray that day will come."

"Why not start now?" My gut twisted as his mental state wavered again. "You said you wanted a clean slate, to start fresh from this point. We can do that now."

"I can't." Before I could react, he tackled me. "I must wipe it all clean and try again."

The blue aura of Rebirth snaked toward my mind from where he strangled me. "Stop!"

"I can't. Not here. I must wipe it all away. No one should know about what I did here, what I made Talib do." Fear filled his face, and I saw him for the frightened child he was inside. "Helike, Oplontis, I need to purge those to start again."

"N-no, I won't … let … you." My power surged forward but did nothing to his arms.

Desperate to salvage what fragments he hadn't taken from me, I turned my power onto myself, commanding it to take my body and devour it. My neck crumbled under his fingers. His face shifted from confusion to panic. Each grasp of his fingers found more and more of my flesh turned to ash.

"STOP! YOU CAN'T!" He reached for my face, and my world ended.

526 AD Antioch

For the first time, the table was flipped. It was no longer me hunting Hotan but him hunting me. He was obsessed; I imagined his mind was filled with questions about how much I remembered. I had retained most of Oplontis, or so I prayed. Helike was a jumbled mess with haunting images of a third entity I knew I needed to find. As for Scotia, I only recalled my arrival and Hotan's panic-ridden face before it all faded away. The headaches were unbearable at times; I had prevented him from messing with my mind, but I had broken myself.

Antioch was a large trade town where information and supplies could be bought. It was nestled between the Orontes River and the mountains of Silpius and Staurinus. Besides trade, it had become a place to entertain the masses with theaters, stadiums, and even a circus for visitors to indulge their time and money. Byzantine soldiers with their pikes, teardrop shields, and flamboyant capes of blue, red, and yellow marched down the street. They arrived more than a hundred years prior, condemning the paganists and forcing servitude to Christianity. Theodosius had made sure of this new reign of religion after the Sibyl of Delphi refused to foresee the future, warning he was a wicked man. I sought her counsel once, but she refused to see me. Her priestess had shared only one verse from the Sibylline Books, and I can still recall her voice etching within me: "*In a circle flow a restless stream of fire; And deathless angels of the immortal God, whoever is, shall bind with lasting bonds.*"

A giggle caught my attention. There, in the brothel's doorway, was a girl so familiar. She reminded me of the courtesan, but that was impossible since she had died hundreds of years ago. It was her lips, the shape of her face, and even the color of her eyes like a field of yellow and orange lilies. On the morning breeze, a hint of rose, cypress and lilies took my memories back to that lustful kiss from centuries ago. I lost my focus and tripped before catching myself on the merchant's table. She was gone.

"Sir, are you not well?" The sun had just crawled out from behind the horizon. "Perhaps there's not enough light to avoid it."

Shaking my head, I cleared my mind. "I was lost in thought, my friend. The past has a way of fogging the present, does it not?"

He smiled and patted me on the shoulder. "Perhaps you're not awake, my friend. Come, join me for tea! Tell me, where do you come from?"

I took the warm cup of herbal tea; a hint of rose hips and sage wafted from the mahogany-colored beverage. "I have just traveled back on the Silk Road."

"Silk Road?" The man's eyes widened. "You must have a death wish, my friend. I hear much bloodshed has painted that road as of late. Spies and backdoor dealings have turned the route into a place for assassins and no place for traders."

I nodded in agreement. "I fear it will only grow nastier if Justinian becomes emperor. His greed to take over the silk trade is known all the way back to China." I felt more awake as I sipped the tea. "Thank you for the tea."

"Ah, it is worth the price of news; there are few chances to talk about these things with the locals here and far fewer are willing to talk at all." He went about setting up his stand. "You should be careful. If the soldiers hear your thoughts on royalty, you might be run through."

I laughed. "They can try, but I doubt it would get them far."

"You're a strange one." He laughed in a failed attempt to hide his discomfort. "What brings you to Antioch?"

"You know, I'm not sure." I finished the last sip and placed the cup back on the tray. "Thank you, I feel more awake."

"What is your name?" We shook hands, starting the ritual of parting ways. "You seem like a worthy resource to have in my pocket."

"It's best you not know." I frowned. "My name brings destruction to those who whisper it."

I turned and left the merchant lost in my words. The sun crept higher, nearing mid-morning. I pulled my hood around my face and shifted the dagger in the small of my back to remain hidden as I walked the streets. They had confiscated my gladius at the gates; considering its gold and silver inlays, I knew it wouldn't be returned to me. It would become a general's new prize or a soldier's pocket money for a courtesan later. I paid well for the weapon, hoping to give the seller needed money for a better life. While it was presumptuous of me to throw coin out in waves like I did, I came across it easily.

Screams and alarmed yelps erupted ahead of me, and I froze. Rodents, cats, and dogs filled the street as they ran for their lives. My stomach turned: *earthquake.* Birds fled overhead, and I spun to observe a mule begin to fuss and neigh. The first and most dangerous quake would come any minute. I scanned around for an open space and ran for the field between the buildings and the amphitheater; it was coming.

Ba-Boom!

The earth roared, and the tremors started to build. Dust floated up, and the first stalls were falling. Dashing between the last two buildings, the walls cracked as the quaking culminated. My ears were filled with the rumbling of earth underfoot. The sound of falling buildings drowned out any screams as the world shifted in unnatural ways. As it peaked, I felt the first sickening signs that this was not a natural disaster.

A surge of power had been sent out from a place not far off. The unmistakable blue aura told me volumes. Hotan had caught up, and the innocent people of Antioch were caught in the cross-fire. My chest ached from the guilt of endangering them. *If I had I stayed isolated, just maybe they wouldn't have...* I swallowed down the regret, refusing to punish myself for my father's rage and ruthless actions. *He is committing this crime, and I have no reason to feel guilty for his actions.*

The earthquake subsided, and Antioch was on fire. All the glorious braziers brought on uncontrollable flames. Their grandiose appearance down the main streets which led to the many event areas came at a cost. Flames were building, and people were dying. Each death waved through me; my power indulged in taking count of the souls leaving the city. It made me sick as I stood on the hill and watched it burn and fade under a blanket of black smoke. Hotan was fast approaching; my hiding would have to end here this time.

I walked through, looking at bloodstained faces, mud-covered bodies, and the burning of all things living. Each time I bore witness to these traumas, it broke my heart further. *People shouldn't have to pay with their lives like this because of one person's greedy desires, rage, and despair.* I found the remnants of a wall jutting above the carnage and took my seat there to wait. Closing my eyes, I could sense his blue aura moving into the city over the rubble, not once slowing his approach. When I opened my eyes, Hotan stood before me.

"Was it necessary to destroy Antioch to find me?" Anger filled me. "To kill innocents for your own greed?"

"I was tired of chasing." He glared at me, those green eyes always piercing and filled with a madness I prayed to never understand. "It worked, did it not?"

"You're cruel. Do you not feel for those you've killed?" I swept my arm to the dead surrounding us as the smell of burning flesh filled the air. "Does this not bother you?"

"I have seen worse happen to my people." It was cold the way the words fell from his mouth. "They deserved this."

"You're over a thousand years old, Hotan." I stood, staring down at the greedy man before me. "None of these people deserved to be punished for people living only in your heart and mind who died centuries ago. When will your bloodlust know an end?"

"Silence!" he roared, shaking his head. "You know nothing! How dare you judge me!"

"All the deaths at your hand have never filled the void in your core or soothed your anguish. All the times you've killed me haven't brought her back, either." My words hit him like venom, and the twitching of his face spoke volumes. "Grow up. Take responsibility for your mistakes and learn to live your life."

"My life died with her," he hissed.

"Then allow me to live my life now." I threw out my arms and spun around. "I stopped chasing, only to find you biting my heels for a fight!"

"Because you might remember," he mumbled, taking a step closer. "I can't stand knowing that."

"Oh?" I lifted an eyebrow. "How greedy of you."

Growling, he launched himself up the rubble. This time, he brought a sword. I laughed. The blade punctured my hand, and it fell to ash. The blue flames seemed weaker than before, unable to deter the power of Death. I pulled my dagger, covered it with my power, and stabbed it into his shoulder. It bit into his flesh, fading a chunk to ash before he pulled it free and tossed it aside. As he gripped his wound, the flesh grew back shockingly fast, but it drained him to heal.

Blue flames roared to life over Hotan's body, and he shot a ball of fire toward me. My body reacted, and flames covered me as I threw my own. The impact from Rebirth and Death colliding sent a surge of power. I stepped back as the force hit me, knocking the air from my lungs. Hotan's feet slid, and he leaped to more stable ground. Debris shifted and dropped, smoke flattened, flames extinguished, and the air grew hot with power.

Seizing the opportunity, Hotan ran forward. A punch to my gut added to the breathless stinging in my chest. Fueled by anger, my knuckles connected with his jaw. He spun away, alarm on his face. I would not make it so easy to turn me to ash this time. I learned something from the little I remembered when I died in Scotia: our powers have overlapping qualities which compete for dominance. When he destroyed Antioch, he made my element supreme on the ground on which we fought. Hotan would have to abandon the Life part of Rebirth to attempt to make a scratch, and that scared me the most. I knew deep down, the moment he figured it out, he would abandon Life and embrace Death.

Hotan clenched his jaw and threw another punch. I blocked, ducking down to land a hit to his ribs. He shrunk back before leaping at me once more. I countered by flashing black flames to his face, forcing him back. Anything I could do to slow him down was worth the effort. The weight of the power we called forth crushed the earth beneath our feet. The flurry of punches was starting to bite away at one another; chunks of my arms and torso turned to ash. My heart raced, he had done the inevitable, and the power shifted to match my own. I was able to heal, and Hotan showed weakness, slowing to my speed.

With power and all my weight, I threw an unexpected kick to his torso. The connection thudded into him, cracking his bones and launching him into a half-fallen wall. The impact of his body left the clay cracked and dented. Coughing, blood dripping from his chin, he stumbled to his feet again. He panted from exertion but leapt inhumanly high above me. He came down, hands clasped and ready to strike me down, but I rushed forward, out of range. The impact of his fists made an explosive hole in the debris where I had stood, and I shuddered.

Before he could recover, I sprinted forward. As we exchanged blows, knuckles bled and bones fractured. Our bodies struggled to rebuild muscle and skin as other parts of flesh grayed and faded on the wind. It was exhausting; I was growing slower, but he was only getting faster. I attempted to strike him again but faltered. Hotan's fingers dug into my elbow, blue flames biting into me. I paled, struggling to pull away and create distance. The half-wrecked joint in my arm fell away to ashes with a pain far worse than muscle.

"Aargh!" Sweat poured across my face. "Was that necessary!"

The blue flames kept burning and crawling over my arm. My power struggled to fight them back. They extinguished, and my arm exploded into ash and was carried off by the wind. I found myself at a great disadvantage. He had changed tactics, aiming to destroy the joints and kill mobility of the limb. If I hadn't caught on, the flames would destroy the rest of the limb like an infection.

"Iapetos, we both know it'll grow back. You need to stop chasing me down in waves of destruction." Hotan was eerily calm as he stood tall, glaring at me. "I am trying to fix this…"

Why the act? Why the accusations and pretending as if I provoked this fight? Has his mind finally gone? Has he lost it completely? And how dare he claim…

"Fix this!" I growled, sweeping my remaining arm toward the destroyed city around us. "How does isolating me help fix this! You cast me off the island! You continue to abandon me despite knowing what you've done to me and this world!"

"You're not the only one I have wronged." Hotan's green glare shifted, and I turned to see silver eyes watching in horror.

I know him. His name is here in my mind just out of reach. I know his eyes and recognize the familiar emotions in them. He may not remember me either, but I know him and have been searching for him for so long.

The silver-haired stranger tensed under my glare. Confusion and recognition mingled on his face. He didn't think we had noticed his presence, but Hotan had seen him and changed his tone. Hotan's lies filled the air, and I wondered, *What memories of the person before me are hidden in my mind? How can Hotan manipulate us both to this extreme without guilt or shame?* The world fell silent. All eyes fell to silver-eyed man. I was filled with the sickening curiosity of one lingering, unspoken thought: *Will Hotan's manipulation win, or can this man break free to some extent and see the truth in this moment presented before him? I pray for the latter.*

"Who … who are you?" I couldn't stop myself from asking. "What else have you done, Father?"

"F-father?" The silver eyes fell to Hotan. "This is… you tried to…"

Hotan averted his eyes, looking to the ground in shame. The conclusion of father and child had come quickly. Hotan balled his hands into fists. I knew the stranger and I shared a bloodline, and the speed in which we connected the dots threatened Hotan. He marched toward me, and I leapt back. He was growing more powerful with his rising ire. He took a few steps closer, and I made another leap back. *He intends to finish me. In this moment, he has decided to kill me and paint more lies to this man who also haunts my dreams.* My head pounded, fighting to restore the stolen memories. *They still must be here: the man's name and who he is.* As Hotan came closer, my movements slowed and my mind became cloudy.

I can't die yet!

"Wait!" The man rushed between us, shielding me from Hotan. "We can work together! Hotan, you should not have to do this alone! This is why it has gone all so wrong in the first place, Brother!"

"Brother?" I asked, panting. Blood still dripped across the fallen walls at my feet. It was draining to grow an entire limb back at this rate. "What else are you hiding from me? From them?"

"Move, Talib." Hotan's voice carried a dark tone as he approached Talib. "I need more time and you both are slowing me down."

"Wait, what?" Talib froze as Hotan closed the gap between them. "You don't intend to…"

"Yes, he does," I screamed. "He would rather we take decades to regenerate, so he has his quiet time. Who knows how many times he has already done this so that we don't remember."

"No, it… it cannot be." Talib looked up in disbelief as things flooded his mind from deep within himself. "Why! Why do this?"

Hotan came within reach, and I gripped the back of Talib's shirt, yanking him back.

"You fool, don't let him touch you!" I shouted, throwing Talib back onto the debris.

Talib looked up at me, baffled. My anger faltered, and he could see the fear on my face. Hotan was hellbent on another attack. This was it; I had to stop him. Talib was back between us, and Hotan's fingers dug into his shoulder. I gritted my teeth. The pain and twist of Talib's face told me he could feel Hotan's power seeping into him. Deeper than just flesh and veins but to the unknown realm where one's soul was kept.

"Stop it," growled Hotan, sweat dripping from his chin as the internal battle waged between them. "I have to do this alone."

"No, no you do not." Panting, Talib eyed me, and I found myself in awe of his determination against Hotan. "If he is your son, then you need to take him under your wing, not battle against him. He is of our blood! At least leave the boy in my care!"

A wave of power pulsed from them. Blue and red auras mangled into a sickening purple. It was nothing my like power when it met Rebirth. We were like oil and water, but theirs merged into one another completely before attempting to take control. Every part of me felt ill. This was on another level, and I sensed Talib's objective.

"No." Hotan's answered harshly without hesitation.

Another pulse. The red flashed louder. It lashed out and graced my power, and I knew instantly what element had such strength over Hotan.

"You're Judgment…" The one thing that could change the tide and what Hotan feared most.

"Yes." Grimacing, Talib grew pale. "Unfortunately, I am losing. Leave this place! Find me somehow in the next life…"

Recognizing his intentions, I would do what was asked of me. "Thank you, my uncle."

Pulling forth my wings, I sneered at Hotan. He couldn't let go for fear Talib would overpower him. It was an opportunity I couldn't pass up. I knew this man's name and who he was. The pieces and fragments in my mind were pulling themselves together. His power waned, and I jolted to leap into the air.

"No!" Hotan roared as his power broke through, grasping Talib's soul and element into its control. "You will not flee!"

As if under a spell, I stopped. My body was no longer mine as I turned and fell inline beside Talib. Horror danced in my eyes, but Talib's eyes flickered with rebellious anger. We both shared the angry thought—*unforgivable.*

Hotan covered our faces with his hands, and his power seeped into both of us. "Please forgive me for this moment and so many more. I am so close to solving this; I need more time. One day you two will meet and become the pillars you need from each other. I, on the other hand, I need to fade from this world. I'm slowly destroying it with this unstable power of mine. Please, brother, my son, understand my intentions when you remember this time."

A searing pain crawled through my body. Searing heat filled my veins with the element of Rebirth. Under my father's palm, tears fell down my cheeks from the pain pushing inside me. Deep in his soul, I could still feel the tangled struggle of Talib's power trying to overthrow Hotan. My fingers grew numb, floating away on the wind. An aftershock shook my legs apart, and I no longer felt my appendages. I was gone—dead—as my body became ash, joining the flames of Antioch.

I woke on the desert beach. A crow stared at me, turning its head and cawing. I could barely remember my name, let alone how I ended up there. Fragmented memories flashed through me with every blink. Again, I found my mind broken, and whispers echoed into my being in the darkness of my mind. *Father. Hotan.*

Taking in a deep breath, I held it in frustration. I knew what I was—the element of Death. Years—no, centuries—of life and experience remained, but it was clear two entities had been scrubbed from my mind: Hotan and a man. My head swelled and ached. Sitting up, I cupped my face. All I wanted was to remember and know a face or a name.

"Talib," The crow's caw whispered like a siren's voice on the wind.

I turned as the black feathers took to the sky and left me naked in the desert sand. I closed my eyes, and I saw an aura.

"Ah, another immortal." I sighed. "It's me, my damned father, Talib, and the crow."

IO

BE SOMEBODY

Groaning, Iapetos found his body sore for the first time in ages. Images rushed through his mind before his eyes fluttered to life, staring at the ceiling fan in a strange landscape as it turned in a steady silence. Taking in a slow inhale, confusion wrapped itself around his thoughts. Flickering moments of anger and hope taunted his emotions one way then the other. Shifting his head to the side, a window adorned with white lacy curtains and generic white blinds kept the sunlight at bay. Snorting, he urged his body to sit up. Muscles were locked up and unwilling. Grunting, his head spun with another wave of memories, vertigo slowing his efforts further.

"The dizzy spells are the worst." Talib's voice cut through his thoughts, catching a frustrated glance from Iapetos. "I thought I heard the bed creak; I see you've woken up."

Iapetos squinted his eyes. "I should be alarmed, but I don't know who I am or where I stand as a person, if I can even call myself that."

Talib walked around the bed and sat in the chair. "I agree. There is no label for what we are, is there?"

"He took so much from us both." For once, the cold, black pools shifted to reveal silver flecks scattered like broken glass on asphalt throughout his eyes. "Still, I feel like a child in an adult's body, vulnerable and naked."

"That is an honest assessment." Leaning back in the chair, Talib glared outside between the slits of the blinds. "Your own father took away every chance you had to be your own person. He even stole times when you were on the verge of becoming something more than lost in his shadow. One can never learn to grow into anything more than a cesspool of self-doubt and rage when gagged, bound, and caged."

"You were always poetic with your words." Iapetos tired of the rebuttal his body gave him and laid back down. "What the hell did you do?"

"I returned the favor." His stare was still elsewhere as if expecting someone to pull into the driveway. "You put me on the verge of death, and it shook it all loose. I knew it would take that much to free you from the same spell. You are welcome."

With a groan, he looked helplessly at the ceiling fan. "And where is the boy?"

"Your son," Talib corrected, turning his gaze back to Iapetos with cold intent. "Your son is somewhere safe for the time being."

"Safe," repeated Iapetos. "So the chaos on Mt. Pelée was all for him to be reborn?"

"You are mistaken." Again, he amended Iapetos's words and thoughts. "Your father is dead. While your son has inherited his grandfather's looks and powers, that is where it ends, nothing more."

Iapetos's stare met Talib's, both of their faces tensed. "Are you so sure?"

"I am absolute on that fact."

Warm fingers shoved strands of silver hair from Hotan's face. The tickling of the touch brought him back from the calm of sleep. Retrieving her hand with haste, Abigail's cheeks were red as she caught his stare. His eyes fell to her lap where the white rose laid. Lifting his brow, he looked to her face with questioning intent, and her entire face blossomed from her blushing. He knew what he was seeing, and it sent a tangled array of emotions into a panic. There was no mistaking her affection, but his skepticism took hold.

"Do you like me, or is it because I look like him?" The words hit like ice against the ground.

Abigail stiffened, the color draining from her face. "Is that what you think is happening?"

Sitting up, Hotan leaned on his knees. "I don't know. It seems weird you followed him for all that time, and now that he's gone, you meander around me. I'm nothing more than his doppelgänger, but since that night when you... when we kissed..."

She closed her eyes, the words pouring from her without hesitation, "I'd be lying if I said I didn't hope to find a way to have the former Hotan love me. At some point, I even entertained pursuing Iapetos."

Hotan shifted, drowning in regret for pressing for answers he realized he didn't want to hear. *Even Iapetos...*

"But that would have been a fool's errand, an empty love." Her eyes opened, stinging as they forced him to accept the answers unfolding. "I saw how you treated Shellie, and I was envious and angry. There was no doubt you two cared for one another deeply, but what you had was a temporary need being filled with someone safe."

His lips parted, but his teeth clenched the words back into submission. *As much as I want to argue, to deny it, she's right. How we ended up together was just a means of security and keeping one another on the path we wanted to be on. It was a way to cover the painful gaps we had in our lives. It hurts to admit it now that Shellie's gone. In the end, I am thankful we made amazing memories for one another. If I had just known how short her time was… if I could have saved her from Geliah…*

"Neither you nor anyone here could have known what would come of the poor girl." Abigail swallowed, her face mottled as tears welled in her eyes. "Don't suffocate in the things you should have done. Be thankful for the time spent. She was fortunate to have you to hold hands with, to talk to, and even lean on when needed. Few get that at her age."

"Then who am I to you?" The muscles in his forearms twitched with building anger.

"You. Simply *you*, Hotan." Tears fell from her eyes like glass marbles. "I didn't know she would lose her life, but that night at Talib's, I wanted to give my first kiss away, and you were the first worthy person. A part of me was still yearning for *him*, but when our lips touched, when we kissed, there was something there. I don't know how to describe it."

"But I kissed you because you looked like Shellie. It was a desperate and small motion you put into play." Hotan's fingers folded into his palms, the white-knuckled fists preparing for the emotional hits flying between them. "You cornered me because you missed *him*."

"Have you forgotten? You asked me to change my looks!" The tears were endless as her face shattered, giving way to heartbreak. "You asked me to look like her! The moment I realized you weren't kissing her the same way I had watched a million times from the shadows, I pulled away!"

"I…" His mind sent him back in time, trying to recall it. *The black cat, the doll-like child, and then I asked that of her. Her lips… she looked like Shellie, but that sensation of loneliness ebbed into me.*

"I pulled away because even though I looked like the person you loved, the kiss wasn't the same." She bit her bottom lip, choking back her sobs to continue her swings of heartache. "You kissed me as a lover would. It was a kiss intended for me. Shouldn't I be asking you why? Was it because I looked like her, or was it sincere that night, Hotan? You tell me!"

Regret slammed into his chest, knocking the wind from his lungs. "I…"

"You have never kissed her the way we kissed that night." Her lips trembled, the heat of her eyes burning into his soul.

"There was something so familiar, so different…" He paused, unsure of what he thought he had felt at the start of all this. "A kindred spirit just as lonely as I was…"

"Was it the same!" Abigail shrieked with eyes closed tight. "TELL ME!"

Hotan's heart pounded. She had turned his rage on him, and his eyes fell downward in shame. Her fingers crushed the white rose blossom. Abigail trembled, eyes tight, waiting for the truth. It had never been about her fascination with the old Hotan. She had lost interest well before the modern day. Hotan's lips parted, but only a frustrated huff fell out. Looking back to his fists, his back ached under the building tension as she whimpered. Abigail waited for his answer.

The news of her fate rattled me, but that wasn't it. She did what I had asked, even though she petitioned a kiss in exchange for healing me. Is this what she meant that night when she said I gave her more than I should have? Is this the warning she whispered?

A flood waved over him, and he needed to know for himself. Closing the small gap between them, his hands cupped either side of her jaw. The heat of his touch made her eyes snap open, and she gasped. He pressed his own lips hard against hers, warm and soft. A rush of emotions from deep within his core came spilling forth. No longer did sorrow ebb from their connection. He pressed harder, the kiss turning passionate for a lingering second before she shoved him back.

They stared wide-eyed at one another as the rose fell to the ground between them. She covered her lips, unsure why he had answered her in such a way. Hotan realized he had twisted everything from that faithful night. Guilt and anger no longer mattered. His exchange with Abigail was different in both mind and heart. It didn't make him love Shellie any less, but someone far more compatible stood before him. Grabbing her hands in his, he leaned his forehead on their hands.

"I'm sorry," he mumbled, breathlessly. "No, I didn't give you the same kiss that I'd given Shellie so many times."

"Why did you…" The tears slowed from her shock.

"I had no other way of knowing. My emotions are so broken from all that's happened, and I needed to know…" He pulled her hands down, and they locked eyes. "You're not a replacement for Shellie, and I'm not a replacement for Hotan. Just be patient; give me time. Compared to everyone, I'm still learning to walk on my own."

Shaking her head, she gave a small smile.

Letting go of her hands, he reached up to her face, wiping the tears away. "I should have never made you cry. I'm sorry I wasn't seeing everything; I can be blind to my own emotions. Perhaps that's always been part of the problem."

II

CARELESS WHISPER

1157 AD Hama

Someone had been leaving me notes. A crow whispered in my ear on occasion; other moments, a black cat appeared, and I would follow it to capture the clues I yearned for. It was difficult to find any hints of Hotan and Talib, but I persisted after the two men who were connected to me and held answers about the dreaded immortal life I lived. We all had never-ending lives, as did the shapeshifter who left me the breadcrumbs behind their trail.

As I searched, I found sparks of power igniting inside mortals all over the world. As the decades passed, they reincarnated, and I kept watch on these individuals. In the last few decades, hints of power seeped from them, and I realized Hotan had done something to them. There were more immortals—or had been more at some point. This was the reason he ran from me or hunted me down. Occasionally, the crow left journal pages with details of this mysterious past.

In my hand, I opened the paper once more. *Hama.* It had suffered foreshocks for over a year, and the chance Hotan's power caused them seemed likely. He hadn't chased me down, but something in my gut told me he had taken what he wanted from me. I stood in the desert's heat, staring down at Hama, wondering if it was the last day it would stand. My desire and want for answers grew, but Hotan's rage and reputation for destruction terrified me.

The crow landed on my shoulder. It whispered, "Talib has entered the city as well. You must find him. Hotan is angry."

Before I could ask anything else, the bird fled like so many times before. Frustrated, I squatted and peered down. Horses at the outer city wall danced, tugging on their hitches. I waited for the impending earthquake. The rumbled vibrated through the sand under me. Columns of dust rose as the shaking grew with alarming speed. I lost my balance, landing on my rump as I watched the city break apart. The Al-Rahba fortress shattered like a clay pot. All of Syria would feel the rage of nature.

As the quake subsided, a few columns of smoke lifted to the sky. I was thankful it wasn't like the fires in Antioch or Helike. Over the last five hundred years, I had worked hard to remember details from those times, trying my best to tiptoe around the parts and details of Hotan. When I dared, it brought mind-numbing pain. It was under Hotan's lock and key. Standing to my feet and brushing sand from me, I took a moment to close my eyes. *There!* I could see blue and red auras together. For the first time, I was the harrowing sign of Death and flew my way to them. *I must be quick.*

As I glided over, people shrieked, fleeing the city as my shadow cast over them. *At least this improves their chances of survival.* None of them knew the real monster was just below me, taking off his mask and dressed like an assassin.

"H-Hotan!" I could hear Talib's shocked voice as I circled in, lower and lower. "Why are you here in Hama?"

"It doesn't matter; I need your power." Hotan gripped Talib, and I dove hard, hearing his words and knowing he was prepared for me. "Sorry to have to do this again…"

"Again?" Talib questioned, but it was too late. Hotan's power gripped Talib's, taking over the element of Judgment.

Fear rattled me; ceasing my descent, I turned tail. I couldn't win against his abuse of the element of Judgment. I feared I was still too close to escape now.

"Iapetos…" The fiery rage in Hotan's voice made it clear I wasn't free from his reach. "You will come back here. Now!"

Against my will, my body did as he commanded. I flanked a hard left and dropped inline beside Talib. Déjà vu washed over me, and I felt ill. This wasn't the first instance. Talib struggled against the soul-crushing control within him, but I felt him pulling everything together. Each time, he knew and didn't feel right. We were the same in this infernal scuffle to reclaim our memories—our identities. Fearing Hotan would realize someone had fed me information, I feigned ignorance.

"Who is he?" I flared my wings and gave an intimidating glare toward Talib. "Is this how you forced me back here?"

"It doesn't matter; I have no time to chase you." An aftershock was causing the debris to creak and crumble around them. Hotan's frustrated tone continued, "Now, come here, grab hold of Talib."

Sweat dripped down my temple. Without hesitation, my body reacted against my will. Talib tried desperately to break the bond. His lips twisted, unable to open. Hotan denied him the right to talk or protest these actions. As our eyes met, I gripped his shoulder. My power surged forward, and Talib gasped.

Tightening my hold, my heart raced as the strings of the element of Death invaded him.

"I'm sorry for this." I looked upon him with pity as guilt weighed down on my heart. "I know what he intends to do, and I will not go down without a fight."

Grimacing, Talib's soul tangled in a battle of life and death as he struggled to push both entities out—Death and Rebirth. I tugged on my end, pushing Judgment out and pulling Death back into myself. We both yearned to be the masters of our own souls. It was exhausting. Muscles tight, my body was growing weaker. The struggle took a toll on Hotan, and we all three fell to our knees. Talib pushed us to the edges of his core. I gave it my all to pull and overturn the direction to aid him. My body ached with the tension it held. Talib panted as he reached over to Hotan's hand, trying to pry it from his shoulder.

Hotan's fingers dug harder, gritting his teeth, glaring at Talib. "You don't understand…"

"I am not your tool to win wars with!" Blue flames were crawling across Talib, his tattoo curling around him like stripes on a tiger. "How many times have you done this to me already?"

Does he remember?

Frantically, I poured my power through Talib, aiming to drive the last of Rebirth from him. It was a risk; the pain it may cause would only be temporary, but I had to try something. Hotan's eyes broke away from Talib and met my heated stare. The element of Death shifted, helping push out the last remaining throngs of Rebirth from his core. When I felt the last piece of Rebirth leave his body, I dissolved my own. Before Talib could catch his breath, I pulled him away, increasing his distance from Hotan. The look he shot Hotan said volumes. Rage filled him, and he broke from my grip. Talib stood tall, jaw muscles twitching from the anger boiling within him. Blue fames taller and wider than the buildings which still stood poured from him. Hotan marched toward us. He had become a monster far worse than I imagined; his power still attempting to destroy his own brother.

"Answer me!" Talib's flames shifted from blue to red. Judgment had overpowered the last of Rebirth and burnt it from his system. "How many times!"

"This is the seventh time." Hotan avoided making eye contact with him as he failed to resist the element of Judgment. "If you intend to ask why, I willingly answer that I intend to kill you both to buy myself more time to fix my element."

I shot Talib a look. "That doesn't justify casting me, your only son, off the island."

"You were a mistake." The coldness in Hotan's reply was painful even to Talib. "I was grieving, aiming to bring your mother back. Instead, I created the element of Death. You shouldn't even exist."

Wrath consumed Talib. Marching up to Hotan, Talib punched him. His fist locked with Hotan's jaw. *CRACK!* Two teeth bounced across the ground. Hotan didn't flinch. *Or was it that he couldn't under Judgment's grip?* No signs of pain or sound came from his lips; he didn't even take a step back from the impact. Instead, his own markings crawled across his skin. Hotan had tired of being under the weight of Judgment and was pushing it from his body. Talib's control swayed, and my panic surged.

"Back away or he will take—" I was too late; Hotan grabbed Talib's throat.

The hand on his throat tightened, and Talib's flames fell away. Desperately, he gripped onto Hotan's arm, hoping to pull it away. He clawed at him, but his fingers burst into ashes. Terror filled Talib. He peered up into the wild madness of Hotan's glowing green eyes, blood dripping down his chin. Talib's body turn to ash and floated away.

"You left me no choice. I can't have you slow me down here, Talib." Hotan turned his attention back to me. "This is your fault."

I couldn't calm the beating of my heart. "You hunted him down and came after me with ill intent. Look to yourself for the blame."

He lunged forward, and I took to the air. Slamming him with a ball of black flames, I fled far and away. *For now, I will hide and wait for Talib to be born again while staying out from under Hotan's glare. At least this time when we met, we remembered. I pray Hotan doesn't find Talib before I do yet again.*

1350 London

My power had grown stronger, and I was losing my ability to control it. The Black Plague was ravaging the masses in my wake. Everywhere I stepped foot, people fell ill, and I knew deep down it was because I couldn't contain the power which poured out from my immortal body. I turned to the only person I knew capable of stopping me—Hotan. The crow had been reluctant when I asked. It stared blankly at me, and it was weeks before it returned with an answer.

"London," it cawed once like a whisper and left.

I wasted no time packing what little things I needed to leave. It was the last time I would see the mountain villages of China, which had been my home for longer than expected. Traveling across the continent, the wake of Black Plague followed. By the time I reached London, the state of the city startled me. The scourge wrecked the lives of the living well before I arrived. My stomach twisted; the answer was clear.

Hotan's powers were barreling out of control and eating away at Life. *Has he fallen too far into the side of Death and sent my own power awry by doing so? Why abandon half your powers for one side which is already controlled by another?*

"Is this why you took so long to answer me, crow?" It flew down and sat on my shoulder. "I see I'm not the only one to blame. What was he thinking staying someplace so populated? Do you want me to do something about his presence here?"

"Yes." It fluttered off.

Leaving the docks behind, I walked the streets of London and absorbed the mayhem. Piles of bodies filled the streets and courtyards. Heavily covered men came by with wagons to carry them off to burning piles elsewhere, far away from the living. Doctors wandered door-to-door wearing inhuman plague masks. Several times, I was stopped on the streets and encouraged to wear one, but I refused. Death was immune to ailments, even ones created in its wake. If refusing a mask provided one to someone who needed it to protect themselves, then I had helped on some level.

Leaving behind the wealthier section, I meandered through the more desolate areas. They burned the piles there, no longer able to keep up with removing the bodies. Men tossed one body after another onto the raging flames of corpses. Pulling my hood over, I pulled up my scarf to shield my mouth from the ashes blowing across the district like morbid gray snow. I stole a moment to watch. Leaning against the corner of a nearby building, I took in the sight. *How could my father allow his power to seep and wreck the lives of innocents to this degree?* I felt death unfolding all over the city and the weight of the departing souls.

Does this make you feel empowered? Do you relish in the high this brings you, you sick bastard?

Hands gripped the back of my coat. A sickening sensation washed over me as I sensed she didn't have long. Turning around, I found the girl, pale and thin. Rosy rings and boils painted her body. It was a wonder she was able to stand, let alone walk out into the street. Her bright, revealing dress caught my attention. Considering I had wandered into an area called Farringdon Without, she had to be a local prostitute for hire. She tilted her head back to expose her face, and my breath caught in my throat. Those familiar lily yellow eyes with orange flecks had found me again.

"Reincarnation?" I muttered, not sensing any power within her.

"Forgive me," she croaked, letting go to lean on the lamp post. "I was, I was…"

Coughing consumed her, and she slid to her knees. She spat blood across the ground and turned her gaze to the fire raging across the street. I squatted, fascinated by her.

"I suppose I'll be joining them soon." She gave a faint smile and turned. "Either the plague or consumption. I suppose it'll be both that kills me."

"And you can still smile?" The stare she gave me told me of the exhaustion eating away the last of her life.

"Ah, were you one of my clients?" A hint of recognition hit her eyes, and my heart stopped. "No, no, you couldn't have been."

"Why not?" I mused, remembering Pompeii's kiss and the life her eyes held in Antioch.

"Because you're…" She searched my face, losing her words.

I offered my hand to her. "Where are you going? I'll take you there."

Sighing, she shoved my hand away and used the lamp post to pull herself up. "I don't need pity from the likes of you."

"Who do you think I am?" The sickness had darkened her mind, but she blushed and laughed a moment.

"Why you're…" She lunged forward, coughing and sputtering for a long time. Wiping the blood from her lips, she found the strength to spin back and finish. "You're the Angel of Death."

I paled, the amusement fading from my face.

"Ha!" She grinned. "I knew it had to be you. It was only a matter of when and where." She lifted her skirts, showing a flashy new pair of shoes. "I put them on. I knew you'd be coming, so I dressed up and pulled myself off the bed, I did. Damn it all to Hell if I die like the other girls."

I couldn't help smiling at the absurd tenacity of it all. "They are nice shoes."

She lost her grip on the post, and I caught her in my arms. "I didn't mean to be a bother."

"Bother? I thought you said I was the Angel of Death?" She trembled, clinging onto me as she pressed herself into my chest.

"You're not supposed to be so damn warm." Muttering into me, she hid her face from me. "I thought you were supposed to be cold as ice."

"Afraid not." I wrapped my arms around her, the soul within her stricken body clinging hard to what little life she had left. "If you take care of yourself, you might last a week."

"I'm scared." Her breathing sped up, panic filling her voice. "But like in my dreams, here you are. If you can take me now, get it over with."

My heart ached; the request was one I had never endured before. "Are you sure?"

"I wouldn't have asked otherwise." She sniffled. After a long silence, she looked up with a mournful stare. "Just promise I won't be left on the street or in a bed to rot. Throw me to the fires."

My fingers brushed the sweat-soaked hair from her forehead. The rings had ravaged her skin and her lips were cracked. Still, under the facade of her dying body, I saw her soul, bright as ever. This was the same woman who had left me stunned and dazed so many times before; there was no mistaking it. Pulling down my scarf, I leaned down, daring to steal a kiss. Her hand stopped me.

"You can't." The trembling started again. "This bloody plague has me smelling as ripe as the dead ones." She dug in her pockets, and petals from lilies and rose hips fell to the ground. A chunk of cypress followed them, clanking against the cobblestones. "I was supposed to use posies, but…"

My lips pressed against hers. Without thinking, she returned the kiss. Releasing my power, I cut the ties between life and death. She fell limp in my arms, and her body went cold as my lips pulled away. Scooping her up, I marched to the fires and tossed her shell into the flames of freedom. I stood, watching her flesh curl and blacken in the monstrous heat.

I wondered as I walked away. *If it had been another life, could we have been happy together?*

I walked down alleys and through streets. Doors to houses were ajar, revealing the scenes inside. Beds were emptied; some of them were stripped, burning with their dead. Night had fallen, and the skies glowed orange with fire; the dark shadows cast across the streets made London a living nightmare. Some of the sick did as the girl had done—wandered around, hoping to bring enough attention so not to rot in secret in some hovel. It was more of a plea. Some even walked silently into the fires without a scream leaving them.

A black cat skirted out from under a broken pile of crates. It circled back, weaving between my legs. The yellow eyes and the ebb of the shapeshifter's powers caught my attention. I squatted down, curious where it came from. As I reached for it, it scampered just out of reach, tail flicking in annoyance. I stood and followed it through the streets. We came down a quiet section where doctors patrolled, checking the houses.

She dashed through a cracked door. Someone had left it open in a rush. I lost sight of the cat, but I could see where the steps fled down the flight of stairs. The first floor was bare, but a light glowed above. Easing my way up the steps, I paused at the door. Peeking in, no one was there. I spun around the room in hopes of anything catching my eye. A journal lay on the floor, half hidden by the bed. Picking it up, my heart thudded in my ears. This was Hotan's journal. The cat peered around the door frame, mewing for my attention.

"You're not really a cat, are you?" I huffed. "Thank you for helping me find this journal."

Afraid Hotan would return in search for it, I headed back the way I came. I froze at the top of the stairs. A man stood before me, wearing plague doctor attire. I knotted my brow. *How many times did we pass each other in the streets? We were this close the whole time.* The cat leapt to the railing as a little girl's giggling filled the air. I opened my mouth to speak, but nothing surfaced.

Is it Talib or Hotan under that mask?

"Who are you and what power do you have?" Talib commanded at last. "My name is Talib, and like you, I am immortal."

"Talib." I peered down to the journal in my hand, its red leather cover catching his eye. "You're Hotan's brother…"

"Yes." He softened his tone. "Is that written in that book there?"

"That, and more about my father." I mused. *He is far less alarmed than I expect from him.* "My name is Iapetos. Has he ever mentioned me to you?"

"No. I have not seen Hotan since the fourth century." I frowned, and he matched it, both of us feeling deep down that the information was wrong. "Who is your father?"

"Hotan." Again, Talib's eyes dropped to the book in my hands. "But he says nothing about me in this journal. I see he has even abandoned you…"

"Y-yes." I could see it in his eyes how Talib's mind unraveled; the determination pushed forward without understanding the drive behind it. "And, Iapetos, do you know your element?"

My mind filled with flashes of the girl; the coldness of her lips still lingered on my own. I whispered, "Death."

Talib pulled back his hood, unbuckling the leather strap and removing the plague mask. Iapetos stared wide-eyed at the silver-eyed man with long silver hair. He wiped the sweat from his face. Without a doubt, he had been working moments before. I watched his eyes dance side to side as thoughts flew in his mind. The tension in my body released, though the idea Hotan could still discover us had my heart racing. I took another step down, and it prompted his next question for me.

"Iapetos, would it be safe to assume this Black Plague is your doing?" He sighed, sounding like a teacher who had finished his evaluation of a student. "I imagine your element is difficult to control, being it is a segment of Rebirth itself…"

"In theory, this plague started when I got close to Hotan." Swallowing, I dared to explain what I barely understood myself. "It used to be in the form of earthquakes, but something has changed. As I got closer to him, people were getting horribly sick. Not knowing if there were any other immortals in existence, I felt the need to seek him out. I ended up here in London. A small black cat led me here, and I found this journal explaining there are more of us, but I'm nowhere in this…"

"Then how do you know you are Hotan's son?" Talib narrowed his eyes at me, his suspicion growing. "Have you even met Hotan?"

I covered my face trying to recall a memory, but the headache surfaced, biting at my soul. "I remember being someplace dark and choking, the ocean's salt bitter on my tongue and stinging in my lungs. There in that abyss, I heard him calling for my mother, Liora. She looked at me and told me she would give me life so that my father may have the son he prayed for … but then I found myself banished, naked and afraid … alone and angry. I, I feel as if I have seen him, but I can't remember as if it's locked away. It hurts trying to even attempt to look within myself for him."

The plague mask dropped at his feet, tumbling down the stairs. Its potpourri flung across the steps, and Talib stumbled back, leaning against the wall. My words had struck true. He also felt the pain of trying to remember certain moments in the past. Maybe some part of him knew memories were missing—somehow stolen by his brother.

"What has he done to us?" He looked to the ceiling, and I knew he felt the unease within his soul too. "Hotan, what are you doing to us? Have we met many times before and you've broken us apart? Why do we both feel like we've seen one another and spoken?"

"Yes, I feel like I can trust you, as if you've done something for me…" I gripped the book tighter, pouring myself open to him. "Is it possible I have discovered his journals in the past and he's been cautious not to write about me this time?"

"It would be something he would do…" Talib rubbed the back of his neck, pondering this before he realized something. "Abigail, are you still here?"

"Abigail?" I searched the room below, alarmed. "You weren't alone?"

The black cat raced back up the stairs from the shadows again. Giggling like a small child, it weaved through Talib's legs.

"I beg you, please at least talk to me." Furrowing his brow, Talib pleaded with her. "Was it not you who led us here?"

She paused, her little yellow eyes looking up at me then back to him, "Yes, I did."

"Who is she?" The hair on the back of my neck stood on end. It was the first time I had heard the voice of a girl and not the cawing whispers of a crow. "What is she?"

"Iapetos, this is Abigail, the element of Body." She sat and licked her paw. "My dear, why have you brought us here?"

"To give you two a chance to remember." She ran up the stairs pass me and stopped at the doorway. "For centuries, I have watched Hotan destroy you two, hoping to buy more time to undo his power. It has only caused more destruction and is now distorting everyone's power. The journal must stay in exchange for not having your memories wiped. He will return soon enough and wonder who has been in here."

We looked to one another, shuddering at her words—destroy you. The truth of it made my bones ache and my soul twist. Looking to the book in my hands, I turned, marched across the room, and placed it back how I found it. This wasn't the time to be greedy. I already knew the answers I wanted laid within Talib's mind, not the distorted perspective of a broken man who spent centuries covering his mistakes, including my existence. It was clear; I would make this choice for us both.

"I'd rather give up my search for him and join you in your travels." Marching down the stairs, I picked up the mask and handed it to him. "If we can make distance from him, my element should stop killing at this rate. I apologize for my numbness to the damage it causes."

"Understood." Peering down at his mask, Talib agreed. "We will leave London and find a safe haven to exchange information. Perhaps we have answers for one another."

"Something tells me we do." We headed for the door but paused, looking to the black cat. "What about her?"

He pulled his hood over his silver hair, strapping his mask on before he answered, "She stays with him, always. Someone has to keep a record of the damage he continues to do to himself and the world."

The door thumped shut behind us, and I followed Talib's lead. We weaved through the ashen streets with only the eerie orange glow of the fires to light our way. After making several turns and walking blocks away from where we left Abigail, we came to Talib's door. He threw an arm out to signal for me to stop. Locking eyes, he pointed to the ashen ground where fresh steps led inside. A cautious look over the door told us someone had forced it open. We paled, the same sickening twist in our guts. Hotan waited inside for Talib. It was hard to say if he was aware we had made contact, but we couldn't risk facing him.

Shaking his head, Talib pointed to go further down the block, motioning to be quiet. Looking to the windows, we prayed Hotan wouldn't see us pass. The windows were dark, and the falling ash was thick enough to cover our tracks. Picking up pace, we marched toward the harbor. Talib peered over his shoulder at me several times as if surprised I had followed him without hesitation or voicing any rebuttal. *Even if Hotan had watched us walk away, we looked like doctors searching houses for bodies. As of late, he avoided me at all costs.* The dock creaked under our steps. A sleeping sailor waited at the end with his feet propped on a crate near a flickering lantern.

"You there." Talib's voice sounded ominous as it bellowed from within the cone beak.

There was no reply besides the man shifting himself before continuing to snore. Kicking the heels from their perch, the sailor stumbled to his feet, swinging wild and angry. Talib caught the man's forearm, slamming a heavy pouch of gold coins into his palm. The man broke free, opening the bag to count how much it held. I smiled; to see my uncle and I had something in common was entertaining. Part of me felt proud and hopeful.

I see he chooses the same concept—throw around enough coin, and everything comes to you easier. I wonder if he feels like he's helping them too?

"You two looking to get the hell out of London?" Placing the bag inside his coat, he whistled long and loud. "We've got ourselves two more bunkmates!"

"Aye…" grumbled someone on the ship.

After a long moment of silence, a plank banged against the dock. It didn't matter whether this ship took us to Spain, Italy, Africa or even India; all that mattered was gaining distance from Hotan. With discipline, Talib could help me stop the spread of the Black Plague. The deck of the ship was filled with barrels marked with the ship's guild mark on them. I lifted an eyebrow, running a finger across one. Many of the guilds didn't allow backdoor deals, let alone last-minute passengers without the guild master's approval. Not even a captain had the authority to sign off on anyone, no matter how high they paid. It was a sacred trust between the crew and the guild master. Strict tracking of the people on board was a way to protect funding and supplies. It also guaranteed everything ran smoothly and the trade would be profitable.

A sailor with a lantern coughed under his bandanna, waving them into the Captain's Cabin. The weathered old man popped the cork off a bottle of scotch, cursing under his breath. He glanced up groggily as he finished filling his glass. Taking down the sharp liquid, he banged the glass against the desk, sending a rolled-up map tumbling to the floor. I grabbed Talib's shoulder, but he motioned to leave it to him.

"Exactly who do you think you are you that you can buy passage on a guild-owned ship?" He snorted a grotesque sound deep in the back of his throat. "Not to say I don't blame you for wanting a ship out of this hell hole."

Talib unbuckled the coned masked, a coy smile across his face. "What if the guild master wishes to ride his own ship?"

The old man squinted his eyes, and Talib let the hood fall down on his shoulders. "Well, by God, it is you."

"You're a guild master?" I had carried a lot of coin, but Talib had taken it further and was running full international operations. "Why on earth would you bother?"

Rasping laughter came from the captain as he rose to his feet, shaking Talib's hand. "It's been a while. I can't thank you enough for the investment and chance you took on me, sir."

"I see you are taking my advice to heart, old man." Chuckling, Talib sighed before turning his attention back to me. "This is … my apprentice. I wish one day for him to take my place. Until then, he will need many years of hands-on experience in all parts of the business."

"Aye, aye." He shook my hand, looking me over with great interest. "Is he your nephew?"

Talib blinked, peering over before answering with caution. "Why, yes. How on earth did you know?"

The old captain tapped at his temple with a warm smile. "These eyes aren't as good as they used to be, but the genes in your family are strong. You two are built from head to toe like toy soldiers meant to stand side-by-side. Even your chin and browline match."

"We will leave you be, Captain." Talib opened the door, motioning for me to follow. "Sorry to disturb you at such an hour."

"It's not every day I meet the guild master." Chuckling, he poured himself another round. "Glad to see you in good health, despite the fall of London."

Talib nodded, a grim look across his paling face. He walked across the deck, looking for a quiet spot on the railing on the other side of the barrels crowding the ship. I marched close behind him. The crew members took no heed in where we were going. Making it to the rail, I gripped Talib's shoulder. Part of me wanted to make sure he was there by my side.

"Exactly what is your plan?" I swept an arm to the ship. "Are we to hide on this vessel and pray Hotan doesn't find us?"

"Not exactly." Talib pushed my hand off and leaned on the railing. "We first need to take you some place far from people to master your powers. The wilds of India, Africa, anywhere such as that should be fitting for the task."

"And what if he follows?" I paced, the thought of being chased making me uneasy. "Hunts us down?"

"He will not," Talib murmured. "I think if we stay clear of him and do not meddle in his tasks, we should be safe. He will avoid us, and we will oblige."

"Then what is this plan? What else do you intend to do with me?" I paused, glaring at his back.

"I will teach you everything I know." Straightening himself, Talib locked eyes with me, sunlight flashing in his silver eyes. "Who we were, when we became immortal, how I survived all this time with no one, and how to use that dreadful curse attached to your soul."

I couldn't stop the smile growing on my face. We both relaxed as we listened to the sailors shouting and dropping the sails. Talib had accepted me with little effort, and for the first time, I wasn't alone. There were no other obligations or hidden agendas. Just two immortals searching for answers and companionship in someone who understood the tribulations we faced.

12

HONEST

"Why did you bring me here?" Iapetos followed close behind Talib as they entered the church. "Please don't tell me you think I need saving."

"Technically, yes, but not in the religious sense." Talib sighed, waving Lucius over. "I want to introduce you to a friend of mine."

"I don't think a priest can do much for me." Iapetos murmured, slipping into a pew to sit down. "But this is quite the impressive piece of architecture. It's been a long, long time since I sat in one so exquisite."

"Thank you." Talib shifted his stance and straightened his tie. "I commissioned this in the early starts of the town. Granted, it was a broken heap until Hotan's powers came out for the first time."

"First time?" The expression on Iapetos's face shifted to a colder tone. "Why fix a church?"

"That wasn't the intent." Leaning on the pew behind him, Talib crossed his arms. "He was defending himself against the element of Fear. A young boy being chased down with a machete invokes fight or flight. It was only natural it would shake lose the element of Rebirth since Geliah was forcing his powers onto him."

"So, he was never aware he had powers at the start?" Iapetos tilted his head back, staring at the carvings in the rafters above.

"Never knew. Even after that incident, he didn't realize what was happening to him." Pulling himself off the pew, he greeted Lucius with a hug. "Sorry for the intrusion, Lucius."

"It's always a pleasure to see a familiar face." Pulling away, Lucius looked to the man in the pew. "And who might this be?"

"Iapetos." He stood, reaching over the rows to shake hands. "Lucius, was it?"

"Yes. You look familiar. Have we met?" Iapetos eyed Talib, the atmosphere shifting.

"He's family." Talib's words dropped like a brick into Lucius' ears. "This is my nephew and Hotan's father."

Iapetos's expression went sour. "That's rather bold."

"Then this is…" Lucius's blue gaze shifted between the two men for a minute before he brought his fist to his lips, deep in thought. "Element of Death, I reckon."

"Lucius is the element of Light." Talib walked away. "I'll be leaving you two to talk. I have some matters to take care of over at the high school next door regarding Hotan's records."

"Oh, okay." Blinking, Lucius looked to Iapetos who fell back into the pew with an annoyed look on his face. "Talib's never been good with words, to be honest."

"Or direction." Iapetos said, feeling flustered. "Sorry to interrupt your priestly duties."

"I welcome distraction on occasion." Lucius motioned, asking if he may sit, and Iapetos reluctantly slid over. "It's not that I mean to pry, but I pity you for carrying such a heavy element."

"I never thought of it as heavy." Iapetos snorted, his stare falling on the winged crucifix. "It's a curse, a mark of exile and my inability to be accepted by the world and my father."

Grabbing the rosary from his neck, Lucius pushed on. "I thought having the element of Light was something safe, even harmless. When your father stripped away who we were from us with ill intentions, we were unaware at the time. I returned to this world and found how naïve I had been. Even something so simple can cause a wake of destruction unlike anything you can imagine. Learning about my element all over again with a new understanding of what it meant to embody that aspect of life itself has been difficult. The tribulations you have suffered by discovering your own must have eaten away at who you are as a person."

"You forget I have never been a person." His tone was smooth and bitter as he spoke. "I was born from a cold womb of death and desire, a moment of greed and jealousy cast me out into the unknown. Childhood is something I will never have, life was never mine to claim, and the world hates and fears Death."

"You are wrong." There were no signs of hesitation in Lucius's response. "What happens when light is taken away?"

The entire church fell into darkness. It was a little after noon, yet it was so dark Iapetos couldn't see his own hands before him. There were no signs of where windows, candles, or even lights had been seconds before. Iapetos shifted in his seat, unsure where this was going. Muscles tensed, preparing for a fight. The air grew cold, the pew icy as his teeth chattered. A normal person may have caught hypothermia with the speed in which the temperature dropped.

What has Talib gotten me into this time?

"Tell me what you see?" Lucius's voice echoed in the abyss of darkness, seeming ominous.

"Nothing. Not even a candle flame," he answered.

"And now?"

The room came back to life, but it grew brighter with such speed it made him squint. His eyes burned; everything fell out of focus or disappeared into the blinding explosion of light. Iapetos couldn't tell if the light from the candles or the stained-glass windows were to blame. He closed his eyes, but it still penetrated through his eyelids, making him hiss. Covering his face with his palms, he gritted his teeth. Heat came pouring across him. Sweat trickled down his cheek and breathing became labored within the bombardment of light.

"What do you see now?" Lucius's voice was unmoved.

"N-nothing!" Shouted Iapetos, alarmed.

The heat retreated, and he took in a deep breath of relief. Blinking, he worked his eyes to adjust back to normal. He glared at the priest with a newfound wariness.

Lucius is right. Even the element of Light can have frightening effects on a person. If I had faced him on the rooftop, I would have lost in an instant. Who is this man?

"Whether you devoted yourself to the light as your father had done or continue to devote yourself to a path of darkness, neither of these will let you see the world around you. You willingly allow yourself to be blind." The priest sighed, twilling the rosary in his fingers before continuing. "We all have to find the right balance to allow us to walk a path fitting for who we want to be. Plants can't grow in the dark; plants can't grow in only light. It's the art of day and night that allows life to grow. Iapetos, we all have our own version of day and night, but we aren't normal people, and that makes it far more difficult to see. Life is full of trials. Without those moments, we can't find our place in this world."

Iapetos stared in awe at the priest. *This is an incredible friend you have, Talib.*

Lucius broke his stare on the rosary and patted his back. "I'll leave you to your thoughts. I have to clean the holy water fountain before service tonight." His smile was bright and harm-less as he slid out of the pew.

No words could create a response that would reflect Iapetos's feelings. Emotions stirred, and the priest had flipped his under-standing of his own life upside down with uncanny skill. It was clear Lucius had become a priest because he enjoyed giving guidance. He was good at it; he knew what to say without ever receiving a word from those he approached. Iapetos watched as the blonde man made his way back down the aisle. Turning in front of the podium, he disappeared to the discreet corner where the trickling of water echoed from.

I see why Talib considers him a friend. How the hell am I going to figure out who I am and what I want to do? I was born into darkness, but that doesn't mean I have to stay there. He's right, I was happier when I let myself be here, in this world where light and dark alternated without blinding me to what was in front of me. The fingers of his right hand fidgeted around a single gold band on his left ring finger. *Olivia, I should have never given up my life with you, but I was so afraid of watching you grow old. Knowing you were with child… knowing it was mine… knowing I would have to live in this world was too great of a weight for the broken man I was.*

Sweat dripped from Hotan's chin. The sun beat down on him as he leaned on his knees. In front of him, a Roman marble column was adorned with a blossoming vine of white roses. The image obstructed the backdrop of the junkyard. Catching his breath was proving hard after pushing his element to alter the cars that had been there. Stumbling backward, he fell onto his back in the shade of the camphor tree. Closing his eyes brought back flashes of Abigail's distraught face, and the kiss he gave her stung at his lips.

It was the wrong way to handle it.

Deep and slow, his breathing regained normalcy. Inhaling, he held it there to lull his heartbeat to slow down. After another round, his heart quieted in his ears and his muscles released their tension. Thoughts collided, none still enough for him to grip and focus. Abigail had shoved him away and rushed out of the room. A week had dragged by with no idea where she went or what form she had taken. Cracking his eyelids, he stared up at the swaying branches, and a mockingbird tilted its head at him before taking flight.

Standing back up, he went for the next tower of broken cars. Palms flat against twisted metal, he steadied himself. Pushing power into everything, he changed directions. His spine stung as if the element was trying to deter him, continuing his struggle, resisting his want to create only urging him to destroy. Fighting through the pain, Hotan focused on the flames flowing out from him and wrapping around the debris. He focused his thoughts on an image of a garden he once saw in a book. He listed out the plants, mapped out the look of the landscaping, and demanded it to come to life.

Like he had witnessed with Lilly, the tower melted and condensed. Spilling to the ground, the blob reshaped itself, stretching in purposeful directions to form more recognizable things. The border of the planter came into being, the soil dark and rich, and soon the plants grew. His muscles screamed, but he knew not to cave. His power was like a spoiled child screaming for the wrong attention. He wouldn't let it stay on the path his predecessor had taught it. This was his life, and he would work at turning it around so that the two sides of Rebirth no longer had a wall between them.

Flowers came and went, turning into ripened fruit, and he pulled away from the stalks of corn he found his hands grasping. His knees buckled, and he sat drenched in a cold sweat. A red tomato lay fuzzy and out-of-focus inches from his face. He wobbled as he attempted to sit upright, his body feeling like a numb noodle. A shiver rattled through him. Eyelids threatened to close under their newfound weight. Reaching out for the red fruit sent him falling backward, the ground warm under his back. Eyes closing, he failed to grasp the fruit that looked so enticing to eat.

"I pushed too hard." Hotan gasped for air like a fish. "Too … much…"

"Hotan." He couldn't get his eyelids open, but fingers brushed his hair from his face. "You can't keep putting your body through this."

"Why?" He knew Abigail's voice and touch well. "Why is it … so hard?"

"Life isn't easy." Her power ebbed into him, taking away the breathless sensation. "Death strikes quick, for it finds no value in lingering as life does."

"I can turn all of this to ash with no effort." Hotan hated the sting this truth had about his element. "But I feel like I am being ripped apart when I create something living."

Sighing, Abigail stared down at him with the empathy of the world. "Dying means a release of life so other life may grow. Living means working to maintain the life that has been given. Perhaps there is a reason we are nothing more than survivors until we rest in peace."

"The way you see the two sides of this curse of mine … is beautiful." He gripped her fingers, staring into her eyes.

Her face flushed. Tugging her hand free, she left him sprawled in front of the garden he built. A secret garden in the middle of the labyrinth of broken machines. Decisions still needed to be made, emotions settled, and time was slipping by so much faster in this new stage of immortality. He could live forever, but it didn't mean he had that long to settle his feelings for her. The pain in her eyes made his chest ache. Shellie's smiling face flashed in his mind, and he bit his lip.

It's not the same—the way I feel when we touch and look into each other's eyes. I know it's different; it's not meant to replace Shellie. But why? Why do I feel so damned guilty about wanting to be with Abigail? I keep making excuses, questioning her feelings, and second guessing my own. I don't want her to think it's just a phase or a poor attempt to fix a bleeding heart. Am I scared? Are we scared of what's unspoken between us?

13

WAKE UP

1450 AD Toulouse

We traveled by sea and by land, and in those private moments, Talib taught me what he knew. It was strange to feel the tendrils of Judgment slide through my body to help turn the tide. After some time, I realized the plague, the earthquakes, and even floods had subsided in my presence. I was haunted and numb to the wake I left and the lives taken with it. By foot, we passed through France and into Spain where we left Tarragona for North Africa. From sea, we ported at Palma for resupply before departing for Bejaia.

The city was beautiful; white walls overlooked the sea from where it nested in the steppes of arid land. Bejaia rested on the west side of the gulf named after it. The water was as bright as a turquoise amulet, and the manned lighthouse made it an invaluable main hub. Trade ships came and went in droves. Most of them dealt in spices, fabric, and treasures made from talented hands using the local vegetation. Even gold and salt became huge exports there as thirsty merchants hoped to make themselves rich beyond their imaginations.

Decades swept past as we wandered the arid mountains, traversed the desert sands of the Sahara, and made our way to the Niger River. I quickly learned the limitations of the element of Death and what resulted from interacting with nature. There was no need to explore its ability to disconnect a soul from its body, or that I could sense the remaining life on every man, woman, and child within a large city's span. This came as natural as breathing for me. Rebirth was spiraling my powers out of control with each attempt to overlap it with its own version of Death. We were fighting for dominance.

It had limitations. Yes, it could cause natural disasters, but it was limited to the ways of the basic elements—earthquakes, floods, storms with hellish gusts, and even wildfires. I couldn't command the locusts, but I could kill them with the power. It could spark disease, but it couldn't stop the spread or make it cease without claiming the lives of those with infected bodies. Just as I had failed to stop the fall of the cities like Helike and Antioch, it was only the cog in a greater war machine.

We took leave in Bamako, fortunate to have evaded battles spurred by the falling Mali empire. The Songhai had taken over in their stead, but there was still unrest. Satisfied we had overcome the worst of my affliction, we aimed to return to Europe. The imbalance involving the element of Death had been soothed; however, how well I would maintain when faced against Hotan remained an unspoken fear. With changes in the trade routes and civil wars disrupting what had worked for decades without trouble, we aimed to head back to France.

Toulouse, a small capital in south France, was as far as we managed. To the north, the battles and unrest over the nobility for rightful heirs still waged. News came through word of mouth about Joan of Arc and the siege of Orleans. The power she held to sway the people's hearts burned the ears of the people gossiping there. When I first traveled through Toulouse, I had the misfortune of bringing the Black Plague to the great city, but long after I left, the sting of famine and flood remained. I was sickened knowing I was to blame, but they would never know the weight of the fact.

What mortal man would believe I brought death to an entire city for so long and to such a scale?

They lost over ten thousand people in the seventy years since its start. This was one of France's largest cities, and I had brought it to its knees. Talib purchased a villa near the main road where traders traveled, including his own company. It became a refuge and resting place for many of the unfortunate caught in the wars waged between selfish men. We hadn't decided our next move or even goals. I opened his office door to find him finishing business with a foreman passing through with reports. He motioned for me to enter, and I sighed.

Closing the door behind me, I took my place standing behind Talib's chair.

"And were there any other concerns, Mr. Daughtry?" Talib dipped his quill into the ink and finished scribbling notes into his ledger.

"N-no, sir." The man knelt in front of the desk with his hat in hand. "I appreciate your understanding on the matter."

"I appreciate you watching out for the welfare of the ship and crew. I can make new trades far easier than I can replace an entire ship and crew." Placing the quill in its stand, Talib sprinkled sand on the paper to soak up the excess ink. "Be careful, and may the new contracts I gained for you work in our favor."

"Your father did right, handing the company over to you." The man stood, eager to leave as his eyes bounced between us. "Your family treats this guild right, sir."

The man opened the door and darted out, slamming it in his rush to be free of Talib.

"Do you ever get the urge to reveal it's you, the so-called founder and great grandfather still running things over a hundred years later?" I grinned, circling out from behind him to flop into a chair.

He laughed, shaking his head. "I do not think they would believe me, Iapetos. Which reminds me, I was called by your name the other day when I was in Marseille."

"Oh, really?" I perked up. "What did they say when you told them they were mistaken?"

"I did not tell them." Talib smirked, blowing sand from the ledger and closing it. "They said you had aged well."

"If they only knew how untrue that was." Staring out the window, I watched the tree limbs bounce in the breeze. "You shouldn't confuse them like that, Talib."

"What are the chances of you visiting Marseille within the next decade?" He dropped the ledger into a drawer and locked it. "As I recall, you called it, 'a cluttered pile of buildings meant to be as useless as a peacock's tail.'"

"Because it is, and no, I don't want to set foot there again." Huffing, I stood when he did, a common sign of respect drummed into me at this point. "What are your plans? Now that the reports are all done and handled for the time being, I imagine you have something in mind?"

"*I* will be here nursing the sick." Talib eyed me, his words making me slump my shoulders.

"And what errand am *I* to run on your behalf, beloved Uncle?" I mused, earning a snort from him.

"I need you to go to Tona in Spain, my dear nephew." He walked around to the front of his desk and leaned against it, palms gripping the edge. "There is a local dispute involving the village blacksmith, and a seasoned guild master's input should put the conflict to rest. Are you up for the challenge, Iapetos?"

"Blacksmith?" Scrunching my face in confusion, I realized a more pressing question needed answering first. "Where is Tona?"

"South of Vic." Talib took in a breath, and he relented, "North of Barcelona."

"Ah!" A sparkle came to my eyes. "Barcelona! Now there's a city I adore."

"I believe it is like Marseille, just with a Spanish flair is all." Talib huffed, quashing my excitement. "You should visit Vic on your way back, especially if you miss the Romans."

"Romans." My tone dropped, and I curled my lip in disgust. "They stamped their temples everywhere as if pissing on land claimed for themselves. So, tell me more about Tona?"

"It's suffered much like Toulouse has. Plagues, floods, famine, and now, is short of able bodies." Straightening, Talib pulled away from the desk, and we walked out of the office. "The blacksmith fell ill or may even be dead already. The trouble is with whom replaced the man."

"How so?" I scratched my jaw as I considered the odd conflict.

Talib smiled, "I have seen how you handle this. Though I wonder if the person in question is a reincarnated immortal."

"Can't you sense them?" I winced at the shift in his eyes.

Talib's smile fell away. "I assume, yes, but part of me wonders. Hotan's power is so unstable, I can only assume it hampers my own abilities."

"May I take a horse this time?" We paused under an archway, watching a servant eat her lunch in the courtyard. "Or am I expected to walk?"

"Go by horse." Talib watched the girl with a pained look on his face. "I would hate myself if you returned with news of a lynching … or worse."

"Quite the mess to sort out indeed." I turned. Not another word was needed between us.

Marching into the stables, I eyed the two horses left in the stables. With so many traders and reports coming and going, there had been many exchanges. None of the horses I had doted on over a few weeks ago remained. Instead, I had a light riding Cheval Navarrin and a bulky Auvergne draft horse. I glared at them, and they snorted back as if acknowledging why I had come. The Cheval danced in place, high-headed and full of energy. In the stall next to him, the Auvergne mare flicked a single ear back and huffed.

"I agree; he's quite annoying." Whistling, the stableman appeared. "Jacque, saddle the mare. I'm taking her to Tona."

"Yes, sir." He pulled tack from the nearby beam. "Do you want me to pack your saddlebags, sir?"

Weighing the question for a moment, I nodded. "Yes, do that for me while I change into something more suitable for riding."

By the time I made it back to the stables, Jacque had her brushed, and her mane and tail were trimmed and free of tangles. He wrestled with a back hoof, finishing with checking her hooves and shoes. The old mare flicked her tail at him, and he gave up trying any further. He offered her a sugar cube for her patience and not kicking him for messing with her feet, and she didn't refuse.

"Are the shoes okay?" I patted her across the neck, and she shuddered in delight.

"For now." He scratched his forehead as he looked over the horse. He circled one more time until he made it back to his starting point. "The shoes should hold, but I would see a black-smith when you can to get them replaced."

Smirking, I pulled myself onto the saddle. "Then I will see the blacksmith in Tona about it."

Making a clicking sound with my teeth, I urged the mare forward. The whole ride along the mountain paths and roads, I could feel one shoe bothering her. She would sidestep, avoid placing too much weight on it, and break the pacing in her gait. It made for a rough ride, though draft horses weren't known to be smooth to begin with. By the time I strolled into the edge of Tona, I was happy to dismount and give us both a break. My back and thighs ached, and she let her back left hoof rest.

Sighing, I ran my hand down her rump and hock, tugging gently and she lifted her hoof. "Damn, the frog looks swollen, and this shoe's shit. I'm sorry, girl. Looks like we both need to see the blacksmith for business."

I continued down the road toward the center of town. Digging into my pockets, I found the sugar cubes and gave my horse one. The path became wide and hard-packed, taking the strain off her bad leg as the old mare balanced her weight. My unintentional tugging of her lead only resulted in a demand for a sugar cube as an apology. Arguing voices echoed off the build-ings. If they had sent me to resolve an issue, it made perfect sense they would be fighting as I arrived. It didn't matter; with the influence of money, I could orchestrate their opinion elsewhere. The closer I came, the louder the shouts and curses became. They were screeching like sirens leading me to the forge. One last turn and we came upon a small stable and the blacksmith's quarters in an open area of town.

"I already told you, he's too ill to work." There was a loud clanking of iron and the hiss of white-hot metal hitting water.

"He may never get well enough to work the forge, let alone throw the hammer."

Outside the shaded workspace, a large group of men mumbled to one another. Their postures tense, arms crossed, and brows low. This had the inklings of an angry lynching mob. I looked to the mare, and she snorted at me, flattening her ears as if to say, *This is your problem*. Rubbing my jaw, I kept walking with eyes and ears open. A large man stomped into view; he had been in the workspace where the blacksmith should have been. He joined the group and spun on his heel.

"There has to be someone else who can do the work!" he bellowed like an angry bull, face red with rage. "It's shameful having you do this. Does your father know the shame you bring to your family name?"

"You never once complained about me helping him with the work, Antonio." A woman with a fiery stare came marching out from behind the forge. "And you dare to make an ordeal out of this while he lies on his deathbed!"

Her voice barked with authority, and the crowd of men dispersed in a hurry. Again, I paused with a smile on my face. *They've taken their share of lashes from her tongue if they can't defend their comrade at this point.*

"Look, we allowed it. It was cute, but this… this puts even me to shame." He faltered, losing his will for shouting. "I've called for someone to settle the matter. You'll see. This game of playing in men's work will end soon enough."

She ripped off the leather padding, exposing the sweat and black smudged skin underneath. Antonio stepped back, hands raised in defense. She twisted back to the forge, and Antonio's eyes widened as my brows raised. By the time she emerged from behind the forge, her cotton dress was nothing more than a frail nightgown. Her hair was balled on her head and clung to her face. She scowled, producing a hot poker in her hand. Antonio turned, paling as he ran full steam in the opposite direction.

"You run, you coward!" She tossed it in a barrel of water on the edge of her area. "Bastard."

"I take it you're the blacksmith?" I mused.

"What of it?" She swiveled her head, and my breath caught in my throat. "Uh, you're … not from around here."

Her yellow and orange eyes made every cell in my body freeze. The courtesan in Pompeii, the girl at the Antioch brothel, and the dying girl in London—here she was again, in front of me a hundred years later. I covered my mouth, taking in every detail. Her brown hair was a nest on her head as she pulled a strand from her lips. I could still feel the icy bite of our last kiss. Sweat slid down her cheek, rolling over her neck and between her breasts. My face flushed. Without the layers of leather pads and her blacksmith's apron, the soaked gown did little to hide her figure.

"Are you here to take my father?" Her voice was husky, losing the bite it held only a minute before.

"What?" My eyes jerked back to her eyes. "No, he'll be fine; he has plenty of time left. I'm not here for… I'm here for you, apparently."

Her brow folded. "I'm sorry; I thought you were someone else."

Closing my eyes, I scrambled to regain my focus. "Let me back up a moment. My name is Iapetos. They sent me here on behalf of the guild master from Toulouse."

"Is that so?" The dangerous edge crept back into her voice. "I take it you intend to give my father's forge to someone else?"

Patting the neck on the mare, I mustered a smile. "I haven't decided anything just yet. My first concern is fixing the back shoe on this mare."

Searching my eyes for a moment, she walked around me. Like I had done earlier, she ran her hand across the horse and felt the foot. She reached to her hip and scoffed, realizing she had dropped her tool bag when she gave chase to Antonio. Instead, she spit in the hoof, digging her fingers in and around to get a better look. Her stern face didn't betray a thought running through her mind. She let the foot drop and watched the mare flinch, resting it with no weight on it. When her eyes caught mine, she seemed angry.

"How far did you ride her with a bad shoe like this?" She brushed past me, and my heart fluttered. "You're lucky she doesn't have thrush."

"Toulouse?" I replied, leading the horse to the hitching post by her workstation.

She pulled on her apron and tool bag, loading and unloading it with various tools from the table. "How is she?"

"Calm?" I shrugged. I had never bothered to learn much about horses, let alone this one I took on a whim. "Forgive me; the stableman had a look before I left and said it needed to be replaced, but—"

"It should have been done before you left." Marching around me, she focused on the job and had the hoof back in hand. "You're lucky you didn't make her lame crossing the mountains."

She tapped a wedge between the worn-out horseshoe and hoof, coaxing the nails to come out. Dropping the hammer into her bag, she grabbed another tool to help pull and tug it off. The last nail wiggled out, and she tossed the shoe back at me. It bounced and hit the side of my foot, but she paid no heed to me as she cleaned the hoof and frog. Another exchange of tools followed, liquid and smooth in motion as her hands dipped in and out of her bag. With each stroke of the file, clippings fell to the ground. The intensity of her stare and the nimble actions told me she had done this task a number of times. Her muscles pulled and pushed her arms from pure memory and confidence.

"Take that worn-out shoe and add it to the barrel on the other side of the forge," she commanded, and I did what was asked of me. "When you get over there, you'll see a bucket of new shoes. Bring the bucket if you can lift it."

It was challenge. She had stolen a glance at me when she said it. I reached down, retrieving the worn-out shoe. Looking it over only added to my guilt. The shoe was complete shit, and she was right. *It's a wonder the mare didn't go lame on the way here.* I dropped it into a barrel of decrepit shoes and found the clean shoes beside it. I grabbed the handle, lifting it with one hand. Protecting my pride, I swallowed down the grunt as the weight of it pulled on my shoulder and sent my muscles burning. A normal man would have needed two hands for fear of throwing out a shoulder.

When I dropped the bucket beside her, she snorted. "It does no one any good to throw out a shoulder to impress a girl."

"I hoped to impress the blacksmith," I retorted, grinning.

It was enough to earn a smile as she lined up shoes, trying to find one big enough. At last, she had one long enough, but the horns would need hammering to match with width of the hoof. The mare was happy to reclaim her leg as it watched me follow behind the girl. She paused at the forge, picking up the hammer. She spun around and grunted to see me in the way.

"Are you lost or daft?" Pressing the hammer against my chest, she shoved me against the work table. "Stop following me; you're in the way."

"Well, put me to work." I pulled off my coat and rolled up my sleeves. "I can stoke the fires."

She paused, assessing the look in my face. "Pump the bellow then. I need it hot."

I didn't hesitate pulling and pushing on the handle to bring air across the forge's fire. With each stroke the heat slammed against me increasingly. I cursed under my breath, amazed she'd been working and handling all of this on her own. She retrieved her poker as more heat exploded from the fire before she placed the shoe in. The metal grew red, and she pulled it out, placed it on the anvil, and hammered it out. I paused from my task, admiring the muscles in her arm as they lifted and dropped the hammer. Sweat trickled across her skin, and I became lost in thought.

I want her to be mine. I want her like I've never wanted anything in this world. Is this what they call love? Am I falling in love with this girl?

Turning away, I leaned against the forge. In the panic, I hadn't paid heed to my actions. Flesh seared and clung to the brick, and I paled. The pain hadn't alerted me; it was the smell followed by her shriek. The hammer and shoe thudded against the ground. She gripped my shoulders and pulled me away from the forge. Strong-arming me, she forced the injured hand into the water barrel. She was so pale and wide-eyed.

"What in the devil is wrong with you!" Bewildered, she searched my face.

"It's okay," I whispered, unsure how to explain it to her. "I'm not hurt."

"The hell you're not." Her eyes hovered back to the forge.

I turned to see the flesh still sizzling on the bricks. "Sorry, I wasn't paying attention."

"I can't believe you didn't react." She turned to my arm in the water. "Unfold it; it does no good to ball it up in a fist."

Sighing, I pried her hands off my arm. I pulled my fist out, water dripping. Looking at it, I didn't want to open it. If I did, she would know I wasn't a normal man. My heart ached and my throat burned to think she would think of me as something more. Echoes of the past whispered in my mind. Her voice from long ago and the names I had heard: *Angel of Death, harbinger of Death, Iapetos.* My heart fluttered as I peered up into her tiger lily irises.

Deep down, she already knows I'm not normal… not a man… something immortal.

In a leap of faith, I opened my hand but closed my eyes so I could not see her face in that moment. There was a long silence. My beating heart was deafening as I waited for her words. The heat of her fingers slid across my palm. I waited for her to jerk them away, but she didn't. I opened one eye, curiosity goading me to take in her face. She peered down at my hand, her face stern. Something deep within her stirred, and her eyes shot up. I swallowed, eyes wide at the reaction.

"You lied." Her voice was low, a harsh whisper between us.

"I didn't lie." I searched her eyes, hoping for a hint of what thoughts raced through her mind.

"You said the guild sent you," she hissed.

"He did. Master Talib sent me here to see the blacksmith," I remarked, her fingers squeezing my hand tight. "That's why I'm here."

"Don't you mean you're here to take my father to the grave?" The words slammed into me, cold and hard. "You're… you're the reaper."

My chest ached as I digested the word, my spiteful nature rising. "And if I am?"

Hurt wrecked her face. She let go, turning away. My breath caught in my throat. Reaching out, I gripped her arm and tugged her into me. Her face swiveled, ready to voice her disapproval. Pressing my lips against hers, I wanted what I had tasted in Pompeii under the heat of Mt. Vesuvius and the glow of burning bodies in London. It was her tongue that pressed past my lips, fingers snaking into my hair. Some part of her soul remembered too—the exchanges, the want, and even the regret. Breaking away, I stared at her with renewed wonder.

"I feel like I know you…" she confessed. Her face filled with confusion as she looked up at me.

"In another life," I mumbled. "Many times before."

14

GOOD ENOUGH

Iapetos stood in front of Hotan's apartment door. Opening his right palm, a brass key glared back at him, waiting for him to decide. Snorting, he rolled his shoulders and unlocked the door. The air inside was stale and reflected what he already knew—Hotan hadn't returned for months. Slowly and quietly, he shut the door and locked it just in case. His eyes spanned from one end to the other.

Why the hell did Talib give me the key?

Scowling, he walked cautiously into the living room, careful not to disturb anything there. The radio had collected dust, the bathroom was still dabbled with black spots of dried blood, and nothing had been packed before leaving. Frozen in time, the room was still in the moment Hotan had left after their encounter on the rooftop. A pigeon fluttered away from the windowsill, alarmed to see movement in the sleepy apartment. Spinning around, he was lost as to what he came for. *What did I hope to find?* Frustrated and confused, he sat on the couch, leaning his elbows on his knees. Breaking his empty stare from the window, his focus fell on the open photo album on the coffee table. He saw himself, and his chest ached.

This can't be what I think it is. Olivia, you were always one for taking pictures, but to keep remnants of me seems pointless after I left. Why would someone torture themselves like this? I was dead to you. I even said those words to you when I turned away. Sometimes, when I close my eyes to rest, I can still hear your choking sobs and feel your fingers grasping at my jacket. A photo album even now...

Pulling the album closer, he blew dust from it. His own eyes glared back at him from the image of himself next to the smiling woman whom he once called a lover. Pain boiled up inside him; emotions he had swallowed so long ago resurfaced as if he were reliving the memory in his mind all over again. The muscles in his cheek twitched. Unable to ignore the album, he flipped to the front page and traversed through the memories she had left behind.

I didn't realize she had so many pictures of me. How often did she come back to these and dream of the time we spent together? Did part of you hope I would come back and remember you this way? Has he been looking through this? Wondering where I was after... after... Olivia...

He paused, each page flip feeling like a slap against his cheek. He looked at a young, smiling Olivia, nuzzling his side in a photo taken shortly after they had become more intimate. She had graduated high school, and he could no longer ignore her advances. Her eyes shined bright blue under a curtain of chestnut brown hair. The smile she wore was meant for him. How she found where he lingered at the dive bars or late-night diners made him wonder. She had invited him countless times to hang out with her and her small group of friends. With no inkling as to why, he found himself there. Occasionally, in those quiet, secret moments alone, he would smile for her and her alone.

It had been one fateful night together which would make him question everything about himself, the world, even his quest to find his father. It all unfolded so suddenly, and the throbbing ache in his chest made one thing for certain—Olivia's memory never faded. Her laugh, the sparkle her eyes held, and the way her fingers caressed his cheek—all of these and so much more stung at him. Chills ran across his skin from memories of her gentle whispers in his ear and the way she would tug at his shoulder. He would lean down to indulge her since she was shorter than him.

It feels as if it were only yesterday. I would have never been good enough for you. Why did you love me so deeply, Olivia? Even after I told you everything, you simply told me that even Death deserves to be loved, to be happy, to be a father of life. You never questioned my words. You didn't doubt the idea, and it rattled me in ways I never knew possible.

His fingers tightened their grip on the album, and he forced himself to turn the page. A wordless story unfolded with each flip. The sparkle in her eyes faded away after his image no longer appeared by her side. Images of her growing belly followed by newborn pictures stirred something deep inside him. *Not only did I take Olivia's sparkle of life from her when I disappeared, I gave my child a husk of a once wonderful woman.* The faint smiles and tortured little boy who grew with each page were haunted pictures of a past life he should have been part of. Blank pages brought him up for air as anger and frustration ate his soul. Gripping the album, he fought the urge to throw it across the room.

I never meant to hurt you, Olivia. Instead, I did something far worse; I broke your soul like my father broke mine. How am I any better? How am I different from him! You gave me a chance to change my life for the better, and I abandoned it because I was too afraid to live. Would I have been more willing if I my memories were intact? Maybe I would have tried instead of running away from all I could have had—something that not even my father could have.

Jerking himself off the couch, he unlocked and opened the door to find Hisota waiting for him. He gave him a hardened look, but the young man was unmoved by the stranger in the doorway. Iapetos took a step forward, but Hisota lifted a hand, demanding he stay where he stood. Looking him over, Iapetos couldn't gauge the emotion written on Hisota's face. It was stern, blurring anger and courage on his tight-lipped face. Sighing, Hisota folded his arms, peering into Iapetos's dark eyes without fear.

"Did you find what you were looking for?" Hisota's eyes dropped to Iapetos's hand which still gripped the photo album. "I don't think Hotan would like you stealing the only pictures he has of his mom. He only found it recently, so you can imagine how taking it away now would be a bad idea."

Flinching, Iapetos had unknowingly failed to leave it behind, his emotions blinding him to walk away with the precious momento. "I was wondering…"

Hisota lifted an eyebrow, and his words revealed something Iapetos hadn't accepted. "This realization he is your son and that you abandoned them frightens you, huh? It's what brought you here in the first place."

The muscles in Iapetos's face tensed. "So, you're the element of Fear now?"

A smile came across Hisota's face, feeling less afraid of the undead monster before him. "For now."

Looking to the album, Iapetos pressed further for information. "Did Olivia leave anything else behind?"

"Olivia?" Hisota was invested in the conversation unfolding. "I don't think Hotan's ever spoken her name since she died. You say it so easily. Why do you care if she left anything else? What are you looking for?"

"I…" Iapetos's voice caught in his throat. "I don't know. Something tells me I might find an answer if there was more. She was that sort of person, a person unafraid of the past and the future, no matter how broken it seemed."

"You know, they say it's best to leave the dead in peace." A sour expression gathered on Hisota's face. He gripped onto the fear he sensed inside Iapetos, pushing it to rise, wanting to see how afraid the element of Death was of his own past. "I'm not letting you go near shit without knowing your full intentions. I don't care if you can kill me. I do care that Hotan's father has shown up, yet he's been missing for months."

Iapetos's head spun with the weight of the element of Fear. Memories of Olivia overlapped with memories of his own of his father banishing him from the island of paradise. A cold sweat crawled across his skin as the physical torment of fear invaded him. Glaring at Hisota, he fought the fear building within him to no avail. Hisota's stare was cold, and Iapetos leaned on the wall behind him to keep balance. Despite being a new immortal, he had harrowing control and instincts for the element they had charged him with. It still made Hisota's legs weak, but he had intended to try his luck from the moment he sensed Iapetos there.

Cold fingertips gripped Iapetos's shoulder, and a woman's voice whispered in his ear, *"Why did you abandon us? Why did you become like your father, Iapetos? Please come back, my love. Come back to your son…"*

"O-Olivia?" Iapetos spun around, his swinging arm meeting nothing but air.

He lost his balance and fell at Hisota's feet. Hisota looked down with a knowing expression. "If it's any consolation, Hotan fears becoming *that person* as well. I had to see and feel for myself what is at the center of your actions, and it's something I can't argue with. Whoever that man was, he was the real devil in all this."

Wide-eyed, Iapetos looked up at Hisota's stern face dabbled in sweat. "Hotan…"

"You two are more alike than you realize. You and your son, not that other asshole. To answer your first question, Annie and Jacob would know if there was anything lingering around from Hotan's mom." Satisfied no harm was intended, Hisota relinquished the information to Iapetos.

Hisota walked away, but Iapetos gripped his leg. "Wait!"

Keeping calm, Hisota glanced at the hand before looking Iapetos in the eyes. "Yes?"

"How did you do that?" Iapetos's brow creased as he let go, aware how threatening being touched by him might seem after the fight. "How did you make her appear?"

A mischievous glimmer came across Hisota's dark eyes. "I just plant the seeds; it's your own soul that does the worst of it."

"Well, this is unexpected." Lilly was standing at Hotan's head, waking him from his nap on the ground. "I knew you wanted to practice, but you've made a patchwork forest in here."

He opened one eye. "Is that a complaint or a compliment?"

She pondered, tapping her lips with a thoughtful fist. "Both at this given moment."

Sitting up, he pointed across the way. "I planted a garden."

"You planted nothing," she said and snorted.

"You got me on that point." Climbing to his feet, he stretched. "I suppose I should take a shower."

"Please do." Lilly was spinning around, marveling over the walls of greenery. "You can't even tell this is in the center of a junkyard."

"That was the goal, I suppose." Yawning, Hotan rubbed the back of his neck as he took in his work.

Grabbing his arm, Lilly demanded his full attention. "Is it getting any easier?"

Hotan's eyes fell to his hand. Balling it into a fist, he waited for her to look down. His fingers unfolded, and a tiny finch fluttered out of his palm. Lilly stumbled backward, following the tiny fluttering of wings until the sun obscured her line of sight. Twisting around, she paled. He was breathing a little harder, but the exhaustion he had experienced was fading. Before, he would have been wobbling, but in the breeze, he didn't sway once. He had broken down the walls between life and death in a matter of weeks.

"I suppose life gets easier if you're willing to work hard enough for it." He smiled, and Lilly laughed. "What's so funny?"

"You sound like some kind of philosopher suddenly." She slapped his shoulder. "Please, go take a shower; you've done enough damage to my property."

He grunted; Hotan had no energy left to argue. Shuffling his way back out of the junkyard and into the garage, his mind was circling over how everything had fallen apart between him and Abigail. He paused in front of the door which led into the tiny living quarters. Taking in a deep breath, he forced himself into the room. Abigail straightened her posture where she sat on the couch, reading one of Lilly's books. He paused just inside the doorway.

After a minute of exchanging hardened stares, he broke away and headed to the back where the shower waited. He turned on the sink and splashed his face with water, wanting to refresh himself. Thoughts washed away with each droplet that fell into the basin.

"Clean towel and clothes should be in a bag hanging on the back of the bathroom door." Lilly paused from where she stood at the doorway. "Uh, I've got work to do…"

The tension in the room sent her rushing back out. Lilly didn't know what happened between them, but she could figure it out. Picking up a wrench, Lilly paused. Her cell phone was buzzing around, still on silent. "Jacob" flashed across the screen, and she knew he could put some light on the situation. Looking to the door, she answered it with a coy smile.

"Just the man I needed to talk to."

"Is this where I should be worried?" Jacob asked. He had not expected her to pick up.

Pacing back out into the sunlight of the parking lot, she peered over her shoulder and lowered her voice. "I think there's something happening between Abigail and Hotan. If anyone can figure it out, I am betting it's you."

"Oh, are they there now?" Jacob was intrigued. "Don't tell me they've had a lover's quarrel."

"Actually…" She covered her mouth. "I think so."

"Wait, what?" Jacob went quiet for a solid minute before he spoke. "I entertained the thought, but I swear it wasn't my doing."

"I know it wasn't your doing." Lilly was flustered. "You swore after *that* debacle to never play matchmaker ever again. I just worry they are falling for one another for the wrong reasons."

"I see…" His voice trailed off. "What if I—"

The door opened to the living quarters, and Lilly barked across the receiver, "I got work to do. I don't have time for this right now."

"Uh-oh, you've been caught." Jacob chuckled as she shoved the phone in her pocket.

Abigail closed the door with gentle care. She froze there, staring at the door as if it were saying something to her. After a few minutes, she broke away and glanced at Lilly who was walking back into the shade of the garage. Abigail's shoulders slumped forward as she took a seat on a work stool. Her unfocused stare on the dismantled car and frown on her face spoke volumes. Depression was weighing her down far more deeply than simply feeling sad. She seemed in pain, disconnected from the world around her.

"You want to talk about what's going on between you two?" Lilly dropped her cell phone onto the toolbox, and the screen lit up, ticking away on a timer. *Jacob hasn't hung up—typical of him.* Avoiding bringing attention to it, she picked up the wrench. "By the look on your face, it's important to you both."

Blinking, the focus came back to Abigail's face. "What is it like to be in love?"

Walking up to the car, Lilly gave a half smile. "Like the world around you can shatter at any moment."

"But how do you know you love that certain someone?" Abigail spun the stool and faced the door, making sure Hotan wasn't coming out anytime soon. "What is it like to love someone?"

Lilly crawled under the car and began her work. "Well, you care so deeply for someone who can make you feel so frustratingly fragile. That's how it made me feel. I was angry and happy all at once. In fact, terrified and confident at the same time. A mess of emotions you can't decipher or even fathom to untangle. When you look into each other's eyes, you can see their secrets and know who they are without ever speaking a word. It feels like … fate."

Abigail spun the stool back around. "But how do you know when you love a certain someone? How do you know when it becomes more than friendship?"

The wrench halted for a few seconds and started again. "When it's more intimate than loving and caring for someone, it becomes a reaction against your will. You don't have any say in it. That doesn't mean you can't push love away or abandon it. Sometimes life gives us no choice. I… I've had that happen to me, loved and abandoned. I've had it where we kept crossing paths, neither of us willing to speak our affection, but the kisses said otherwise. I've been given love and ruined it. The only thing they all had in common was a reaction."

"How so?" Abigail stared at Lilly's legs dangling out from under the lifted car. "What kind of reaction?"

"Shouldn't you be asking Jacob about all this?" Frustrated, Lilly tossed a rusted nut across the shop floor and scooted over to the next one, wrenching away. "He's the element of Love. He can give you better advice than I can. You're asking the woman who chose to be single forever."

"I want to know from your perspective." Abigail's voice had a stinging resolution; she refused to back down.

"Fine." Crawling out from under the car, she sat up with a face smudged in grease and dirt. "When I was in love with Jacob…"

Abigail paled, realizing what she had been asking of Lilly. "I didn't mean to pry…"

Lilly raised a hand, her eyes demanding Abigail's undivided attention. "When I was in love with Jacob, it was the most wonderful and cursed thing that ever happened."

Hotan had walked out, his eyes wide, but he remained silent.

"He fell in love with me long before this immortal chaos and long before he ever had powers." Lilly looked to the ceiling as if begging someone to forgive her. "He was all I had left, so I stuck with him for so long because I had no one else to turn to. It was wrong, I wasn't honest with myself or with him. He saved my life, and I thought… I thought I could pretend to love him back as thanks, maybe even out of obligation. You can love someone for all the wrong reasons; feeling pity for one another can do that to a couple. At the end of the day, you have an empty relationship that is already cracking at its foundation."

Both Hotan and Abigail had opened their mouths to speak, but Lilly lifted a hand. Abigail was still unaware that Hotan was standing at the door. Lily had squeezed out the answer, and she continued sailing her point home.

"It fell apart. He went one way, and I went the other. I realized that I had fallen in love at some point with someone else. I was in denial for a long time. I didn't understand... No, I didn't *want* to understand the feelings I had rolling around in my heart and soul. As for Jacob, I had already let him go, and as for the other man, I never confessed I had fallen in love. It would have been cruel for me to speak up considering the situations involved, especially since he left me behind so easily the last time we were together. There are many regrets. A regret for dragging out an empty love and the regret of not being brave enough to voice my love. It doesn't mean it would have changed anything, but I would have been happier with myself for being honest with my feelings. I suppose what I am trying to say is that it's damn near impossible to see clear lines of when you are in love or not. Feeling good and feeling love are the same sensation, depending how you're gauging everything in your life. Most importantly, be honest with yourself."

Abigail creased her forehead as she stared down at her clasped hands in her lap. "Be honest with myself?"

"Yes." Lilly shot a look to Hotan who was sliding down to sit on the steps. "You both need to ask yourselves some important questions and answer them honestly, with yourself first, then each other. When you do that, you'll be able to determine what is between you."

Glancing at Lilly, Abigail realized her stare focused on something behind her. "Hotan…"

He heaved a heavy sigh, pulling himself from the steps, feeling too restless to sit longer than a few seconds.

"I didn't mean for you to hear…" Tears were rolling down Abigail's face as he marched past without saying a word.

"She can stay here with you, right?" he asked Lilly.

"I guess…" She blinked, baffled by his reaction.

"I need to clear my head." They watched Hotan march out of the shop, strap on his helmet, start his bike, and soar off.

Sniffling, Abigail whimpered, "Do you think he's mad at me?"

"No." Lilly pulled herself off the ground and leaned over the toolbox, the call minutes still rolling on the screen. "He needs time to sort his feelings out. You both do."

The call ended; Jacob had heard everything. A text came across the screen as Abigail slinked back into the home office.

[JACOB: WELL SAID, MY LILLY. LOVE YOU ALWAYS.]

15

DUALITY

1587 AD Roanoke Colony

I woke from my dream, sweat and fever wrecking my body. The creaking of the boat's bow and sloshing of waves reminded me I was far from my time in Tona. Despite it being well over a hundred years ago, I could still feel her warmth, the taste of salty sweat on her skin, and her voice whispering in my ear. *Lilly.* I had spent a week in Tona, quelling the town's rage over having a woman work the forge. Smiling, I swallowed back the nausea of seasickness and clung to the memory.

The looks on those men's faces when I filled a table of tools and shoes was priceless. I had asked them to choose the ones made by a woman's hand, and they looked at me as if I were mad. They knew there was no difference; the tools were all made by a blacksmith—nothing more or less. The barriers had fallen between Lilly and me. She was not the first woman I laid with, not by a long shot, but it was the first time I felt love. It scared me, and I left in the middle of the night.

I couldn't allow myself to become a man like my father—unable to live his life after losing someone so precious.

The boat rocked, and with it, my stomach. Sitting up, I pulled my boots on and dressed, though haphazardly. This wasn't like the rides across the Mediterranean or the straits and routes along Africa, India and even the Orients. The Atlantic Ocean was taxing; some of the crew would not live to make it back home to England. They called it the Americas, a land wild and free, full of opportunity. That wasn't the reason Talib and I headed there with this expedition to settle.

Rumors had come fast—a result of mistaken identity. Someone thought Talib had been on an exploration ship and reported him missing; it was assumed he had fallen overboard and was most likely dead. It seemed Hotan was on the move, but we didn't know why.

"Come on. If you stay under here any longer, it will ruin you." Talib was on the ladder steps, one hand on the hatch to steady himself as the boat tilted with the waves. "Come out, get some fresh air, and keep your eye on the horizon. We made it through the storm just fine."

I groaned, not willing to risk opening my mouth to attempt speech. I had held up fine at first, but the moment the storm hit, and we packed inside the tiny space, I lost my battle to seasickness. I wasn't alone; a few seasoned sailors had similar trouble. Eager to escape the putrid sour smells of the underbelly of the ship, I followed Talib out.

"Morning, m'lord." A sailor nodded his hat to us. "Looks like the other two ships beat us to shore by a few days."

Pausing, I steadied my stomach before fussing, "How can you tell?"

"We were hit by the storm first and pulled sails." The sailor nodded to the crow's nest. "Jimmie said the other two might ride the outskirts and ride the wind ahead of schedule. Far as we can see, that's exactly what they did. It just means we get to rest proper once we get our feet on some dirt."

"I'd love to be on dirt again," I said, and Talib laughed at my statement, slapping my back.

"Let us go chat." He motioned further down the deck away from prying ears. "I hate to say it, but he is coming for us. At my core, I cannot shake the feeling that he wanted us to be here waiting for him. Perhaps there has been a change of heart."

"You can't be serious?" I leaned on the railing, my eyes locked on the line where sea and sky met. "What if he plans to undo this time we've been together?"

There was a long silence. We both dreaded that he might take this time away from us. We had become like brothers, learning from each other. Talib knew more about the powers, the origins, and Hotan. On the other hand, I had the experience of using it in battle and knew the limitations of being immortal. The pain never lessened; I just learned to ignore and recognize it differently when I lost a limb or crushed an organ. It would heal, but immortals couldn't tend the wound like a normal person. It was best to behave as a wounded animal would—scurrying off to a dark cave, healing for a few days, and returning with tail wagging.

"Are we sure he's not already there?" My question made Talib flinch. "Talib, are you ready to face him?"

"I doubt we will ever be ready." He stared across the endless horizon of navy blue. "At least this time, we can attempt to prevent another disaster like so many times before."

And there was our other concern. Why should we let him scar this new land like he's done the old?

"I can't help but feel each day that we get closer to this new land…" I paused, my hands still tingling from the dream, still feeling the past as if it were yesterday. "I feel he's already there."

"If that's the case, we have a plan intact." Talib turned, marching away before I could say much more.

Yes, we had discussed it, but the growing fever throughout my body made it clear Hotan was there and knew we were coming. It wouldn't be long before I would feel the shift; I would struggle to keep the power bottled in or risk unleashing hell upon those we traveled with. My mind bounced from earthquakes, floods, volcanoes, fires, and plagues, wondering which it would be this time. *What price will these people pay for this if we fail or if Hotan unleashes his own wrath upon them?*

"A day or so." I heard the Captain's words as relief and anxiety mingled within me. We were out of time to steel our nerves on the matter. "You may want to check on the young lad. That's a look of fear if I ever saw one. My men said seasick, but that's the look a man gets when he thinks he's facing the end of his existence or going to Hell."

The captain didn't understand how insightful he could be. Talib joined me once more, his hands gripping the railing tight. He was just as frightened as I. His own brother scared him. A shiver rattled me, the idea of it unsettling. We met eyes, the same grave expression written on our faces. Talib's lips parted, then froze. There were no words to comfort me. We both knew I would pay the heaviest price for chasing Hotan to the shores of the Americas.

Roanoke Island was just beyond the horizon. What Hotan intended to do with us was beyond our understanding. Over two hundred years had passed with no signs of him, yet he waited for them on the shores of a wild, untamed land. He had all but written an invitation by hand. In the ship ledger, he had written "Talib Bithloa." It was loud and clear we had never escaped his watchful eye. He had known their whereabouts for every decade.

We assumed we were giving him a wide berth, but as my power rattled within me, I knew we had been horribly naïve.

"If I fail, use your power to send me away, Talib." A cold sweat swept over me; I could feel the bite of Rebirth and Death recognizing each other. "We are about a day out from where I can feel him."

"I wish I had wings like you, so I could just fly away from it," Talib confessed. "Are you going to be able to keep it under control?"

"I, I think so." A drop of sweat trickled down my cheek. I clenched my teeth at the thought of how agonizing it would be to endure. "But I must admit, I never thought it would be this painful. Then again, I can see how in the past, I would have fled to the point of interference or being angry and ready to fight."

"We can only assume it is something he designed. Just like how I keep getting drawn into the areas as soon as your elements meet." The sun was fading, falling behind darkening waters. "Let us try to remain sharp. Neither of us know what he intends to do by cornering us here in the Americas. I can assure you he has known of the closeness between us on our travels. He is far cleverer than either of us. Honestly, he's outwitted me plenty of times…"

***

The screeching of gulls was a warm welcome, and the sun rose high in the sky. I could still feel the bite of sea sickness. My complexion pale and movements dull. The crew suspected I'd been stricken with scurvy or even fallen victim to dehydration. Many had died on the trip across the Atlantic from both and far worse. With an arm against my stomach, until at last the sensation shifted. The moment my body set foot on land, a wave of power surged within me, and the agony of choking it back left me breathless. Talib kept peering over, his eyes speaking volumes. He knew what ailed me, and he felt helpless. Part of me wondered if he felt guilty for bringing me here, but we both knew I would have come anyway. Neither of us would allow the other to face Hotan alone. It was dangerous to even consider the idea.

Each person had a task awaiting them in the Roanoke Colony. Captain White's first order of business involved venturing out to the natives to establish trade and peaceful relations—essential for surviving the first winter in this new place. The more experienced and stronger hands set to work clearing trees and staging the walls of the colony to create a safe barrier between them and the wildlife. Women and children had also come with us, including the captain's daughter. They had their own tasks—managing the supplies, mending clothes, organizing equipment for the men. Once settled, the captain and the core crew would resupply and head back across the Atlantic with no guarantee of returning.

Within a week, they had finished the walls and built the governor's lodge. Several individual cabins were completed for the families, providing shelter for most of the settlers; they could start calling this place home. Still, there were no signs of Hotan beyond the struggle raging at my core between the element of Death and the influence of Rebirth. I confined myself to a cabin; Talib warned the others I had fallen ill and quarantined. For fear of death, no one dare enter but Talib.

Most of the tasks and needs had been achieved except one daunting detail: the lack of supplies to last through a hard winter. Determined to maintain peace with the natives, raiding them for their winter reserves was out of the question. Perhaps Talib's influence had something to do with this goal. Being a guild master brought a lot of pull; we had the ships, the money, and the supplies to support a colony like this. Regardless, winter was fast approaching. The leaves had changed to brilliant reds and oranges and the wind carried a chill.

Months passed without any signs of Hotan, but I lived in the constant wake of his power, sensing it rolling ever higher, closer like the tide. The natives spoke of a winged man passing through the area. Finally, someone had seen him, but it did little to comfort me. Excruciating pain would dull only to rise again. It was as if he were allowing me the time to adjust. The moment I gained rest by culling back the torrent of clashing powers, I would wake, screaming. The colonists dubbed me possessed after witnessing fevers, vomiting, and screams from the cabin for weeks on end. I could hear them gossiping outside the door. Food supplies were low, and their hunger added to the superstitions building in their minds and heart.

"He will bring death to us all." It was a harsh whisper.

"He must be possessed." Ah, now the preacher added his two cents on the matter. "Mister Bithloa won't let me see to the man. It's the devil's work; I am sure of it. Each passing day we allow this to fester, the worse our situation becomes."

"Fools," I muttered, shivering at the table, and glaring at the door. "Superstitious fools."

"Have you spoken to him?" The woman's voice sounded alarmed. "About sending him with the captain back to England?"

"I asked the captain to convince him to do so." They were walking away, his voice trailing off. "But he seemed unsure about allowing someone who's contagious…"

A smile crept across my face. *I wish it was that way.*

Grunting, sharp pain pulsed through me. It was as if Hotan had set foot inside the colony walls. It burned at my core like a hot coal. Trying to breathe, I rasped for air and tried to muffle the scream wanting to escape. He was close. Tendrils of the element of Death desired to seek Rebirth. Chills shook through my body, fire filled my soul, and it took all my will power to keep my powers inside the cabin walls. I gave up on keeping it within the boundaries of my flesh. I had to wait to leave; the chance of running into someone was too great, and I didn't want to harm anyone.

Pushing onto my feet, I tried to step away from the table. Like a sword to my gut, the burning ripped through me. A scream escaped me, and I doubled over on the table again. It differed from previous encounters; my power rebelled, betraying me. Tattoos snaked across my skin. Gritting my teeth, I pulled it back like the reins on a bucking, fighting wild stallion. The power shifted, all of it sucking inward and knocking the air from my lungs. Gasping, my wings exploded into existence. The weight thrust me forward, and I caught myself, leaning on the table.

What is wrong with me? Why can't I stop it?

The door opened, and my eyes shot upward. Talib slammed the door, wide-eyed as black feathers fluttered in the air between us. The burning in my core was like a wildfire. Sweat dripped off my chin. The chills I had abhorred were replaced by fever as my muscles and joints ached. Talib locked the door, his eyes filled with worry.

"He's horribly close." It was a struggle to talk, and I found myself annoyed. "I'm… I'm going to have to leave in the cover of night. I can't get them to go away." He followed my eyes to the feathers across the table.

Forcing my wings closed freed what little space remained. Talib had seen them a few times but not this close. His expression was a mixture of envy and admiration. The feathers were black as a crow's, but the bulk of them seemed tattered, broken, even rotting away. They were worthy wings for the harbinger of Death. A flash of off-white reflected in Talib's eyes. I had forgotten that they were harrowing from the sickening aspect of exposed bone. They were decrepit appendages that looked barely capable of carrying a man in their true condition.

Shaking himself loose for the glare on my wings, Talib replied, "Understood. But can you wait for nightfall?"

"I pray so." I gave him a grave expression. "If not, I may risk leaving in front of them in hopes of not repeating a decade's worth of deaths."

Talib swallowed. I couldn't hide the pain washing over me like waves smashing into the shore. With each peak, my wings flared, and I gripped the edges of the table tighter. My breathing had become laborious, and I felt so ashamed. *How pitiful. With all the work we have done to help master my abilities and power, to fail in front of Talib's eyes is unforgivable. I have failed him.*

He shifted and reached a hand toward me. My pride bit at my soul, and my wings opened wide, the tips scraping the far walls.

"Don't touch me!" I roared. "If you use your power, I will lose what little control I have. I must manage this alone, or I'll never learn to control it in Hotan's wake."

Retracting his fingers, Talib turned and unlatched the door. "Lock this after I leave. I intend to do something about this. Do you suspect he's in the colony?"

"Y-yes." The door smacked loudly behind him.

Fear jolted me into action. I rushed the door and slammed the lock. It would be dangerous if the ruckus of my wings and screams of pain enticed a colonist to enter the cabin. I sank to the floor, gasping and staring at the fire. Part of me wondered if crawling into the orange flames would cool me down. Peering down at my hand, I remembered the burning of the forge. Through the agony, I smirked. I hadn't flinched then, but now, I looked like a wilted plant too close to a campfire.

She would laugh to see me like this.

Pulling myself to my feet, I stumbled past the table and made it back to my chair. I straddled it, leaning on the back to lose myself to the dancing flames. A strange calm came over me as I imagined her tiger lily eyes. Closing my eyes, I focused to find blue and red auras balled into one cabin. *Hotan is here.* My eyes shot open. *Rebirth is gripping Judgment.*

"No…" My heart raced.

Another wave of pain kept me from climbing to my feet. He had intentionally separated us by manipulating my powers for weeks to eat away at my stamina. Hotan knew what he needed to do. Talib couldn't overpower his brother, but it wasn't because he lacked the strength with his power; Talib could easily defeat Hotan. Rather, it was his unwillingness to harm his own brother that held him back. The crushing force of frustration grew within me as I sensed the losing battle. In this helpless moment, I understood the expression Talib made back on the ship when it all started.

<*I know you're here. I know you intend to unravel every bit of happiness I've ever known*>. There was silence, but I knew he could hear me as he took hold of Talib's power, stealing its control for himself. <*Spare these people. Talib and I will deal with what has happened, but if there is any heart left in that husk of a being, spare the lives in the colony. I've fought long and hard to master this dreadful element. Please don't release it here and now.*>

It pained me to plead to a monster. Scoffing, I glared into the fire as if it were the physical embodiment of my rage. He was stripping away decades that I had treasured. Finally, I had learned kinship, love, and the beauty of life. Hotan planned to rip it from me, but these people deserved better than unmarked graves in a foreign land. Swallowing my pride, I begged again against my better judgment.

<*Please, do me this one request. Please, I beg of you, Father.*>

The silence was unbearable, but then Hotan's voice came forward. *<It will take a great deal out of Talib to make this feasible. I need his power to achieve this. Do you understand?>*

My fists tight, I relented, *<I understand.>*

<In that case…> This was the moment I dreaded, I knew the result of his next words. *<Iapetos, leave here now. Leave behind the memories you have of me and Talib along with this place.>*

I couldn't stop the hot tears from falling. For a moment, I fought his command, struggling to not move. Then my mind became cloudy, and I couldn't remember why I was there. Like waking from a drunken stupor, I stood and walked out. The world around me was empty, and the ship was pulling away as I flew away without my regrets to remind me why I should have stayed—why I should have been so angry.

16

LOVE ME 'TILL IT HURTS

As he yanked on the string, the old bulb flickered to life, revealing the shelves of decaying cardboard boxes. What little Olivia owned and what Hotan could no longer bear to stare at had been stored away in the apartment's underbelly. Iapetos spun around, taking in the scribbled permanent marker labels. Boxes were stacked in unordered chaos all around the basement; some were on shelves, and others were piled on the floor.

"How accurate are these labels?" Iapetos grumbled to himself.

He walked over and used a finger to lift the lid on a box labeled "Xmas" to find broken Christmas ornaments and decorations. *At least one box is accurate.* He surveyed the room, taking in the dust-covered stock. Closer to the stairs was inventory meant for repairs and maintenance. Halfway into the basement were seasonal or rarely touched items, including a misplaced air conditioning vent and shower rod. It was in a shadowy corner where he found something of importance. It was so dust-covered that he almost failed to notice the elegant label written in cursive: "Good Old Days."

Iapetos froze, his heart speeding up upon recognizing Olivia's handwriting. She was always a romantic—sending letters under a diner table, leaving notes in pockets, and snapping photos despite his rebuttals. He placed a hand on the crackling cardboard and rubbed it with affection, dust balling up where he scraped. Taking in the musty air of the basement, he glared at it as he would an opponent on the battlefield. Every muscle had grown tense, the seconds ticking by at an agonizing pace. He sucked on the inside of his cheek, shuddering away the hesitation building inside him.

Gripping the box, he pulled it under the buzzing lights and steeled himself. Opening the flap, his eyes fell on various items wrapped in decaying newspaper. Curiosity bit at him, their shapes giving him a sense of nostalgia he wanted to chase further. The first item was Olivia's cheerleading trophy from her last year in high school. The corners of his lips fell as guilt pushed down on him. The plastic trophy cup was loose in its marble slab with its broken corner.

"That's right." He squatted, leaning on his knees as he cupped it in both hands. "I was angry the night I left. I cleared the countertop, and this went flying against the wall next to you. You flinched, tears across your face, but you pushed…"

He set it down and dug back in, unraveling the knick-knacks that were next to the trophy. Most of them held no signs of damage like their companion. Pom-poms lay just under those, rustling in hushed whispers as he tossed them aside. Again, his body locked up as his eyes met the carefully folded item underneath—the worn-out, black leather jacket he had abandoned there the night he stomped out of the apartment and never turned back. Many of the photos featured him wearing the favored item, and a few showed Olivia sporting the relic.

A chill crawled up his spine. Nerves in his elbows wound themselves tighter with anticipation of what he knew awaited him. Fingers wrapped around the collar, unraveling the jacket as he lifted it from its dusty tomb. He pumped his freehand in a fist a few times as if trying to get the sensation back into his fingers. Holding his breath, he dove into the left pocket. *It was always in the left pocket.* A folded paper slid across his fingertips, and goosebumps waved over his skin. He was used to the past haunting him regarding his father, but this was different. The aching of his heart was harsh, leaving his chest stinging.

"What have you done, Olivia?" He was gentle with the aged notebook paper as he read his name written in his lost lover's handwriting. "Why would you go this far to think I would…"

He dropped to the floor, his heart beating loudly in his ears. As he flipped and unfolded the letter, each glimpse of random words his eyes fell upon filled him with a sense of longing. Pausing, he lifted the paper to his nose. Though faint, her perfume wafted up from the page. *As always.* Closing his eyes, memories of her smile and touch flooded him. An echo ripped him back to the present. "*Why did you abandon us?*"

Flustered, he gripped the paper tighter, pushing himself to read:

Iapetos,

If what you say is true, that you can never die or grow old, I hope this letter finds you well. Thank you for leaving your jacket in my care. As I write this, I imagine you sitting there, looking no different than the day you left.

Iapetos paused, swallowing. It was hard to think he had opened up to a stranger after all the centuries he had walked the Earth. He had shared every tale of historical moments for her entertainment, revealed his identity, and told her what he remembered of the story of his life. She never once doubted it; instead, she thirsted for him to tell her more. Biting his lip, he read on.

> Part of me still hopes you will walk in the door at any moment, but we both know you won't. Instead, let me tell you how thankful I am to have been part of your life and that you were part of mine. We have a brilliant son who bears a striking resemblance to you. There are days I watch him from the kitchen, marveling over this gift and understanding how frightening it must have been for you to know the impossible happened. Your battles, your tribulations, and even your anguish all fed a fear that drove you away. I don't blame the child, myself, or you, my love. I write because you need to know that I forgive you.

He covered his mouth, biting his lip harder. He read the line over and over, letting it soak in and baptize the inner fears and demons haunting his soul. She knew. She was the only soul on Earth who knew him as a person and not Death itself. She saw life within him, and he gave away that precious gift. He dared to destroy it.

I have no way of knowing if our son will be immortal like you. Perhaps by the time you find the courage to come seeking this box, we will both be gone. Regardless, know that you are more than the discarded ruins of your father's lamentation. I forgive you, Iapetos, my love, and I will always love you through this life and the next.

He shuffled to the next page, her voice whispering with his own as he read her words, her thoughts, and her hopes.

Considering we are here, time broken apart, I so desperately hope you are reading this and understand that I know who and what you are: a cursed man. I beg of you, learn to forgive, not forget, so one day you can move forward. Don't allow the past to haunt you. Learn to love yourself as I have loved you. Most importantly, think of the future you want for yourself.

I named our son Hotan after your father. Why? Not to hurt you for leaving me. No, never for something so spiteful; you know me better than that. My hope is that you learn to love who you are and where you came from. Move on, let go of vengeance, and learn to face a child before having to face yourself or your father again. Life, never-ending or not, should never be wasted on anger, fear, or even guilt or jealousy.

Remember, I forgive you. These are the most powerful words anyone can say to someone as haunted as you are, my beautiful Angel of Death. You can learn to say I love you again.

Forever yours and always,

Olivia

Crumbling the paper in his fist, he stared at the concrete floor. Emotions collided with one another, none of them capable of clawing themselves to the surface. Pulling himself to his feet, he reached back into the box and picked up the jacket once more. He paused; he had so much to consider with new and old forgotten memories melting together, redefining who he thought he was. Sighing, he pulled the dusty leather back on like he had done so many times in the past. This was her parting gift, a reminder she had forgiven him.

Pulling the light string, he left the broken, scattered remains of his past on the floor in the darkness. Climbing the stairs, his mind swirled, lost in a sea of indecision. Light blinded him as he reached the top steps, swinging the door open with a violent thud. A silhouette greeted him—one he wasn't ready to encounter just yet.

"What are you doing with Mom's jacket?" Hotan's voice growled through his clenched teeth. "Where did you find that?"

Blinking, Iapetos's eyes adjusted to the fluorescent lighting flooding across him. "It's my jacket."

"No." Hotan nodded to a patch, a souvenir from Benny's Diner. "I tore a hole there on the shoulder…"

Iapetos glanced down; the new addition was vivid compared to the worn-out leather it was stitched onto. "So, it seems you did put a hole in my jacket."

Hotan stood in the doorway, the muscles in his face taut. "Give it to me."

Iapetos lifted an eyebrow, assessing his opponent. "She left it for me."

"Says who?" Hotan's face flushed, anger building in his voice.

"Your mother." Iapetos opened his fist, revealing the crumbled papers. "Here, see for yourself."

Hotan looked at the ball, unsure as he reached for it, as if a cat luring a mouse into taking the bait.

"I won't bite; I promise." Iapetos took in Hotan's features and mannerisms. Somewhere on that distraught face, he saw just a little of Olivia. "You can read it, though it wasn't meant for you."

Shaking fingers took the paper and unraveled the mess. Lips bounced with the words as he read it silently. His flushed face paled with each line. Flipping the papers sent Hotan stumbling backward. The gap increased, and Iapetos slipped by. As he marched down the hall, he glanced over his shoulder to see Hotan lean against the far wall, his hand covering his mouth.

You're right, Olivia, we are alike. What you didn't see is that he has some of you to guide him. He's both stubborn and patient; I imagine that's what got him this far.

Hunching his shoulders, Iapetos shoved out the doors and exited the building. Both hands dove into the pockets just like the old days, and in the right pocket, his fingers met another note. Pausing, he pulled out the folded paper labeled "Hotan." Grunting, he put it back.

Now isn't the right time, Ollie. He's hurting and lost. I would know; I wore that look in my eyes for a long time.

17

BACK AGAINST THE WALL

1902 Mt Pelée

All I knew was rage after I woke. I was walking aimlessly through a countryside in Portugal when I came to my senses in 1587. Why I was there and what had happened to me only caused agonizing pain. All I had was the rage for a name and face—Hotan. I searched the world for him, always a few steps behind. I had caught a glimpse of the monster in Yokohama in 1866 before the fires consumed everything. From Japan, I discovered him on the Mary Celeste, but I lost him when I drowned with the ship on that faithful day in 1872. It took nearly ten years before I discovered his trail in Haiphong, Vietnam. He left a letter with only one sentence:

I need more time.

The storm surge swept me away despite being three miles from sea. Typhoon flattened the coast. My feet landed on the dock, and my fist crumbled a letter inside my coat jacket. He had done the unthinkable—he sent me an invitation. I pulled it out, reading it once more:

> Come to St. Pierre, Martinique. I'll
> be waiting at Etang Sec.
>
> Hotan

It was abrupt, and every cell in my body was on high alert. If he wanted to kill me—if he could kill me—he would have done it centuries ago. The fear felt instinctual as it twisted in my guts. As my feet hit land when I stepped off the docks, I paled. A surge of familiar power waved over me. A smile crossed my face. *He's here.* At first, I wasn't sure where to go. Grabbing a sailor, I pointed to the place on letter, Etang Sec.

"Where is this place?" I demanded.

He frowned, his eyes rising over my head. "On Mt. Pelée."

I spun to see the smoking volcano. A haze of memories, disjointed and broken, came to mind and I mumbled, "Mt. Vesuvius."

"No, sir," he spoke louder. "That's Mt. Pelée. She's been brooding for days on end, shaking the town and raining ash. We're trying to prepare for the worst, but the trading companies aren't willing to pull the locals out for their own safety. Etang Sec is in the thick of the activity. No man would dare go to that place now." He pointed, one eye squinting. "It's there, you see. Right where the smoke and fire keep popping. It's a death wish."

"Perhaps I came looking for one." I abandoned him, marching through the town.

I had my target in site and aimed to make my way there. Silence fell over the people I passed. They watched me like a dark phantom headed to a place designed for death. Climbing the last ascension, I reached a plateau. Large columns of steam plumed into the air, the stench of sulfur overwhelming. Heat rose from the ground and waved in the air between vents. Hell had formed itself on Mt. Pelée. Deep down I wondered, *Is his power causing the chaos? Will my power tip the scale and wipe out the lives below? What does it matter? At least I can face the man who gave me this haunted life. I am Death, and the bodies left in my wake are nothing more than a rite of passage.*

Peeking through the steam, I caught glimpses of what made Etang Sec a worthy landmark. Boiling sulfuric waters filled the once dry lake crater to the rim. It was surreal seeing a lake spit and hiss like a pot on a stove. Everything was dead or dying. The sulfur, the heat, the ash, and hints of lava all were a recipe for impending doom for the flora and fauna. If I had been a normal man, the burning and withering follicles in my lungs would have killed me way before reaching the height.

The wind carried voices, and I squinted, searching along the edge of Etang Sec, hoping to find the source. My heart fluttered. Two figures stood before me, one silver-haired and the other like obsidian, skin black as coal. The element of Death seethed, roiling in and out of my body. My stomach knotted. Pain surged as I felt my power flare, as if they could draw my power from me, consumed by this new power of Death. My knees buckled as I watched; a cold sweat did nothing to tame the raging heat tearing through me. Veins on fire, I pulled myself back to my feet.

I recognize Hotan, but who is the other man?

I marched forward with labored breath. The ground shook underfoot as Mt. Pelée roared louder. Our powers lashed out, tendrils clawing at each other across the divide as nature screamed her disapproval. Hotan turned, his green eyes gleaming like emeralds against the dark abyss of his skin. I flinched, seeing he had opened the floodgates of his power completely. It terrified me. I couldn't imagine how he was able to hold his mind together, knowing I could never do the same. How he could stand without being consumed by his power and turning to ash in front of me was beyond comprehension.

Can he retract his power again after releasing it to this degree? Is this what it means to let the power do as it wishes?

"Who in the world…" the man before Hotan whispered, panting.

I needed to know why he had summoned me to this land of fire and sulfur where at any moment Mt. Pelée may consume us in her wrath, red and hot like the flames of Hell. Swallowing back the pain and forcing my body to move against its tightened muscles and aching joints, I met them at the summit at last. The black-skinned demon was undoubtedly my father; his power painted him in the sins he had committed for so long. I didn't recognize the man with the hair and face so much like Hotan's. Regardless, the features were strikingly similar to both myself and Hotan, and I knew we were related in some way.

Fear filled this other man's eyes, his breath catching in his throat. He could see the power escaping me and clashing with Hotan's. Again, the ground rumbled underfoot. Pain surged in parallel; my body and the earth were both in agony from the imbalance Hotan had caused. It wasn't *if* Mt. Pelée would blow, but a matter of *when*. As the two versions of the element of Death fought over supremacy, it could only be a matter of minutes.

The town below will be decimated. It's Pompeii and Mt. Vesuvius all over again.

Fear shifted to anger in the silver-eyed man. My heart fluttered as a stir of immortal power grew within him. He was like me, like us. I had never stopped to think there were more of us and panic shook me. *I have wasted so much time chasing my father's shadow when I could have found someone more willing, more understanding.* My chest ached. There were so many secrets, and in this one selfish moment, I had risked it all.

"What is going on, Hotan!" the man shouted, his anger spilling forth into words. "Who is this, and what do you intend to do with him?"

I wanted to say something. I wanted to tell him my name. I wanted to know his, but first, I had to be sure. Forcing several steps closer, my legs gave way. My knees slammed into the dirt as agony took hold of me, and I muffled my screams. Powers were colliding, and we all wore expressions to match the vexing feat of it all. Markings crawled across my skin; I couldn't contain it any longer. I had tried so hard, but I couldn't stay conscious without letting some of it vent against my will. The rage in the silver-eyed man continued to build. Catching Hotan's glare, I pushed to find my voice.

"Your name … is Hotan? You've plagued my dreams for hundreds of years…" I drew a breath, turning to the other man. "Who are you?"

Sighing, Hotan answered, "I'm your father, Iapetos. Today, I intend to make things right by you and give you the life and opportunities I squandered and denied you."

I saw the other man's anger waver as he looked to Hotan's hand. Fear filled me. A ball of power pulled the element of Life and Rebirth into it. Only Death remained in the body before me.

What horrid thing does he intended to do to me?

"What will it do to him?" His voice fell out like a warning toward Hotan, eyeing me as he asked, "What will *you* do to him?"

"Talib." Looking down at his hand, Hotan smiled. "It will give him a single opportunity to create life. Being the element of Death, he's only known a life of rejection surrounded by the destruction I have forced upon him. It was your efforts that aided him in his renewed ability to control his powers, but I don't know what will happen once…"

"It is the same concept; someone from our lineage must be involved for a reincarnation to be successful." Sweat trickled down Talib's cheek. "Why does Iapetos have to carry your seed in particular?"

"I think you already know…" Closing his eyes, Hotan's face tensed, and my stomach twisted. "Only two people are capable of carrying this seed: my brother and my son. I thought and hoped that Saphellia would awaken. I was afraid to force it myself. I realized that between you and him, the one I have wronged the most is Iapetos. My son has never experienced childhood, a mother's touch, a father's guidance, falling in love. To repent for my mistakes, I will give him something we have been denied."

"No, you cannot…" Talib asked the questions filling me before I could piece them into words. "Is he even strong enough to contain it?"

They looked to me, and the agony in my body gave way to terror as I stammered, "I, I don't know."

Everything dulled. Pain had taken the reigns back into its greedy hands. I couldn't move. My vision blurred as I listened. I wanted to run, I wanted to shake him and tell he that he was a mad man. *If this rendered me to this state, how is he able to stand with half his power balled into one hand, despite its tendrils manipulating everything around me? How powerful is the man who called me son?*

Hotan continued. "As I thought about it, it made more sense for Death to give birth to the reincarnation of Rebirth. From the ashes, we will be born again. It is mentioned in multiple folklores and religions. The true meaning of life comes after death; therefore, I chose Iapetos. Fate guided me this time, not my selfish wants like in the past."

"Why am I here?" Talib demanded. "It seems my advice is not needed."

"You're wrong." Hotan's voice sounded ethereal in my ears. "It was your advice which led me this far…"

"And how much and for how long did you ignore my advice before heeding it?" Talib balled his fists tight, anger fueling him. "Why do I not remember giving you this advice?"

"I took those memories away." Hotan's words brought forward a rage within me like no other. *The bastard has been taking memories!* "I apologize for abusing my powers. I still want to hear what decision you would make. Which immortal would you choose to take this once-in-a-lifetime gift to bear a child?"

"Do you realize your powers have made the other elements unstable?" The fiery gaze from Talib chilled me to the bone. "How many lives have been claimed because of it?"

"I never had control of my powers to begin with, Talib." I could barely breathe, barely stay in a stable state to hear my father's confessions. "And worse, he is stable until I am near. Perhaps he holds a key, but again, your abilities have grown beyond what I gave you."

The powers shifted, the two auras of death tangling and knotting in unknown ways. I wailed in agony, and the earth shook and screamed with me. The sound of fissure bubbling and hissing to life nearby made me envious. I wanted to release this searing pain and bring a calm to the unstable surge of the element of Death. It hungered for the end to come. I could feel how it ate away at Hotan's body, bringing his death closer. The sulfur in the air thickened. Mt. Pelée was on the verge of wreaking havoc across this land and its people. Again, the ground rumbled underfoot, and rocks rained down. I didn't need my vision to know that Mt. Pelée was erupting.

"Who should be chosen: the childless brother I hurt or the child I rejected and abandoned on multiple occasions?" There was an eerie lack of emotion in Hotan's voice as he pressed Talib further. "I'm confident both of you can handle it. As for how it will become stable, I can't promise anything."

There was only a quick pause before Talib answered, "As grandfather begets father, father begets a son, son begets the new generation. If you wish to pass down your legacy, this is your only chance to honor the memory of the life you longed for while giving him a piece of humanity he would never have been able to experience…"

I could sense a surge of power, its aura red and calming. In the darkness, where a blue ball glowed between the walls of Death and Judgment, I watched him shift the power. Siphoning the red aura, the small ball of Life shifted to a purple hue. Swallowing, I stared at it with daunting realization.

<He's lost his mind. Forcing Life into Death, even with the aid of Judgment, will never work. It'll tear me apart. Please, please don't do this! I've suffered enough! MAKE IT STOP! PLEASE STOP HIM, TALIB!>

My body was running out of stamina. I fell, slamming my back against the ground. Not a finger would lift nor, could I find my voice. I gripped to what little awareness I had, still fighting in the veil unseen where I knew Hotan still watched. That look, that pitiful expression of sorrow and guilt was insulting. This was all his doing; if it pained him so, why wouldn't he come to his senses on the matter. With stolen memories, I can only imagine I had tried, and even Talib had tried in the past decades? Centuries?

"I want part of this reincarnation to have some of you in it." Hotan spoke, a surge of his power engulfing everything in the bleakness of where my soul watched. "Perhaps the next version of me would have a better sense of self and not repeat the mistakes I made. As for my son, I pray he finds someone to love, to know the excitement and fear of becoming a father has on one's soul."

Talib's voice revealed he now suffered alongside me as he asked, "How are you not in pain?"

Hotan sighed, "I am, in many ways. Physical, emotional, mental, and even in my soul as it lies here in my hand, embracing a small part of you."

"How does this work?" Talib demanded. "The seed... how do you give it to someone else."

"With the help of your element." Hotan's answer filled me with dread. "He will take it from me and swallow it."

"S-Swallow it?" The simplistic answer was terrifying. Asking anyone to swallow someone's soul was demonic, and Talib's voice reflected my own emotions. "What will happen then?"

"I simply don't know." I could feel the strings of Rebirth pulling out Talib's power, forcing it to do its bidding. "Iapetos's element allows him to swallow souls, Talib. Frightening, isn't it? Regardless, I pray this will be the last one he ever devours."

With that, Hotan took control of Judgment. It surged into me like a thousand needles. In my weakened state, I couldn't refuse or fight back. Against my will, I would become the vessel for this seed.

<When will you ask me what I want out of life, Father?>

I gave up. Tired of the resistance, tired of the pain, I took in the command tied with the tendril of red power.

<If you're so hellbent on doing what you want with my life, here, have it.>

"Iapetos, I give you the soul of your father and the seed to make a new life of your own." Hotan's words were bitter promises I never wanted. "Please accept this as reparation for all the sins I have committed against you and others in my life."

<*I can never forgive you for this. You deserve the death I feel taking you, but I will not create a life for you. I will not atone for your sins on your behalf. I am not you.*>

As if under a spell, I rose to my feet and didn't resist. If this was Hotan's soul, then I would swallow it and rid the world of this terrible plague. My only wish was to watch him die, but my eyes wouldn't allow me to see. I reached out and took the seed of Hotan's reincarnation into my palm. My jaw fell open like a gate. I raised the ball of power with its purple aura and inhaled swiftly. I drank in the power, eager to take his life and snuff out the last of his blue flames. Hotan grunted as death gripped him. His soul devoured, I imagined his body falling to ash.

They always do when I consume them…

The power hit my core and bore its fangs. It bit into my soul and tore it apart. Fear shook me. I fell to my knees, screaming as a new pain took hold. My sight came back, and the red flares of lava matched the mixture of terror and anger inside me. Black and blue feathers exploded from my back as wings stretched out, no longer derelict and rotten. My soul and the seed were reacting and fighting with one another. I was Death, and it thrust Life into me. Mt. Pelée rumbled and smoldered heavier from its fumaroles, matching my turmoil. Stumbling away, Talib watched helplessly as blue light blinded me and dared to silence my cries of torment.

Unable to breathe, I rolled forward as the surge waned. The wings were on my shoulders, their shadow wide and contrasting against the chaos brewing from the volcano underfoot. I saw Hotan falling to ashes, but he wasn't dead just yet. I crumpled under another surge of power. If this continued, I wouldn't be able to flee before Mt. Pelée erupted.

"Talib…" rasped Hotan, leaning heavier onto him. "He's struggling to stabilize it…"

"What can we do?" Talib came for me, but Hotan grabbed him. "We must help him!"

"I will do this." Half his other arm was turning white and flaking off in the wind. "Listen closely…"

Panic filled Talib's face. "Please don't do this, Hotan!"

"Leave this place," Hotan demanded. Again, he had hijacked the element of Judgment. "Do not remember this place or the whereabouts of myself or Iapetos. You will have a full plate since this will break the reincarnation spell further. Iapetos was in bad shape when he arrived, so I doubt he'll recall you being here. I will do everything I can to stabilize him. Now go!"

<NO! You can't do this to us, to me, you bastard!>

Talib gripped Hotan's shoulder as anger filled him. "No… I cannot…"

"You must." Hotan's brow folded upward in desperation as he pleaded, "He is my son, and as you said, he is my responsibility. I will stabilize him before I let my soul be swallowed completely. Please leave, for I fear the task may cause an irreversible explosion like that of—"

"Mt. Vesuvius," Talib answered. My body was breaking down, and Talib's words haunted me. *I was there too.* "How do you propose I leave?"

"Lend me your element…" Hotan leaned his forehead onto Talib's shoulder, "And I will prove you have your own wings."

"Fine." My heart sunk as he allowed Hotan to take control. "Do what you will with this last moment of Judgment."

"Forget this place, and fly back home on your own two wings, my dear brother." His grip released, and with one great whoosh, Talib left.

"What of me?" I rasped, watching his obsidian flesh crumble away.

"You stabilized quicker than I expected." There was a faint smile as his crumbling body came closer. "Can I ask the same of you?"

He leaned his forehead against mine. "Ask what of me?"

"Fly from here, and forget me, forget all of me."

Mt. Pelée roared, and the ground shook. Hotan fell away, his ashes mixing with hers as if she came to reclaim him. A tinge of Judgment had left him. As I fled the volcano, its destruction destroying everything, my mind wandered.

Why am I here? Who was the man with the red aura?

18

FALSE ALARM

"I don't understand." Hotan heard the clicking of the apartment doors closing. "All this time?"

Taking in a deep breath, his mind echoed parts of the letter his mother had written. She left it behind for the man he had labeled a monster for so long. He was confused by how Talib was handling the situation and Iapetos's change in behavior. Before, Iapetos wanted to rip out Hotan's throat, but the man just walked away, sharing a look in his eyes he knew well—pain, confusion, and even the calm anger few understood. His straight face, solid and unmoving, reflected his own.

Are we not that different? Does he miss Mom as much as I do?

Hotan flew out the doors, but Iapetos was gone without a trace. The letters in his hand stared back at him as they fluttered in the breeze. It felt different from when he had left after the fight on the rooftop. All these weeks, he had prepared himself for an instant battle when and if they met again, but this changed everything. His mother had known everything, including the possibility he might become immortal.

Did she leave something behind for me?

A car slowed down on the street, the tinted window rolling down to reveal Jacob. "Hotan, are you okay?"

"I…" He looked to the letters, folding them with care and sliding them in his back pocket. "I need to see Talib."

Jacob gave a smile. "Hop in. I'll text Annie and let her know I've got ya."

"So that's why your timing was on point." Hotan slid inside the car, rolling the window up. "You've been trying to keep tabs on me for them, Annie and Hisota."

"Yeah, but we understand you have a lot to digest." Jacob finished typing a text message and threw his phone in the cup holder. "Annie had called in a panic and said… well, I suppose it doesn't matter."

"Said Iapetos was here." Hotan and Jacob locked eyes. "He was. I ran into him."

Jacob swallowed. "And you two didn't go after each other's throats?"

"No, it was as if…" Hotan's mother's written words echoed in his head, *I forgive you.* "I need to know what happened between Talib and Iapetos. There was a sensation like the last string attached to my power was cut loose, and it has been calm ever since. I need to know why."

"Fair enough." Jacob nodded. "I suppose the old man will have answers on that topic."

Hotan leaned the back of his seat down. "I think I'll take a nap."

"Not so fast, I still have a bone to pick with you." Turning the car, they were gaining speed on a bigger highway toward the outskirts of town.

"With me?" Hotan raised his eyebrows. "What did I do?"

"Abigail." Jacob's purple eyes shot him a side glance, and Hotan turned away.

"There's nothing I want to talk about right now." Closing his eyes, the muscles flinched in Hotan's cheek. "Not at this point. Lilly gave us a lecture; I don't need a second."

Sighing, Jacob shifted in the driver seat. "Well, in that case, all I have to say is … never feel guilty for loving someone, as long as you love them for who they are, not who you want them to be."

Hotan remained silent.

Jacob grunted and focused on the drive. In a matter of minutes, Hotan was asleep, losing his battle to the weight of mental exhaustion.

Jacob parked his car close to Talib's back door. Hotan didn't stir from his sleep. Saphellia opened the door, waving for him to come in, and he motioned for her to come to the car. Her brow furrowed as the screen door made a loud slap behind her. A few steps shy, she noticed his unexpected passenger. Jacob opened the driver's side door, leaning over the top of the car.

"I brought a visitor." Jacob smirked, nodding in Hotan's direction.

"I see." Saphellia crossed her arms. "Was he hurt or forced to come here?"

"Ugh, no." Jacob's face flushed. "He demanded to come talk to Talib."

"I see," Saphellia repeated, looking over Hotan. "He looks thin and exhausted. I'm shocked he would come here and risk running into Iapetos."

"He ran into Iapetos." Jacob gauged her paling face. "When was the last time he was even here, Saphy?"

"It's been a few weeks. Talib dropped him off in town, and that was the last I saw of him." Walking around, she opened the passenger door. "Is he okay? Did they get in a fight?"

"No and no." Rubbing his shoulder, Jacob confessed what little he knew. "He seems baffled by his encounter with Iapetos. On top of that, I think Abigail and him are falling for each other. That's a lot to swallow on top of all this supernatural bullshit."

Sighing, she nodded. "Hotan. Wake up, Hotan."

Jolting upright, Hotan realized he had arrived at his destination. Leaning forward, he crushed his palms into his eyes, rubbing the sleep from them.

"Come on, Talib isn't back yet." She stepped back, giving Hotan space to climb out of the car. "For now, you can finish your nap in the guest room, or I can brew some coffee."

"I-I think I'll crash on the guest bed." Hotan's cheeks flushed. "It's been a while since I've let myself sleep. I kind of miss it."

"Go on, you know where it is." She shut the car door, watching Hotan shuffle inside. "Abigail, you say?"

"Yeah, it seems genuine, but I don't think either of them know how to explain it and express it." Snorting, Jacob smiled to himself. "I suppose the real problem is they have to find a happy median with their own emotions. No one can tell them how to do that; they have to work through it themselves."

"True." Saphellia crossed her arms again, tapping her arm with her fingers as she thought. "Normally, I wouldn't question their connection, especially after the one night here over a year ago." Her fingers paused, and she looked over the top of the car at Jacob who raised his eyebrows. "But they are so different. She's nothing like Shellie, even if she can look like her. Then there's the fact that he looks like Hotan, who we now know she followed for so many centuries. In the end, that's all that connects those two. The way they see their world is a completely different beast."

"Here's hoping mistakes won't unfold that harm them … or us." Jacob climbed back in the car.

"Wait," she said. He stood back up to meet her gaze. "I thought you were staying?"

"Nope, got to head back to Annie's." Jacob glanced at the closed back door and lowered his voice. "Iapetos and Hisota also had a confrontation. I need to gather information however I can about this guy. It's weird that none of us except for Talib knew who or what he was … or that he existed." Jacob turned back with a dangerous look on his face.

"It doesn't sit well with me either. Would you believe me if I told you the old Hotan ripped away memories by force?" Saphellia's arms dropped, and she waited for his reply.

"I believe it." Swallowing, his expression softened. "But to do that over and over to your own brother and child is…"

"Unforgivable." Saphellia's voice hit hard as she stomped off toward the kitchen. "Let me know what you find out, Jake."

"Yes, ma'am." Jacob shook his head, relieved to be leaving.

Hotan's head sunk heavy into the pillow. The bed was a warm welcome as he laid there on his belly. There was no desire to test out his power here, no complicated emotions stirring every time he saw Abigail, and no sensation of Iapetos coming in the door. He had avoided the church but found a nostalgic comfort in the tiny room reminiscent of a small countryside hospital room. His head pounded, still swimming in the abyss of confusion created by those few minutes with Iapetos. Reaching in his back pocket, he pulled out the folded letter and glared at it.

"She knew this whole time and never said a word." A bitter twist ripped through Hotan's soul, the unshakable affection for his mother feeling stained and distorted. "How could you not say anything?"

He fought the urge to crumple it and throw it across the room. Instead, he tossed it on the end table and crushed his face into the pillow. The darkness lured him into a deep sleep, and the tension in his muscles loosened their grip. He made out the muffled sounds of Saphellia coming through the door of the room, although her words were mangled and slurred as he had lost himself to the want for sleep.

Blinding light brought Hotan to a familiar place in his dreams. A vast space, flat and never-ending with cracked soil like the Bonneville Salt Flats. Heat rose from the white ground at his feet, and the sharp horizon cut across the divide, splitting the white land from the blue sky. Last time he was here, a figure matching Geliah—no, more so Iapetos—had slashed him down. He had endured this dream time and time again. As if habit, Hotan spun around, looking for the incoming attacker. His ears filled with the beating of his heart and sweat stung his eyes. Frustration added to his growing tension.

"I thought I was over this." Hotan spun again, the searing sunlight obstructing his ability to focus. "I suppose I have options this time." Looking to his palms, he sighed. "Let's make some shade."

He crouched and slammed his hands to the ground. Clay crackled with blue flames, and roots boiled up from the dust. Satisfied that he had seeded enough power into the ground, he stood up and took a few steps back. An old, majestic oak created a shield against the blinding sun. The shade provided a startling chill to the air, and the sunlight no longer interfered in his ability to scan his surroundings. Something fluttered in and rested on a branch. A black bird bounced in the limbs above him. Where it came from doesn't matter; it's only a dream.

Walking around his handiwork, Hotan watched the crow follow above, cawing occasionally. He circled one more time, confirming no signs of anything approaching, and the bird stayed close by. Rubbing the back of his neck, Hotan furrowed his brow at the black-eyed, feathered pest, and it cocked its head in reply.

"I suppose it's just the two of us," he remarked.

The crow shrieked, launching off the limb and swooping low. Hotan ducked out of its way and turned around. There stood Iapetos. Muscles tightened across Hotan's body. Iapetos stopped at the edge of light and shade, as if it had created a barrier between them—a line he dare not cross. Despite the blinding sunlight, he was a foreboding shadow, unmoved by the bright world they stood inside.

"It has been you this whole time, the one who comes and cuts me down, hasn't it?" Hotan's anger and frustration drowned the fear which used to overwhelm him at this point in the dream. "The father coming for his son, how biblical."

Iapetos's face was no longer the fuzzed and shadowed blob from before. His irises were like large pupils, but they fell to the ground in shame. Hotan flinched.

Why would he feel shame, and in my dream?

"Does this mean you've been hunting me in my dreams and in real life?" Hotan's stomach knotted. Do I even want to know the answer?

"Yes." Iapetos's eyes lifted, and his cheek tensed. "I thought perhaps talking here would be best."

"Bringing me back to a place that has haunted me for years about my death isn't ideal." Hotan scoffed, crossing his arms. "I tried talking to you in person over an hour ago, what made you change your mind?"

"First, I must confess, your mother left you a note as well." Hotan's arms dropped, and he opened his mouth to respond, but Iapetos spoke louder, sterner. "But I don't think either of us is ready to learn what she has to say to you. Did you read—"

"Yes." Hotan's fists balled tighter as he glowered at Iapetos. "She forgave you, but I don't think I can. Even knowing we aren't so different, I can't forgive you."

"What makes you think we're the same?" Iapetos's brow lowered, glaring deep into his son's eyes. "Can you compare my past to yours?"

"Our fathers tossed us into a sea of despair." Again, the twitch of muscles in Iapetos's face let Hotan know his words were slicing through the tough exterior. "Not only that, but we both had to figure out how to live and thrive under the shadow of our father's sins. The difference is, I learned to accept people in my life. I was me and not this person and thing I am reincarnated after. I lived the way I wanted despite my immortality. You let your vengeance devour your soul. You became no different from the person you sought to kill."

"You're right. I reflect my father's mistakes." A smirk crept across Iapetos's face. "Hotan, I can't go back and rescue your mother, and I can't become the father you wish you had. In fact, I still don't know what I want for myself. Like your mother said, I need to learn to live for myself. Part of me wants to chase vengeance, but who or what to aim this weapon at is not so clear now. Lines have been blurred, truths have been revealed, and I am just as lost as I was the day he created me."

Taking in a deep breath, Hotan closed his eyes. "I don't want to be your enemy. That person spent their last moments on Earth atoning for centuries of mistakes and selfish decisions. Like Mom said, I don't have to forget about the past, but I can't forgive you either. Instead, I can move forward, and maybe someday, I'll learn how to forgive even you."

Iapetos smiled. "She meant it when she said you were brilliant."

Opening his eyes, Hotan stared at the ceiling fan spinning above him. The dream had ended. Perhaps Iapetos was satisfied with what he had to say. Sitting up, Hotan balled the sheets in his fists. Blinking, he hadn't awoken in a startle or cold sweat like so many times before. There was no lingering sensation of fear and anxiety, only the mottled mixture of unsettled emotions.

What was the purpose in telling me about the letter for me? Did he feel guilty?

The door opened, making Hotan jerk out of bed. Talib froze. Hotan's tension fell away, and his face flushed from having swung out, ready to fight. Clearing his throat, Talib raised his hand, holding the handwritten letter he found on the end table.

How long was I asleep?

"Where did you find this?" His silvery eyes demanded an answer. "It is from your mother, is it not?"

"I-Iapetos gave it to me." Hotan shoved the sheet and cover back on the bed. "And she wrote one for me, but he's holding it hostage."

"Really…" Talib stared at the pages again, placing his knuckles to his chin. "Saphellia made coffee; let us talk at the table."

"Okay…" Hotan was nervous; something about Talib's reaction to the letter made every nerve in his body tighten. "Are you okay?"

"Yes." Talib seemed absent-minded as Hotan followed close behind him. "Just… I never expected this. She knew who and what Iapetos was, and now, I wonder how this letter impacted him. In fact, I cannot help but question if she had figured out who I was or suspected me to be immortal."

Hotan sat down, rambling off everything running through his mind as Saphellia poured him a cup of coffee. "I never knew she left anything behind. As many times as I went through all her things before, I should have found something like this. It seems like Iapetos knew where to look. I don't know how I'm supposed to feel about any of this, especially knowing how much my mother was involved without ever speaking a word."

"I see." Talib laid the pages on the table and took a sip of coffee. "You said there is one for you, a letter from her? What was his reason for not giving it to you?"

"He said I'm not ready to read it and neither is he. He's not ready to see what she had to say, so I don't think he's read it." The coffee was warm and sharp on Hotan's tongue, spurring him to continue his thoughts on the matter. "I told him I can't forgive him for not being there, for everything he's done to me, to her, to everyone."

"I can understand that. No one is asking you to forgive him, and I do not imagine he has asked you for forgiveness?" Leaning back in his chair, Talib drummed his fingers on the table. "Has he?"

"N-no." Staring down into the cup of coffee, Hotan watched the steam swirl upward and fade away. "I just… I needed him to know. Mom forgave him, but I never can. He had so many choices, and she knew, *she knew*, and she never said a damn thing about it all."

"How does one tell a small child he may never grow old?" Saphellia interjected, leaning on the kitchen counter. "Tell her child that he will watch his own mother grow old and die and then walk this Earth alone until his father could escape the curse laid across him? She wanted you to be free of those burdens until she was absolutely sure of your immortality and you became old enough to understand the weight of what you had inherited from your father. I know…" She paused, searching her cup for a moment. "I know that's what I would have done."

Grimacing at his reflection, Hotan furrowed his brow. "Still, how was I supposed to know she left a note in *his* jacket for me?"

"I think she wanted him to find those notes first." Talib huffed, inhaling deeply before he continued. "She wanted him to come back but knew it wouldn't happen while she was alive. Her words in the letter make that clear. And, to be honest, this was a test for Iapetos more so than for you. If he returned, he would want to revisit those memories, so she made sure they were there waiting for him. It was as if she knew Iapetos was capable of that much. She knew he could break free from the self-destructive path he had been walking before they met."

"I don't know…" Hotan started but lost his words.

"Iapetos and I had many years stolen from us. We have recovered them thanks to the events from the fight, but I do not know." Talib stopped talking, pausing the drumming of his fingers. "I do not know who I am anymore, and I imagine he feels the same way. It is like regaining control of your body but being burdened with the consequences left behind from a stranger." He leaned on the table, locking eyes with me. "If I am having a tough time deciding whether to embrace the person I used to be and who I think I am now, Iapetos has a far rockier path ahead. He did not have a childhood. He was born from the element of Death itself. What little he had of a normal life was stripped away and used against him."

"Is it that hard to choose to live your life over destroying everything?" Hotan spat, slamming his cup on the table. "I don't understand how you all keep making this out to be a—"

Talib raised his hand, eyes like daggers. "Did you not struggle for over a year over Shellie?"

Hotan paled. *I would have allowed myself to wither away, but I had become immortal… undying,* he thought.

"Knowing that my brother took so much from me and even more from Iapetos has not made the matter easy. I have come to terms with accepting the mistakes I made without realizing what was happening or knowing who I was. Forgetting the past can make you lose sight of where we want to go in life." The muscles in Talib's face tensed. "Deep down, I cannot help but think it would not have changed those turning points where my emotions decided the path I chose."

"I see." Hotan admired how intimidating Talib's eyes could be. "In short, we still don't know if he'll make the same decision to fight and come after me?"

Closing his eyes, Talib spoke clearly and concisely as he searched memories. "If he is the man I recall, he would rather redirect his rage onto me rather than an innocent child. It may be hard to believe, but at some point in his life, the idea of settling down with a girl was something he deeply yearned for. Granted, this was 1450 AD and in the middle of wars raging all around."

Hotan took another sip of his coffee, calming his nerves. "We're all still waiting to see what Iapetos will do. I get it, we don't know who we are dealing with anymore, but the letter… That's why my mother…"

Saphellia picked up the letter from the table, "She really loved him for who he was, huh?"

"Y-yeah." Hotan huddled his cup. "Even I knew that. The way she would look at his picture in the photos told me more than she ever spoke about him."

"I'm shocked he gave you this though." She gently laid the paper down. "I would imagine this is all he has left of her."

"The jacket." Hotan placed the cup down. "She gave him the jacket back that he always wore in the pictures, what she wore in the photos, and what he was wearing when I saw him."

Talib and Saphellia exchanged glances.

My reflection wavered in my coffee, and I smiled. "She said it was like having him close to her again. I can't tell you how many times I heard that and nothing more about him. If he really loved her, then I hope he's wearing it and thinking about how close she is to him once more by doing so."

Relaxing, Talib leaned back in his chair. "If the Iapetos I admired most is in there, then that is exactly why he walked out wearing it."

19

DARK ON ME

1996

Immortals were popping up everywhere. I followed one to the city, and he hadn't left yet. He looked like the man who haunted my dreams, the ones where Mt. Pelée burst in red ribbons and hot ash.

He knows what happened; he was there.

I had no name. Just the businessman front he used to juggle resources and influence the area. For some strange reason, no one questioned it. The old historian at the library remarked how generous his family was ever since helping found the town back in colonial days. Why he had rooted himself deeply here wasn't understood.

It was getting late, pushing well past midnight, and another storm gusted down the empty streets. The only place open was a twenty-four-seven diner, Benny's Place. The small joint looking inviting, and I was eager to not spend another night lurking in the rain. The door closed behind me with a loud bang as the wind slammed it shut, and the waitress behind the long counter jolted.

Smash!

She dropped the glass cup in her hand. "Crap!"

"Olivia…" The cook appeared in the order window. "Was that another glass?"

She bit her bottom lip, eyes big and filling with tears. "Maybe?"

"It was my fault." I slid onto a bar stool, waving to get his attention. "That wind slammed the door, and I think it frightened her."

The cook eyed me a moment. A rumbling of thunder drew all our eyes to the glass storefront as the wind kicked up and rain fell in dark curtains of gray. Olivia was sweeping up the broken glass by the time I swiveled back, and the cook had vanished. I spotted a menu tucked on the other side of the bar top and leaned over to grab it. She eyed me, cheeks blushing.

"Hi there." She stood, emptying the dust pan in the nearby trash can. "Let me go wash up. Look at the menu, and I'll be back to take your order in just a few."

I lifted an eyebrow and smiled at her. "Sounds like a plan."

Her face flushed once more, and she rushed out of sight. She was young, fresh out of high school. Her auburn hair fought to come loose from her bun, which had been done in a rush. Long strands of hair framed her face and neck, trailing in the air with each movement. She was petite, likely a cheerleader based on the shoes and muscling in her legs and arms. I sighed. *This isn't the time or place to have fun. The whole reason I am here is to figure out who the man with the red aura is. He is certainly not my father.* My eyes fell to the menu filled with classic, burger-and-waffle-themed meals.

So American… I miss France and Germany already. Oh, even Japan or Thailand would be quite the treat.

"Did you figure out what you wanted?" She came back all smiles, her bun wrapped up tightly, all the loose strings gone.

I frowned.

"Uh, what's wrong?" Her eyes widened. "What happened? Did I take too long?"

I shook my head and smirked. "I liked your hair better before." Her face turned a new shade of red, and I burst into laughter. "Coffee for now. I'm not hungry tonight."

She puffed out her cheeks, her brown eyes cutting him to pieces if they could. "Coffee."

"Sorry, I can't resist giving a pretty girl a hard time." There wasn't much else to do with the storm raging outside. "You work late nights like this often?"

She lifted an eyebrow, sliding a cup over and grabbed the pot off the warmer. "Maybe, why would a hot guy like you be asking?"

Now it was my turn to lift an eyebrow. "A hot guy?"

She smiled, snickering as she filled my cup. "You called me a name, so I called you one to be fair."

"Well, I suppose I know your name and should have used it, huh, Olivia?" I pointed to her badge. "And sadly, I don't have one of those cool, shiny tags like you."

"Right, and the cook yelled it a minute ago." The pot clunked into place. "Are you new in town?" The last word lingered, her face expressing she wanted my name.

Sighing, I added sugar and creamer to my coffee. "I'm new here, yes."

"And your name?" She was leaning on the counter behind her.

"Iapetos." I stirred my coffee, eyeing her a moment. "As in the Greek God, Iapetos."

"That's rather dark." She twisted away, grabbing the broom to sweep again. "Ugh, I always miss a piece."

"What's a girl like you doing in a dive like this?" My spoon clanked on the counter, and I watched her as I sipped my coffee.

She scowled. "Because unlike most of my friends, I need the money."

"Ah, plans to escape?" Another sip.

"No. I wish." Grabbing the dustpan again, she squatted down. "I need to help my parents out, to be honest."

My smirk failed, and I stared at my reflection in my coffee. *You jerk.*

"Mom's been real sick and Dad…" She stood, dumping the last of the glass shards into the trash for good. "Dad's gonna kill himself if he keeps working doubles."

"Sorry," I mumbled, gulping down my coffee.

"Nothing to be sorry about." She shrugged. Her eyes lifted, staring into mine, and somehow, she mustered a big smile. "It's part of life to struggle. Just makes those good days that much sweeter, memorable for someone like me."

I opened my mouth, but found I wasn't sure what to say to her. Never in all the centuries had I accepted that we were meant to struggle. *Life isn't meant to be easy but a fight for those sweeter moments.* Swallowing, I dug for my wallet and pulled out cash. In mere minutes with her, I had become ashamed that I never slowed down and pondered this one simple aspect about nature, lives, and even on my own immortal existence. The bills scattered next to the coffee, and she gave a baffled look.

"For the glass." I gave her a pained expression. "For the trouble tonight."

"B-but this is too much." She rushed the counter, trying to hand it all back.

I shook my head, smiling as I folded her fingers over it. "You're a kind girl, and you deserve to be happy."

Turning, I left her speechless. The wind whistled across the streetlights and signs. Rain stung across me like a thousand angry bees. She ran to the door and opened it to call me back, but I wouldn't dare turn around. Closing my eyes, I enjoyed the moment—having a woman scream my name, intending to want me back. It was the first time I heard it in that tone. Smiling, I turned down the dark alley to continue the investigation I came to pursue.

I stood across the street from the diner, the windows bright from the fluorescent lights within. It had been weeks since I had been there, but for some strange reason, I was curious. There behind the counter, Olivia was helping another customer. It was almost one o'clock in the morning, and soon, waves of drunken customers would come and go. I turned to walk away, but the owner of the bookstore came out and glared at me.

"What do you want?" I blurted, ill-tempered. "We've already tried talking, and that didn't bode well for either of us."

"I can feel it." The Cheshire cat grin and glassy look in her eyes made me flinch. "You're driving yourself crazy; it's so wonderful."

Covering my face, I sighed. "Tina, you make me feel better about being the element of Death every time we meet."

She came closer and whispered, "Between you and me, I prefer the insanity over being sane."

"Isn't that the same as confessing you'd rather be drunk than sober?" I couldn't stop the smile forming on my face as I thought about it. "You would rather stumble through life drunk than acknowledge reality when sober? Am I right, Tina?"

"You get it." She hugged me and sighed.

I patted her head. "Did you tell anyone I was here? Who I am?"

"No, I like seeing them freak out and lose their minds." She nuzzled my stomach, giggling. "And this flavor of driving yourself insane is amazing. What on earth are you tearing yourself apart over?"

"A question that haunts me often." My eyes fell on Olivia wiping down the tables in the diner across the way. "Does Death deserve a chance to be loved?"

She broke away from me, scurrying back to her shop and slamming the door. The sound of locks sliding into their resting place made it clear Tina had finished messing with me and my sanity. My hands felt heavy as I slammed them into the pockets of my leather jacket. Shoulders slumped, I relented to crossing the street. The bell on the diner door seemed louder than the last time.

"I'll be right there." Olivia was too busy wiping down the table to notice who had walked in. "Just have a seat wherever you want."

I chose the same stool I sat in before. Behind me, I could hear the clanking of the salt and pepper shakers sliding back into place and the mild squeak of her sneakers against the floor. Silent and patient, I watched her come behind the bar and wash her hands. I waited for her to turn, wondering if recognition would strike her face. Part of me hoped she wouldn't remember, while the other half prayed for it.

Will she smile or frown? I wondered.

"Sorry about that." She turned and flinched. She put her hands on her hips and puffed out her cheeks. "And where have you been?"

Neither. She was frustrated, relieved even.

I smiled, feeling sheepish. "I didn't think you'd miss me that much."

She twisted, grabbing a coffee cup, and setting it in front of me. "You asked if I worked late, so I took more shifts at night. I assumed you planned on coming in more. You never came back after leaving that ridiculous tip, so I gave up hope."

"Is that so?" She filled my cup, sliding sugar and creamer over. "You shouldn't assume things about people's intentions. It can be rather misleading." I propped my elbow on the counter, pouring sugar into my cup. "What made you think I wanted coffee?"

The pot clunked into its spot, and her face flushed. "It's what you ordered last time."

"And if I wanted something else?" I mused, the metal spoon ringing like a bell as I stirred.

"You wouldn't have added sugar." She pulled out menus, her eyes peering over my shoulder, outside into the night. "I'm sorry, but drunk rush is coming in, and if I don't get them in and out of here, they get annoying."

I shrugged, sipping my coffee. She narrowed her eyes at me, but the bell on the door called her attention. The drunken crowd stumbled in, filling three booths with their loud slurs. One table was a couple, the quietest of the three. Then there was the band, not completely drunk but hungry after playing live music at a nearby club. It was the third table, the one with three young men, who seemed to make Olivia tense every time she approached.

Swiveling on my stool, I watched her fingers tighten on the menus and, later, the apron. One man tried to reach out and grab her arm, but she spun around to take the money from the couple. As the night ticked away, even the large food order for the band members was delivered, eaten, and paid for. Olivia glided back, topping off my coffee, but her eyes stayed on the booth of rowdy men. Only one ordered food; the rest slurred cat calls, but she ignored their efforts.

Again, she fluttered back to fill my cup, and I slid it out of reach, making her look me in the eyes. "Are they giving you a hard time, Olivia?"

"They always do." She slid my cup back and topped it off once more. "Don't worry about it. They should be leaving soon."

I watched her leave my side and ring up their tab. Her tension increased the closer she got to the table. Placing the check on the table, she collected the empty plate and cups. The man closest to her reached out and placed a hand on her thigh. She slapped it away, scowling. Leaving them behind, she brought the dirty dishes back to the window and turned back to me, glaring at the booth over my shoulder.

"If he lays another hand on you, all you have to do is call my name." I gave her a hardened glare, and her breath caught in her throat. "I mean it, just invoke my name."

She bit her lip, her eyes watery.

"Oh, miss waitress!" A roar of laughter erupted from the drunken batch of degenerates. "I have your tip!"

Sighing, she broke her stare away from mine. I watched her come close to the table, stopping out of reach. He was waving a pair of twenties in the air. He glanced at his pals, his grin wide as he snickered. *Nothing good will come of this.* He was showboating, preparing to do something wrong, something he thought brag-worthy amongst his group. I sat on the stool, leering at them with my elbows on my knees. The only man facing my direction caught my stare with his eyes, and his smiled fell in an instant. He nodded and mumbled, and his friends twisted to look my way.

"What the fuck you looking at, Captain Emo?" The man with the money placed the cash down on the edge of the table. "Mind your own business."

Olivia jolted into action, her nimble fingers sliding the money off. She spun on her heel, but she wasn't fast enough, and he grabbed her wrist. With a single, quick yank, he launched her off balance, and she found herself sitting in the drunken man's lap. She pulled away, but he cupped her closer. An arm wrapped around her stomach, and a hand glided over her hip and thigh. His fingers worked fast to lift her skirt.

"IAPETOS!" Eyes closed, Olivia's shriek sent my heart racing. *She remembered my name.*

By the time Olivia opened her eyes again, she was back on her feet and grasping the back of my jacket. I had come between her and the assaulter, rescuing her from his hold in a matter of seconds. The stool still spun, and under my grip, the man panicked as he struggled to free his arm. I shot a warning glance at his friends, sobering them up instantly. He jerked his arm, and I tightened my grip.

"She's already expressed not to touch her," I growled. "Pay up and get the fuck out."

"K-k-keep the change." They rushed out of the booth and fled out the door.

Twisting around, I pulled Olivia's hands free. She was trembling, her knees going weak. I caught her before she crumbled on the floor. Choking sobs were escaping her lips, and I found myself at a loss. I slid an arm under her legs and carried her to the closest chair and sat her in it. She had a death-grip on my jacket that she was unwilling to release. I knelt before her, unsure what to do next.

"What the hell happened?" The cook had come flying out from the back. "I heard the ruckus and saw the asshole grab her, but by the time I got out here, she was collapsing, and they were hauling ass down the street."

"He touched her." I wasn't sure how to phrase it. "I noticed they were giving her a tough time and let her know if she needed me…" I tried again to pull her hands off, the beating of my heart scaring me. "She won't let go."

"Iapetos…" she whimpered, sinking into my chest.

"Are you her boyfriend?" The cook questioned. "Glad you were here tonight."

"I'm… I'm not her boyfriend." My chest ached, almost regretting the answer. "Just a regular, that's all."

"Well, thank you." Slapping my back, the cook turned away. "I'll manage the rest of the shift. You think you can take her home?"

She pressed her face against my chest, and I folded. "Yeah, I can do that much."

"Don't worry about your tab." The cook nodded, clearing the rest of the table. "You eat here free; let them know Uncle Benny told you so."

"Yes, sir." I turned my attention back to Olivia. "Can you walk? I have no idea where you live."

Her fingers tightened, but at last, she let go. Sniffling, she wiped the tears from her mottled face. Bracing herself on my shoulders, she stood. She seemed speechless as the tears still fell. I couldn't stop myself from giving her a look of pity. Her eyes caught my expression, and her face flushed. Looking away from me, she went behind the counter to grab her purse. I followed close behind, feeling helpless.

"Are you going to be okay?" Her back was to me, but she tensed at my question. "C'mon. Let take you home."

She spun with a distraught look on her face and rushed me to hug me once more. "Thank you."

"It's okay; I'm glad I was here." I patted her head, noticing her disheveled bun from the whole ordeal. "Let's go."

She nodded, her fingers entwining in mine. I sighed and let her tug me along. There was silence between us as we pushed out into the street. She led me along until we arrived in front of the bus stop. She let go and turned around to face me. Her expression still showed how shaken she still felt over the events at the diner. Tears welled up, and she squeaked something, her mumbling inaudible.

"What's wrong?" I grabbed her hand into mine, hoping it would give her courage.

"The busses." She inhaled, squeezing my hand. "I forgot the bus doesn't start again for another four hours, and it's too far to walk."

I smiled, tugging her back the way we came. "Good thing I have a motorcycle parked in a back alley near Benny's."

"You do?" It was enough to stop another wave of tears from forming.

"I do," I cooed.

We walked back past the front of the restaurant. She trailed behind me, and a small part of me was glad to feel how her hand gripped my own. There had only been one other in all my immortal life who gripped the hand of Death in that way.

To feel as if I'm wanted, I'm yearned for, that I—

We turned the corner. My body burned at my gut as hot blood spilled forth. A knife had dug deep into my flesh. Olivia's fingers let go, and her lips parted to release a shrill, terrified scream. I focused on the owner of the knife—the man from the diner. Filling with rage, I gripped his arm and smirked as I pulled him and the blade deeper.

My lips at his ear, I hissed, "You need to go deeper if you aim to kill me."

The man let go of the knife and stumbled back, his hands covered in slick blood. He shook, looking at his hands. Olivia rushed me, but I threw up a hand to stop her. She needed to stay behind me, so I could protect her. I pulled the knife from my gut and tossed it at his feet. Olivia gasped, but I straightened my stance. My rage had taken over, and I would enjoy this moment of cat and mouse.

"Pick it up," I demanded.

"W-what?" His eyes danced between the blood dripping from me and the red stained blade at his feet.

"Pick it up!" I roared.

Fear jolted him into action. He gripped the knife in both hands and raising it. He trembled like he had made Olivia moments before. My eyes were wide, relishing every moment of his terror. I lifted my shirt; the wound was closing. Dropping the shirt, I paced forward. The man's legs shook, unable to flee. He lifted the knife in defense.

"S-s-stay away from me!" he screamed.

"Oh, you wanted to fight, you have a fight." I laughed, stopping so that the point of the blade tapped against me. Gripping his hands, I moved his aim to my throat. "Aim here. Go ahead, give it another try."

Dread filled his face. A thin line of blood snaked down my neck where the point pierced my skin. Gritting his teeth, the man wet his pants. His breathing was erratic, and tears streamed down his cheeks. I let go, and the knife fell to the ground in a loud clank. The man ran for his life. Picking up the blade, I turned it to ash and let it crumble from my fist. I turned and realized Olivia was there.

"Olivia, I…" My heart ached. I had lost myself and forgotten.

She stared back at me, eyes wide and hands covering her mouth. I swallowed, and she rushed me, hugging onto me. It wasn't the reaction I expected. I thought she would have screamed or fled back to the diner. Her knuckles dug into my abdomen as she pressed into me. The heat of her body was so different from my own blood. My blood rushed, and I wrapped my arms around her. I was surprised when she didn't shudder under my embrace. The aching in my chest ate at my core.

"Aren't you afraid of me?" I whispered.

"No." Her voice vibrated into me as she wrapped her arms around me. "I thought… I thought you were dead. All because of me, you…"

I squeezed her closer, crushing her into me. "No mortal can kill me."

"But you were hurt." I could feel the searing heat of her tears soaking into my shirt. "It's all my fault. Iapetos, I'm so sorry."

I inhaled, holding it for a second before huffing it out.

"If you hadn't been here." The trembling started once more.

I shushed her. "You surprise me, Olivia."

She pulled away, baffled. "Why?"

My smile brought her shaking to a stop. "You aren't afraid of me. You aren't questioning who or what I am. Instead, you're more upset over the situation. You're a strange girl."

She bit her lip.

"Let's get you home." I pulled her away and cupped her cheek. "Perhaps for the first time, I might be compelled to stay still for a moment in this immortal life."

Leaning down, I caved to desire. Her lips were soft and hot against my own. She grabbed my jacket and pulled me close to kiss me deeper as she wrapped her arms around my neck. Our tongues dared each other to chase after our desires. She had seen the monster I was. She witnessed my wrath toward mortals, my greed to overpower, and my gluttony for pain. She watched my body bleed as I dared to tempt a death I knew my immortal body could never have. Olivia had feared the man but embraced the monster. She reminded me of the girl with tiger lily eyes, but they differed from one another. One had seen down to my soul— identified me as Death incarnate and loved me for it. Olivia saw me as a man who needed to remember how to live.

20

STILL FRAMES

"Ugh, what am I doing, Olivia?" Iapetos was back in the church, watching Lucius extinguish the candles, one by one. He raised his voice. "Wouldn't it be easier to blow them out with your power?"

Iapetos's voice echoed; the building was empty besides the two immortals who found solace in one another's company. He had waited outside for the evening service to end before coming inside, making sure they were alone. He wanted to learn more about the priestly immortal who had taken him off guard a few weeks ago.

"You give me too much credit." Lucius chuckled, continuing to snuff out the candles. "I only control light. Unlike the others, I can't take away the flames, I can't produce the wind to blow them out, or even douse them with water. We all have our limitations, human or not."

Leaning on his knees, Iapetos sat in the church's center to keep a safe distance from Father Lucius. "Are you always this philosophical?"

Lucius paused, looking over his shoulder with a smirk. "Are you always lurking so far away, even if the person means you no harm?"

He opened his mouth but shut it. Pulling himself off the pew, Iapetos brought himself to the front row and sat down. "Is this better, priest?"

"Well, at least I don't have to yell anymore." Lucius turned back to his task. "So, what brings you here this time?"

"I… I don't know." Groaning, Iapetos squinted his eyes at the embellished crucifix behind the podium. The winged statue combined with the heavy wooden cross was an interesting choice. He had never seen one in all the churches he had stepped foot in over the centuries. "Does one need a reason to be in church?"

Putting out the last candle, Lucius turned with a grave expression. "I've discovered people come here for the same feelings and desires."

"Feelings and desires?" Iapetos lifted an eyebrow.

"Sometimes they're lost, but more often, they feel guilty for something they've done or may plan to do." Lucius came closer and took a seat beside Iapetos. "Regardless, everyone comes here in search of forgiveness."

Iapetos's jaw muscles twitched. *Am I here for forgiveness? From myself? You gave me it, but do I deserve it, Olivia? For my desire to kill…* He winced, unwilling to finish the thought.

"I see even Death finds himself here for that reason." Lucius smiled and patted Iapetos's shoulder. "I'm here if you want to talk."

He stood up again, but Iapetos grabbed his arm. "What if I received forgiveness and don't know what to do with it?"

Lucius sat back down, pondering as he stared at the crucifix. "I suppose that's the other part. What if you don't want to be forgiven?"

Realizing he was still gripping Lucius, Iapetos let go. "What if I never thought she could forgive me?"

"Isn't that the same?" Lifting his eyebrows high, Lucius looked at Iapetos. "It's natural to want to be forgiven; anything outside of that is a desire, is it not? We punish ourselves far harsher than the people in our lives. That's part of being human."

"I… I don't consider myself human." Iapetos paused, reflecting the words. "I'll have to think more on the matter."

Nodding, Lucius stood up and went about his chores. Iapetos watched the priest, diligent in his mannerisms, putting the old Bible away. He noticed the purple cloth under the old book with its thick cover. Light caught the pages as he closed it and folded the cloth in a ritualistic manner—he had done it so many times that it seemed as natural as breathing. The golden edges and the flash of colorful illustrated borders were familiar from a time long ago.

"Is that… is that a Gutenberg?" Lucius grinned at the question. "I knew there were still copies around, but to be still basing sermons from one is impressive."

The last fold was complete, and Lucius heaved the book into his arms. "It is, and it was a gift from a dear friend. Thanks to him, I have lived many lives preaching from this book."

"Talib has a big heart." Iapetos sighed and watched him disappear into a corner office before returning with a box for the candles. "So, he made sure you had your book for each reincarnation all these centuries? That's a hell of a friendship."

"He did … except once." Pausing, he stared at the black wick. "You're lucky in some ways, Iapetos. Your father didn't put you under the spell. As for the rest of us, some are still reincarnating, while others, like me…" He took in a shaken breath. "My power awoke with startling new strength. And I couldn't stop it."

"It would have been nice to experience a normal life at least once." Iapetos's tone was bitter. "Being the embodiment of Death itself is maddening."

"True." Dropping the candle in the box, Father Lucius worked his way to where Iapetos still sat. "For four years, I was killing an entire country. Thousands of people and animals were starved and drained of any water supply."

Iapetos fell silent. His lips were taut as he gave the priest his full attention. *Even light can bring destruction of great magnitude. I thought only I had the scars and nightmares from wiping out hundreds—no thousands—of innocent lives. To imagine this priest was capable… even if it wasn't intended.*

"I couldn't contain it; I couldn't turn it off. It was a malicious chain reaction that followed and led to harrowing events before Talib found me." Each *thunk* of a candle in the box made the muscles in Iapetos's cheek twitch. "By the fourth year, those afflicted were eating their own children and lying down in the gutters, praying the packs of dogs would free them from Hell. Despite it, I blame myself—not your father, not Talib for not finding me faster, but myself for not realizing that all elements of nature have a dark side. I was careless. I never realized the responsibility handed to me. It seemed harmless, and I was wrong to think of it that way., I never learned what it meant to be the element of Light."

"The 1770 drought of India was you." Iapetos leaned on his knees once more as an ache hit his chest. He had walked through the aftermath, suspecting it was linked to Hotan but came up empty handed. "I… I saw it firsthand. My father and I caused many of the larger and more devastating disasters around the world. Sometimes, it was the battle between us; other times, his power was so unstable it caused nature itself to become unbalanced. I followed those hints, and India was the one place I never found him. You caused the massive drought, not Hotan. I'm sorry you had to experience that I… I know what it means to carry the weight of so many lives on your shoulders. Entire towns, cities, regions, worldwide pandemics were all started by my hand or my father's."

Thunk.

The last candle dropped into the box, and Lucius kept his back to Iapetos. "Please know, no matter what's happening to you, someone understands at least a little of what you're experiencing. Let me ask you again, do you seek forgiveness?"

"Would it be wrong to ask you that question about India?" Lifting an eyebrow, Iapetos was curious to know Lucius more. "Have you forgiven yourself for that moment?"

Placing the box of candles down, Lucius took in a deep breath. "I suppose I have." Over his shoulder he gave a smile. "It's hard to help others if you can't help yourself."

Fumbling his thumbs, Iapetos pondered on the unexpected grin from Lucius. "I don't have an answer in that case."

Chuckling, Lucius confessed, "No, you have the answer. We often reject it or see it as impossible, but the answer is there at your core if you accept it. It's okay not to know and still need more time to digest your feelings."

Groaning, Iapetos covered his face. "Why do you and Talib have to be so cryptic about everything you ask me?"

Sitting down next to him, Lucius patted him on the back. "Sometimes questions are the best way to get your inner thoughts organized. Don't be so hard on yourself. Know that you're not alone; no one wishes you ill will."

Iapetos gave a snort then chuckled. "Never in a thousand years did I imagine myself seeking advice from a priest. Ha!"

"Ah, but that's what makes life beautiful and mysterious. It's unpredictable, and the paths that open and close can be astonishing." Lucius joined in the fit of laughter, killing the tension between them. "Now, may I ask one more cryptic question?"

"Why not?" Iapetos leaned back, grinning as he stared up at the crucifix. "What harm can a question do?"

"The wrong question can do a lot of harm. One must be sure he's ready for the answer that comes with it." Lucius's expression sobered. "Do you plan on facing your son again?"

"Facing him?" Iapetos's smile faded. *He knows why I came here to ponder.* "I haven't decided if I want to fight him yet."

"Facing someone doesn't always imply a fight." His response was abrupt.

"In that case, I intend to face him again." Holding his breath, Iapetos added, "But in what regard I haven't yet decided."

"Ah, I see you understand today's lesson." Lucius pulled himself away. "I must get back to work, but you are welcome any time, Iapetos. You have a friend here."

Lucius walked away and disappeared into the back room. The cathedral made Iapetos feel small under the weight of God's judgment. Leaning forward, his elbow nudged a bible at his side. He grabbed it; someone had laid the silken ribbon across a section. He cracked the pages, revealing the highlighted sections and a slip of paper with his name scribbled on it.

When did Lucius slip this here?

He read the small verse under its yellow glow.

> Just as people are destined to die once, and after that to face judgment.
> Hebrews 9:27

Iapetos hummed to himself, looking over the chapter a moment. Again, he glared at the one simple line. *Death before Judgment.* He sat up straight, rolling it over and over. His father, the old Hotan, had died. His son was made possible by his self-sacrifice, only to become a person identical in appearance. Iapetos had to decide whether to take the soul which once belonged to his father or somehow change the course of the events unfolding.

Could we start again? Am I worthy of happiness after all I've done? If I bring death to him, there is no doubt I must face judgment in the form of Talib's wrath.

Slamming the bible closed, he abandoned it on the pew. Marching out the doors, he froze. He didn't understand what he wanted anymore. Months ago, when he felt the power of Rebirth surge into being, he had a goal, but it all had changed. With the restored memories, he wasn't that person anymore.

It was sinful to have such precious parts of me stolen. Worst of all, I became something monstrous and blood hungry. Where do I go from here, Olivia? We both know I never wanted to be that person.

Pushing his hands into his pockets, he wandered down the sidewalks and streets. His emotions, his desires, and his guilt were tearing him apart. Fingers brushed against the note for Hotan from his mother. Again, he winced and stopped his steps. Pulling it out and seeing Hotan's name, he relented.

If you are so insistent about this, then let me give it to him.

He turned and headed back to the church. Coming through the doors, he saw Father Lucius sweeping around the holy water fountain. He waited for Iapetos to approach and gave a faint smile. Lips parting, it was painful to muster the words. A tiny creak in his voice started, but Lucius raised his hand to silence him. Lucius reached into his pocket and handed a cell phone to Iapetos.

"Take it. Everyone's number is in there." Iapetos furrowed his brow, confused at Lucius's gesture as he spoke. "Talib, Jacob, the main line here to the church is under my name, and Hotan's. There are a few others, but I don't think you've met them or know who they are. Regardless, I want you to know that not one of us would abandon you if you need help."

Iapetos paled. "Why didn't you give it to me earlier? Clearly, you planned on giving it to me."

"I needed to see the resolve on your face." Lucius squeezed his hand before letting go.

"Resolve?" Iapetos glared at the phone. It felt wrong to take it. "Resolve to do what?"

"To find the other answer that still exists." Again, Father Lucius grinned.

Shoving the cell into his pocket, Iapetos became flustered. "I came in to ask for a ride to Hotan's apartment complex."

"Why there? I don't think he's back," Iapetos interjected, shaking his head.

"I want to…" His mind was fighting with itself. "There was a kid, the one with the element of Fear. I want to talk to him first."

Lucius blinked. "Hisota?"

"If that's him, yes." Pulling out the cell phone, he scanned the names.

"He's not in there." Lucius's fingers obscured the screen. "But I think you're right; he's there at the apartment, waiting."

"For Hotan?" Iapetos gave Lucius a confused look.

Lucius shook his head, waving Iapetos to follow. "For you." Following the priest out the door, Lucius paused. "Do you know how to drive?"

"Of course, I know how to drive." Keys flew from Lucius's hand, and Iapetos caught them, fumbling with the phone. "Are you sure?"

"It's a car." He grabbed Iapetos's shoulder. "Remember, Hotan isn't your father. You would do well to find an answer that acknowledges this much."

There was a dangerous look in the priest's eyes before he walked away. Unlocking the car, Iapetos muttered under his breath, "A priest driving a beater like this."

The old orange Topaz sputtered to life. His knees knocked into his knuckles in the cramped space. Ignoring the discomfort, he headed back to the apartment complex. He considered flying there, but it was risky during the day and may appear threatening. One blessing was the Topaz was easy to parallel park. Eager to unfold himself, he stood, glaring at the building. He sensed the presence of Earth and Fear inside.

<Hey, you, I want to talk to you.> Iapetos reached out with his mind, making his words known to Hisota.

There was no response. Iapetos turned, leaning on the car. His dark eyes reflected at him, and he questioned himself. *<What are you doing?>*

"I have a name, you know." Hisota's voice was loud as he stood on the other side of the street. "Hisota. What do you want with me, Iapetos?"

They measured one another for a few minutes, and Iapetos spoke at last, "I figured you are the best person to ask what kind of person *he* is."

"He has a name too; it's Hotan." The cold stare was on par with Iapetos's own. "Have you eaten?"

"What?" Hisota walked across the street and opened the passenger side door. "I'm starving. I assume Mr. Money Bags wouldn't let you out the door without packing your wallet with cash. Let's talk over some food."

<Aren't you afraid?> He lifted an eyebrow at the boy.

"That has nothing to do with why you're here." He slid in and slammed the car door shut. The only words he spoke were driving instructions. "Turn here, hang a left, slow down and look for a sign. It's across the street from the element of Insanity."

They parked in the side lot for Benny's, and Iapetos sighed. The muscles in his body tensed as memories of Olivia flooded him, making his chest ache.

I was avoiding this place, but here we are despite it all.

Inside, there was still the awkward tension between them. Iapetos wasn't sure if his own apprehension had more to do with his past than with Hisota. They both had their reasons for meeting one another. Iapetos ordered nothing, but before he could wave the waitress away, Hisota caught her attention.

"Hey, Jess. Wait, I want something." Hisota scanned the menu a moment.

She turned back, giving him a frustrated expression. "Why didn't you say something when I asked, Hisota?"

Hisota smirked, turning to Iapetos, "You buying?"

Iapetos looked to the girl and nodded, acknowledging he was buying.

"Great, give me the cheeseburger with bacon, no tomato, and no pickle. I mean it this time." He shot her a knowing glare. "Just don't tell the cook it's me. I'm convinced he does it on purpose."

"Don't worry; we still remember the rage monster you became last time. Soda?" She sighed.

"Coke." And Hisota waved her off.

Iapetos glared at him. *Not the kind of person I think would make the best sort of friend. He's aggressive and blunt.*

Hisota leaned back, drumming his fingertips on the table, and stared out the window. "You know who used to sit in this booth all the time?" His fingers stopped, flattening as he side glanced at a baffled Iapetos. "Hotan and Shellie."

"That was the girl he loved…" Iapetos had heard the details from Talib. "And lost."

"So, you know." Hisota's eyes sliced into him. "And no offense, calling you his dad would be insulting to Hotan. I've been his friend, by his side, since I was six years old. There hasn't been a moment in his life when his eyes didn't show that he was suffering some anguish or emotional pain which I could never understand. For the longest time, I was angry."

"Angry?" Iapetos leaned forward, weighing the look in the boy's dark eyes.

Shifting, Hisota leaned forward. "Have you ever known the fear that comes from feeling helpless?"

<I have.> Their conversation shifted, becoming a silent banter within their minds. *<I was abandoned.>*

<Not that.> The tingling sensation of the element of Fear writhed around Iapetos. *<I mean sticking around someone you care for and watching the world rip them apart time after time.>*

The heavy sensation turned Iapetos's stomach, a cold sweat making his skin clammy. *<What are you trying to do?>*

<Show you what I felt and how you've left him.> Hisota leaned back, glaring out the window as the wave of fear drowned Iapetos.

Iapetos closed his eyes and soaked it in, opening himself to it. The element of Death could only threaten the owner of the powers, but to be consumed so heavily by fear could spell the end for him. Flashes of Olivia unfolded. It was as if her voice echoed down a long hall, laughing and crying, screaming then silent. His stomach tightened again and Iapetos fought back the nausea. The funeral distorted everything, and he found himself in a classroom, staring at one child's face. His spirit broken, his emotions dead, a smaller version of Hotan sat silently with his eyes out of focus. On a scrap of paper, Hotan glared at his own scribbled words:

> Where are you, Dad? Do you know
> Mom is dead? Do you know I am here? Is
> there no one left who loves me?

Small hands crumpled the paper. Young Hotan looked up and locked eyes with Iapetos. Iapetos swallowed, a sickening knot aching at his core.

"Where were you?" Tears fell as tiny hands clenched and twisted the paper. "Why did you forsake me? Why did you leave me in this Hell alone?"

The room grew darker, the walls closed in, and the sound of the ripping paper was like rolling thunder in Iapetos's ears. <*These aren't Hotan's questions, but my own.*> Holding his breath, he glared at the child as features shifted until it reflected himself sitting there. The questions and fears were all his own from so long ago. He forced these fears upon his own son just as his father had done to him. History had repeated itself.

I pained over being denied a childhood and a sense of mortality. Meanwhile, my son had those things, and I destroyed them. Does this make me worse—worse than my father and his careless ambitions and greed?

"Sir?" Jessica's voice made Iapetos refocus, and he was back in the diner. "Are you okay? Do you want something to drink at least?"

"I'm fine." Iapetos's eyes didn't break from Hisota's cheek where muscles twitched in impatience. <*How are you doing that?*> He asked him silently.

<*I thought this was part of the element of Fear.*> Sighing, Hisota closed his eyes. <*I don't think its last owner understood internal fears are far less forgiving. I wonder if Shellie would still be here if he had. But where would we all be if he understood the element to the extent I do?*>

Rubbing his fingers against his temples, Iapetos fought the nausea until it faded. *<It would have proven a mess.>*

<Agreed.> Jessica returned with Hisota's order. She paused at the table and gave a funny look at Iapetos. "You look like someone I know."

"I'm new in town." Iapetos knew what she was thinking. "Sorry."

"He's Hotan's dad." There was a small upward curve to Hisota's lips, and he lifted an eyebrow.

"Wh-what?" After a few blinks, she nodded. "That's it! He looks a lot like you. Oh my God, I can't believe this."

The heated glare from Iapetos did nothing to keep Hisota from munching on a French fry. "If you don't mind, we're busy talking about a business deal, Jess."

She leaned in toward Iapetos who furrowed his brow. "Nice to meet you, sir." Whispering, she added, "If you ask me, Kyle is Hotan's better friend." With that, she left them alone.

The information wasn't shocking. Kyle had centuries over Hisota, but he couldn't ignore the boy's ability to resonate with the element of Fear. He had mastered the ability to pull someone inward, cause hallucinations, and shape existing fear for his victim to experience. There was an aching sensation at Iapetos's core. Looking around at the table and chairs of the diner, not much had changed from the days he spent there with Olivia. He had been a regular, her protector, and her lover.

"You see." Hisota paused, taking a sip of his soda. "Even people far from Hotan realize how important it is for you to be here, to even show you exist."

"Are you done?" Iapetos's mood had soured, and he didn't hide the annoyance in his voice. "I have my own reasons to speak with you."

Shrugging, Hisota took a bite out of his hamburger. *<I've pushed my point. Your turn.>*

"Am I wrong to think he denied himself a moment to be a child?" Iapetos leaned back in his seat, weighing the look in Hisota's eyes. "Considering his age, he's made some rather mature decisions and undertakings."

Swallowing his food, Hisota retorted, "Isn't the real question you came to ask me whether I think of him as his own person or a reincarnated immortal?"

Snorting, Iapetos relented, "I suppose that's another way to ask it."

"He's his own person." He chomped on a fry and added, "But to be honest, it's not the immortality and powers that made him this way. The circumstances of his life affected his mentality. He had a single mother, working at a dive like this and living in a one-bedroom apartment because that's all they can afford with a deadbeat dad. He had all the smarts to go to college, but no money for special diplomas and the cost of books and so on."

"I see." Iapetos stared out the window at Tina's bookstore.

"Do you?" Hisota paused from eating and glowered at him. "How can a relic of Death know what it means to live and struggle to survive? To want a life or even desire for life to be something more?"

Iapetos narrowed his eyes and spat, "You make me out to be untouchable, boy. In this, you are wrong. If you think I never took the time to dream, fought for my survival against my father, then you're wrong to think so shallow of me."

"Well, you two have a temper to match." Hisota smirked. "I can crawl under your skin as easily as I do Hotan's."

"What good is a friend whose goal is to piss you off?" questioned Iapetos.

"The kind who tires of pity and depression written on their face." Hisota slapped the table, demanding Iapetos's eyes. "In order to fight, to gain a will to live, you need to get angry."

Iapetos couldn't help but smirk. "Perhaps you're right."

"Life doesn't ever flow in a straight line. It's a pile of still frames of both high and low moments." He grabbed another fry. "If you're not careful, they'll bury you, devour your soul, leaving nothing more than fodder of those bittersweet moments. You're in charge of your life, not those shitty moments. Your life is only as happy as you're willing to allow it to be."

Iapetos furrowed his brow. "And there's the reason you're his friend."

Hisota smirked, stuffing his face with more food.

"Thank you." Iapetos sighed, his eyes scanned the counter for phantom memories left there.

"For what?" Hisota paused, gulping down his soda.

"For being a good friend to him." He locked eyes, and with a sad tone, Iapetos corrected himself. "For being there for my son."

21

THE LOVE WE HAD BEFORE

1998

Two years floated by so fast. I marveled every morning spent waking up beside Olivia, curious how she made me forget why I had come here to this town. Everything I aimed to accomplish, my thirst for vengeance, none of it mattered. If I could be by her side one more day, I was content and found myself satisfied for the first time in all these centuries. Our lives were simple, living as one of the lower-middle-class couples of the new world. Every night, I joined her at the diner, and Benny paid me for my time.

I became a peacekeeper, a bouncer to keep the drunks in line. It was far and few between when any got out of hand. We never saw the man who stabbed me; then again, he probably ended up in the asylum. Regardless, she never once spoke of what happened or revealed to her friends that I wasn't normal. Instead, she took every chance to remind me how much I had always wanted this life. Unfortunately, I couldn't help but remind myself that it wouldn't last.

Guilt would rattle me some nights, wondering how much longer I should lead her on. She couldn't expect an immortal to stay and watch her grow old, but it was more the idea of watching her face and anguish as I never grew old that would break me. Staying with me was no life for her. There would be no hopes of creating a family of her own. She had plenty of suitors, but she insisted on announcing me as her boyfriend, and at times, fiancée. Countless times, I opened my mouth to refuse, dared to correct it, but I never did. After saying it once, it felt wrong to not consider it.

SMASH!

Olivia had dropped a glass on the diner floor and darted for the bathroom. Benny peered through the window, both of us baffled by her actions. Leaving my coffee and stool behind, I leaned on the wall by the women's bathroom. Behind it, I could hear how ill she had become, vomiting violently. I waited, knowing she wouldn't be able to answer me until it had run its course. Silence fell, the toilet flushed, a stall door squeaked, and at last, I heard the faucet running.

"You okay, Olivia?" The faucet turned off at the sound of my voice.

"Y-yeah, I'm okay." She sounded miserable. "Just feeling nauseous."

"You need to call it an early night?"

The door opened, and she scowled. "Right. Rent is due this week. I'll tough it out, but if it's not better tomorrow, I'll call off." Olivia pushed past me, still pale.

"Promise?" I followed close behind, wrapping my arms around her. "I can't stand it when you're sick."

She leaned into me, giggling. "I promise."

Letting go, I allowed her to get back to work. She swept up the broken glass and picked up where she had left off with her nightly chores. It was the midweek night shift, the slowest of all the shifts she covered. I watched her rush to the bathroom several times—once more before we rode back home and again after we stepped foot in the apartment. She fell asleep, pale and clammy. A cold sweat painted her skin, and part of me fretted that my element had played a part in her illness.

The next day, she called off work. I offered to take her to the store, but she insisted on going on her own. As the day went on, she seemed quiet, still fighting the nausea. She had gone to the pharmacy to ask questions and was sent home with remedies of all kinds for nausea. I was making soup and had sat down on the couch for a moment when the bathroom door opened and she appeared, her face filled with confusion and uncertainty. She covered her mouth as she stood in the doorway with a ring of yellow light behind her.

"What's wrong?" I stood, feeling alarmed by the tears building in her eyes. "Do you need to go to the hospital?"

"No…" She turned, hiding her face from me. "Is it true you can never have a child?"

My heart leapt to my throat. "Why would you ask me that?"

She reached for something on the bathroom vanity—a pregnancy test. "It's the third one today. They've…" Her words failed her, and she pushed for them to come out. "All of them have been positive."

My eyes lowered, the lines and answer clear. I turned, leaning on the shelf. There was so much I wanted to ask, but I knew it was mine. We had spent every waking minute together. The trophies, pictures, and trinkets all glared back with their praise, their smiles, and congratulations—none of it would stop the emotions pulling me under into a world of darkness. Anger swept over me as one haunting realization gripped me.

Hotan did something. This is his doing…

Sweeping my arm across the shelf, I flung it all to the ground. Olivia yelped, dropping the test and leaning on the door frame. The tears fell in large droplets. I leaned harder on the shelf, seething.

How can I look her in the face? Why would this happen? Just as I was building up the courage to leave, to encourage her to...

Panic filled me. "I can't..."

"I swear, Iapetos." She shook, sinking to the ground. "I've only been with you."

"I know." My heart pounded against my chest, threatening to break free. "I already know that."

She wiped the tears away, trying to calm herself. "Please, don't leave."

I felt sick. My heart was breaking. *She knows...*

"It's scary. For me, for you, but maybe..." Her breath caught in her throat, emotions swallowing her words.

"I can't." Breaking away from the shelf, I avoided looking at her. "This isn't..."

"Please!" She sobbed, and I froze with my hand on the doorknob. "Please, don't go. It's a miracle. Even if Hotan had something to do with this, shouldn't we make the best of it? You don't have to do this alone, and neither do I."

"It shouldn't be possible. I've never been human, and I'm incapable of being someone's father." I pulled the door open and slammed it behind me.

I could hear her wailing through the apartment door and walls. The hallway filled with the shrieking of heartbreak. Bitter thoughts filled me—ungrateful prayers of hoping she would get rid of the abomination that never should have been possible. I had been looking for a reason to leave, but not like this. Still, I couldn't stop myself as the desire for vengeance and malice shoved me forward. In the end, I could only hurt those who had done no ill toward me.

I left the town behind, and despite the surge of immortals gathering there, I couldn't step foot. It would take Hotan's presence to make me return to the place where so many memories were made. I left my humanity with Olivia. Wandering the Earth as the cursed monster seemed fitting for me—a thing that shouldn't exist.

I don't deserve to be happy, to feel as if I lived a mortal life. Olivia, I'm sorry. I hurt you in the worst way. Please, curse my name and let me be the symbol of your anguish if it helps you move forward with your life. I hope you find someone worthier of your love.

22

SAVIOR

The orange Topaz sputtered and squeaked as it hit every pot-hole on the old, industrial road. He stopped in front of the former air hanger which was converted into an auto shop with a junkyard obscuring the horizon behind it. Iapetos turned the motor off and glared at it from the parking lot. A sign rocked in the breeze: "Lilly Pad's Junkyard & Repairs." Leaning his forehead on the wheel, he wasn't sure what he came to achieve. Perhaps talking to Hotan in person would tell him everything he needed to know.

Pushing the car door open, he shut it and leaned on the tiny beater. He heard someone wrenching away on an old F150 pickup truck. Daring to approach, he walked into the garage and discovered a shapely mechanic, half-hidden by the vehicle. He was amused to see a girl working in an auto mechanic shop, but he had seen far braver girls in the past.

"I'll be with you in just a moment," she shouted, and her voice rattled him.

The sign, "Lilly's", and the voice and the job. Iapetos thought and covered his mouth.

"I said, I'll be right with you," she barked, louder than before. "Take a seat or stand there. Just don't get in my way."

"Lilly." The name escaped him, and her wrenching came to a stop.

His heart raced as he stared at the body which only showed from her navel to her toes. Swallowing, he crouched, but her forearm covered her face. Her chest rose and fell, her body covered in grease and sweat. Iapetos searched for a sign, any sign. The lips he first tasted in Pompeii, the fiery gaze in Antioch, the tenacity he had admired in London, and the passion he embraced in Toulouse.

He tried again, "Lilly."

The forearm lifted slightly, and he caught a glimpse of amber eyes he knew well.

"It can't be." Iapetos stared wide-eyed, confused that she recognized him. "Could it be… this whole time you were…"

She swallowed as if fighting the want to cry. Her breath sped up as she kept herself hidden under the pickup. Iapetos's patience had run out. Her gripped her legs and pulled her out. Iapetos pinned Lilly's wrists above her head. Her hair was messy under her red bandana, and tiger lily eyes were wild with surprise. His lips locked to hers, hungry for the love he had yearned for and thought he had lost to time. Her tongue leapt forward with recognition, and he pulled away to take in her face.

"Why didn't you ever…" Iapetos lost his words to the racing emotions and thoughts.

"I didn't know," she whispered, tears welling up in her eyes. "I didn't know what I was, and I had no way to find you once I came free of the spell."

He let go of her wrists. She cupped his face, pulling him to her and kissed him.

"Lilly?" Abigail's voice broke the moment. "Iapetos?"

"Crap." Lilly covered her face again. "Can you give us a few minutes, Abby?"

"Are you sure?" The alarm and fear filling Abigail's face made it clear this was a secret she had never discovered. "You know who this is?"

"I do." Lilly's voice grew sterner. "Go back inside."

Without further delay, she spun on her heel and slammed the door behind her. Lilly peeked out from under her forearm, and they both grinned. She sat up and sighed. There was so much unspoken between them, and neither of them knew where to start. Iapetos looked sad; the conflict on his mind and heart was visible in his body and eyes. Lilly stood up, wiping her hands off on her jeans and motioning for him to follow her. Silently and obediently, he did. She led him through the junkyard maze. As they reached the core, he marveled over the camphor tree.

It was surrounded by gardens and arbors of all kinds. It looked as if someone had cut and pasted all their favorite *Home & Garden* clippings into one scene together. Confident they were far from prying eyes, she turned and hugged him. Burying her face into his chest, she couldn't fight the tears of joy forming in her eyes.

"I can't believe it's really you." She sounded relieved. "When they said you attacked, all I could think is what a mess this situation had become."

"Why didn't you try to contact me?" Iapetos nuzzled the top of her head, remembering those summer nights in Spain together. "If you knew it was me…"

"I was afraid," she confessed, pulling away to search his eyes. "The idea you might not remember me at all… it scared me to think you'd forgotten."

"What part of the way I looked at you in Antioch, in London, and in Toulouse said I'd forgotten you?" Iapetos's fingers stroked her cheek.

She closed her eyes and steadied herself. "No, not even in those fleeting moments did you forget. I know I didn't."

He kissed her again, both wanting to make certain it wasn't a dream. "Then, this means you can never die."

"No, I can't. You're stuck with me this time, my Angel of Death." She made a face. "But something tells me you didn't come here to find me."

Iapetos's face flushed, and he winced. "No, but I'm glad you're here. I need a friendly face right about now."

"What's your plan?" She scowled, and he knew she was very aware what was on the line.

"First, I wanted to give this to him myself." Iapetos pulled the letter with Hotan's name from his pocket. "I'm curious to know what she…" He stumbled on his words as he looked at Lilly. His chest ached. *How can I talk about Olivia? How dare I compare the two in this moment…*

Lilly laughed, burying her face in his chest. "Don't look at me like that. You look pitiful and heartbroken."

"I'm sorry, I…" Iapetos was sure she could hear his racing heart. "Olivia and I…"

"We had no way of knowing if our paths would cross again." Lilly sighed. "Toulouse was over five hundred years ago, Iapetos. That's a long time to be alone for anyone."

"I know, but…" He inhaled deeply, steeling himself. "Olivia loved me for being simply me, but you, on the other hand…" He wrapped his arms around her, his lips tickling at her ear as he whispered his confessions, "You always saw me for what I was, Death incarnate, and somehow, loved me for that." She bit his neck, and he let go of her, confounded. "What was that for?"

"You shouldn't do that." Her face was red with frustration.

"Do what?" He rubbed the spot, furrowing his brow. "I was being honest."

"I know." She crossed her arms. "We'll have to wait for a more private moment; they're coming."

"Who?" Iapetos slumped his shoulders, frowning.

"Hotan, Abigail, Jacob, and even Talib." Her eyes narrowed, her tone stern. "Are you going to handle this on your own?"

Looking to the folded letter in his palm, he nodded. "I'm ready. I think I have the answer I needed."

Abigail paced in the office. Iapetos had shown up, but Hotan was still gone. She covered her mouth and her mind raced about what to do. Iapetos was dangerous, unpredictable, and wanted to get his hands on Hotan. She searched the tiny living quarters for something, anything that may help. A cell phone beeped, and she searched for it. On the counter, she found Lilly's cell phone and flipped the archaic model open to find a text from Jacob. Looking out the blinds of the door, they headed out of the garage toward the junkyard.

Pressing the call button, she waited for Jacob to answer. "Hey, Lilly Pad!"

"It's me," Abigail announced. "Iapetos, he's here."

There was silence before he asked, "Are you two safe?"

"Lilly just walked out into the junkyard with him." She couldn't hide the panic in her voice. "I don't know. He doesn't seem to be violent, but he had her pinned down when I walked out."

"I'll get Talib; we're on our way." The call ended.

Abigail didn't know him anymore, not like she had known him before that last moment in Roanoke. The man she saw seemed different, and she was unsure what he would do. She had seen how desperate he could get and the wake of the violence and death his element could commit. Sitting down on the couch, she couldn't stop shaking. She never worried about the old Hotan, but fear filled her at the thought of Iapetos coming for her Hotan—the one she loved and adored, the one willing to tackle his demons head on.

She jerked up and threw open the door. Seeing no signs of them, she marched out to the parking lot. The orange Topaz was there, and her brow furrowed.

"Isn't that Lucius's car?" She spun around, glaring at the junkyard. "You would call for help if you needed it, right Lilly?"

Holding her arms, sweating under the searing heat of the sun, Abigail waited. The minutes ticked by with no signs of anything happening. She paced, eyeing the road. At last, she saw a car turning down the last stretch. Her heart raced, and she bit her thumbnail as she waited for the car to approach. Finally, she could see the passengers, recognizing Talib, Jacob and Hotan. The car skidded to a stop and all three poured out. She rushed to Hotan, clinging onto him.

"Are you okay?" He seemed rattled by how she clung to him. "Did he do anything to you?"

"N-no." She buried her face into Hotan's shoulder. "But he took Lilly out into the junkyard."

"You realize she has the advantage out there, right?" Jacob shot Talib a look. "And the vibes I'm getting from here tell me nothing nasty is happening."

"But the way he had her wrists pinned…" She was crying, pulling away from Hotan to look at them. "He seems so different from before."

"I cannot disagree with that," Talib confessed, marching for the gate. "We should at least check on them."

By the time they made it to the gate, Lilly stood on the other side with a tapping foot. There was a disapproving glare in her eyes as she scanned over them. She crossed her arms, waiting for them to be within earshot.

"I see the cavalry is here." Lilly said, flustered. "But only Hotan is coming through that gate and stepping foot in my yard."

They all looked to one another. At last, Talib asked, "Are you sure?"

She glowered. "Do you think I'm joking?"

"Uh, okay, Hotan." Jacob stepped back and gave him room to go through the gate. "You heard the lady."

Hotan took in a deep breath and walked through the gate. He didn't know what waited for him at the center where he felt the element of Death. As Lilly implied, it wasn't threatening, and she didn't seem alarmed like Abigail. Something was amiss. He paused, giving a half-hearted smile to Abigail and the others. This was between him and Iapetos. No one else needed to come into the fray—if there would even be one by the way things were unfolding. Swallowing, he started again, but Lilly gripped his shoulder.

She leaned in and whispered, "Go in there with an open mind. Just do that much for me."

Her tone made him flinch. "What happened between you two?"

She smiled. "I'll tell you later. He's not here for a fight, so don't be on guard."

"Right." He knew that; he felt that much already.

He didn't feel the choking pressure of the power struggle they'd had on the rooftop at the start of all this. No, this was as calm and non-threatening as the element of Death could possibly be. He marched through the shadows of the towers of cars.

He saw the leaves and branches of his camphor tree above them. He would be there, just like the dream, waiting to talk. He had intended in prepping him visually for this moment as he had prepped his alarm for the battle. As much as it pained Hotan, it had worked then and now.

Breaking through into the garden, he found Iapetos squatting under the tree, leaning his back against it. He swiveled his head in his direction and huffed. They couldn't hide the tension they felt in one another's presence. He saw the folded rectangle of paper in Iapetos's fingers, and his heart fluttered. Seeing Hotan's eyes lock onto it, Iapetos held it up, offering for him to take it.

"It's yours. I think we're both ready to see what she had to say." It was a peace offering. "No strings attached. I swear I didn't read it."

Sighing, Hotan came closer and flopped on the ground beside him. As he took the letter, it seemed strange to be so close to Iapetos. Part of the tension broke as he unfolded the paper. Iapetos leaned in, just as curious to see her writing as Hotan. Glancing over at him, he weighed the hardened look on Iapetos's face as his way of expressing uncertainty. His eyes fell back to the letter, and he swallowed back his nerves.

Hotan,

I should have been braver. For this,
I'm sorry.

Hotan stopped, steeling his anxiety and heartbreak. He missed her, and never did he think her a coward. Then again, he still didn't understand where her feelings and decisions laid.

If you are reading this, then I am gone. Out of fear, I didn't find the courage to tell you, and here's my confession, my beloved son. Your name is that of your grandfather, and your father's name is Iapetos. If you take after them, then you should be aware that you may never die. Your conception should have been impossible, but by some miracle you were given to me. Your dad left because it scared him, but I pray your paths will cross someday.

Your father has a big heart, and I will never forget the first night he protected me. The fearlessness and fierceness of his actions spoke volumes. I was just a washed-up high school cheerleader working as a diner waitress. He took a knife to the gut and should have died. In that moment, I thought it was the last I would see him, but he still took me home that night. I invited him into my home, into my life, and into my heart. There was no room for another love in my lifetime, even after he left.

Hotan's fingers tightened on the letter. Iapetos's eyes were just over his shoulder as they pushed forward as one, and he flipped to the next page.

You were so angry with him. Please, I beg you, if you ever find your father, be understanding. You're a brilliant child with a heart as big as his. The two of you will need each other. I want this vicious cycle to break. Fight for something better and weather the storm of life together. He's been alone for so long, and there were times he seemed pained to be here, to accept that someone could love him. Please, break this curse.

I know you could never forgive him for how he abandoned us. No matter how many times I tried, you couldn't accept that someone could fear a miracle, fear their own child so much that he ran away from the only good thing in his life. Trust me, it's possible and has happened to him and now you. I don't know if your grandfather will ever be found. He's been missing for a long time, but your father will forever walk the Earth. If you find yourself no different, immortal, know you have family out there.

Learn to live for every moment, whether it's for a minute or a century. Always choose life, my son. It's difficult, not always rewarding, but it makes those good moments so much sweeter. Know I love you, forever and always.

Your mother,

Olivia

Clenching his jaw, Hotan stared at the last page. She pleaded with him from beyond the grave to accept the man next to him. He remembered the arguments and had regretted them after she died. Repeatedly, he ridiculed her over her heartbroken state over a man who had fled without hesitation. She never mentioned the past—the hurt and abuse he had endured. Looking back, Hotan wondered if he would have been more forgiving or just as angry. Iapetos leaned his head against the tree, staring up into the branches.

"She was always like that." Hotan heard a hint of nostalgia in Iapetos's voice. "From that first night I met her at Benny's. She was always preaching that no matter how crappy life seemed, there were the good moments worth looking forward to."

Hotan folded the paper and held it there, staring at his name. "I can't tell you how many times we fought over…"

"Me?" Iapetos read every word, soaking it in. "I'm sorry."

"I don't need your apology." It all seemed so unfair. "And I'm not here to make you feel Iapetos'better."

A smile came across Iapetos's face. "I don't deserve forgiveness, and I don't want it. I wasn't as strong as I thought I was.

Just like him, I repeated the same mistakes. Though they were on a smaller scale, I still feel the sting. I hate knowing I caused her so much harm, and it carried down to you. Of all people, I should have known better."

"How old are you?" Swallowing, Hotan wanted to know more about the stranger next to him. "Exactly why did you choose her of all people? How many others were there?"

"Valid questions." Iapetos nodded, welcoming the conversation blossoming between them. "I suppose I am well over two thousand years old… maybe older. In the beginning, I was lost and unsure of what I was or even how to speak. Time can skew when you're not aware of who you are."

"And?" Hotan's eyes were like daggers. "Why her? Were there others?"

"The way you ask makes me out to be an adulterer." He lifted an eyebrow, looking into Hotan's frustrated eyes. "But if you insist, if you mean women I genuinely loved, there were only two. Your mother was one of them."

"Why her? What made her so special?" The tension in Hotan's face made his cheeks twitch.

"Despite seeing me at my worst, she never showed fear. She loved me as the monster and as a man." He thought for a moment and continued, "She taught me what it meant to be mortal. That life has deeper meaning than whether your life had ended. There are things to look forward to and yearn for within someone other than yourself. She taught me how to be selfless."

Hotan turned his gaze back to the letter. "That sounds like her."

"I still miss her," Iapetos confessed, "But our time together was doomed to be short and fleeting. Understand, I was already panicking before her pregnancy."

"Panicking?" Hotan furrowed his brow. "About what?"

"If I could handle seeing her grow old, be able to take care of her." He leaned on his knees, staring at the ground. "It seems shameful to admit, but I know nothing about being a mortal and growing old. I don't think I could have watched her life come to an end, watch the time she had to live shorten before my eyes."

"Ah, and the pregnancy was the breaking point." It felt wrong; it wasn't the answer Hotan had hoped for. "You're a piece of shit, you know that."

"Yeah, I am." He inhaled, releasing it through his nose. "But I can't help it. In a lot of ways, I'm just as lost about my emotions as you can be at your age. I don't understand my feelings. I haven't allowed myself to explore them, but maybe…"

"Who was the other woman?" Hotan wanted to turn the tide, respecting the raw confessions spilling from his father. "What kind of girl was she?"

He laughed, standing. "Stubborn and bull-headed. She can strong arm any man if she wanted."

Hotan gave him a look of disbelief. "You're making this up."

"No, really." Iapetos was all grins now. "She wasn't petite and fragile like Olivia. No, this one held a fiery stare, and she saw through me. Every time we crossed paths, she called me by name, by my element, and wanted me more for it."

"What was her name?" Hotan stood, wiping the dirt from the back of his jeans. "Do you even remember?"

"She'd crush me under these cars if I didn't." Iapetos winked, seeing the paling expression on Hotan's face. "Her name has always been Lilly."

Hotan covered his face, groaning. "You've got to be kidding. How long have you and her…?"

"Look, last time I saw her was in 1450." He patted Hotan's back, laughing. "I discovered her today. All this time, I had no idea she was one of us."

Confused, Hotan asked, "Why didn't you know?"

"Well…" Iapetos thought a moment. "I can't sense others like you and Talib. Or should I say, I have a hard time trusting what it is I feel. How could I trust someone? Ironically, now that I think about it, Talib was never there with me when I saw her. It explains the weird coincidence in Pompeii."

"Pompeii?" Hotan repeated. "As in Mt.-Vesuvius-wiped-out-of-existence Pompeii?"

"The day of the eruption to be exact." Iapetos sighed as if soaking in the memory one more time. "Come on, let's let everyone know we're okay, or at least you're okay."

"Wait…" Hotan gripped Iapetos shoulder. "What about this?" He placed a hand over his chest. "I thought you wanted to kill me, to take Hotan's soul from me?"

Iapetos stared at Hotan's hand before meeting his gaze. "That's not my father's soul anymore. That one belongs to my son."

Iapetos rolled his shoulder and left Hotan to digest his words. Walking to the next fork, Iapetos realized he wasn't sure how to leave. He huffed, crossing his arms, and waited. It took several minutes before Hotan ventured around the bend and saw him there. He paused, confused.

"Were you waiting for me?" Hotan lowered his brow and scowled, "I'm not a child, you know."

"Actually, I'm not sure how to get out without flying, and, well, I prefer not to do that in daylight." Iapetos gave him a disconcerting expression. "How does waiting for you come off as labeling you a child?"

"Never mind." Hotan brushed past Iapetos, flustered. "This way."

After several turns, they saw Lilly and the others at the gate. They were arguing in hushed tones. Abigail caught sight of Hotan and pointed, breaking the debate in an instant. She shoved through the gate and rushed to him, gripping onto him. Relief washed over her, the tension and fear melting away. She glanced to Iapetos and lipped, *Thank you.* Everyone froze, glaring at Iapetos.

At last, Talib spoke up. "Did you decide?"

"Yes, I have." Iapetos scanned over them, weighing each of them in his mind and heart. "I think I'll let you all save me, since you seem so hellbent on it."

"I like that idea," Lilly said, smiling, and Jacob winced.

"You can't be." Jacob laughed, leaning on Talib's shoulder. "Did you know about this, old man?"

"About what?" Talib was confused, and Hotan's face reddened. "Abigail and Hotan?"

"No, not that. Everyone knows about that." Jacob blew air between his lips as he pointed at Lilly and Iapetos. "Those two being a thing!"

"W-what?" Talib pushed his glasses on his nose and took in their expressions. "How long have you… I don't understand?" He was speechless.

Laughing, Iapetos pushed through the gate and threw an arm around Talib. "My beloved uncle, did I ever tell you about the blacksmith in Toulouse?"

"Wait, I sent you to Toulouse because…" He paled. "But how?"

EPILOGUE

O *'Lord*
The club had changed names through the decades, but it was a tradition to stop in and play a cover or two. They kept the band going by changing names and moving towns often. It was one of the few small pleasures they all thirsted for. Kyle still played the drums, Hisota was the main singer, but they had gained a new bassist, Iapetos. Hotan never forgave him, but it didn't stop either of them from moving forward with their immortal lives.

Hotan handpicked the next number to end the set. It called for acoustics, and he insisted on singing the main lyrics with Hisota and Iapetos to back him on the chorus. "O'Lord" by Smile Empty Soul was one of those songs on an album only a fan would appreciate. The lyrics resonated with all they had faced in the past and still had to deal with.

In the crowd, he locked eyes with Abigail and grinned. His fingers trailed across the neck of the guitar as he sang. They had come to terms with their inner emotions and resolved what they saw in one another. She wasn't ever Shellie's replacement, and he wasn't just Hotan's stand-in. It became clear none of their affection had been intended to cover or replace their pasts. Instead, they found kinship and love in someone who understood one another's hardship without ever needing to speak deeply on the matter.

Whistles rang out, and Hotan was glad smoking had been banned. Without the obscurity of the smoke, he could take in this generation's faces and wonder where their own lives might take them on their own journeys. He prayed that they would take in life's lessons and push forward. To go through this world alone was a tribulation you brought down upon yourself. The song ended, and the audience roared.

"Thank you," Hotan cooed over the mic. "Remember to always keep good music, good company, and good moments in your life, now and always."

THE END

BOOK CLUB DISCUSSION QUESTIONS

1. Why do you think the author chose to bounce between Hotan and Iapetos when telling this story? Is it reflective of death versus life?

2. Second chances happen often in this story. How significant are these events in each character's life?

3. How impactful were memories? Do you think losing them caused more tragedy? Which would you prefer to deal with, the memory or forgetting?

4. Who or what do you feel was the true villain in this trilogy?

5. Hotan is divided between two loves: Shellie and Abigail. How has his relationship with each girl made a significant impact on him?

6. The past, present, and future collide hard in this final book. By the end, what is the significance of the choices made by Hotan and Iapetos?

7. Discuss your thoughts of how the following phrases are reflected throughout this book and the trilogy: "Family tradition," "Learning to love yourself again," and "Choosing the path you want to take, not the one chosen for you."

8. Talib and Iapetos became rather close at some point in history. Explain how that impacted Talib's feelings about the old Hotan versus the new Hotan? What about Iapetos in the past versus present?

9. Do you feel Iapetos started making the same mistakes as the old Hotan? Defend your decision with examples.

10. Again, we find ourselves thrown into real historical events. Which of these events were the most impactful for the readers versus each character? Do you think adding dark history and disasters aided in capturing the character's mindset at any given time?

AUTHOR BIO

Valerie Willis is the COO at 4 Horsemen Publications, Inc., an expert digital typesetter, co-host to Drinking with Authors Podcast, and an award-winning Fantasy Paranormal Romance author. Her works include a workbook series, *Writer's Bane*, starting with *Research* and *Formatting 101*, and novels inspired by mythology, superstitions, legends, folklore, fairy tales, and history such as in *The Cedric Series*. Many have experienced her hosting workshops or being a guest speaker at events where she shares her expertise in publishing, novel writing, research for fiction, worldbuilding, character development, book design, reader immersion, foreshadowing, and more.

www.WillisAuthor.com
https://linktr.ee/WillisAuthor
OR
Instagram: @WillisAuthor
Facebook: facebook.com/ValerieWillisAuthor
Twitter: @Valerie_Willis
TikTok: @willisauthor
Email: Willis.author@gmail.com

THE BACK STORY

Tattooed Angels Trilogy has been a labor of love project. It's responsible for my drive to become an author and the desire to share my work with others. There are profound moments in a writer's life, and this trilogy had a large part in my own.

Throughout elementary and middle school, I was a tenacious reader with a love for fantasy books. I wrote my first novel in fifth grade. I still have the composition book I filled front to back; it's covered in assorted stickers from the 1990s, and the map I drew is glued in the back cover.

On one faithful night during my high school days, *Tattooed Angels* was born. The clock was pushing past midnight as I tried to lull myself to sleep by listening to some rock music. The DJ came on, talking about this new release from a band called Tool. In the black abyss of night, I took in the heartbeat intro to the song "Lateralus."

The first few lyrics played out the idea of black and white shifting to colors, and it started a chain reaction in my imagination. It was here, lost to the music, when I started asking myself a series of questions.

What kind of character would be like that? Someone who normally sees in black and white but on occasion might see something in color. What if his colorblindness was a result of hidden, secret powers he gained from reincarnation? Wait… I got it. What if he's a failed reincarnation? Hmm, what kind of powers…

I continued to brainstorm, and before I knew it, I was jotting down ideas, doodling some sketches, and the morning alarm was blasting. It all started with the creation of Hotan. What kind of character was he? What was his story? What did I want him to share with readers?

During high school, I faced a lot of complicated situations. My parents were getting divorced, my father was lost to alcoholism (he's sober, and we've made amends), my mother's verbal abuse became physical (we don't talk and attempts for counseling have failed), and I felt broken. While my friends fretted over boyfriends, parties, and being popular, I felt all alone in my own goals. I needed a job, I kept good grades, and my aim was independence as soon as possible.

In a lot of ways, Hotan reflected me—an adult trapped in a teenage body. I earned the nickname "Mother Hen" because I took care of my friends by keeping them out of trouble and helping them with their schoolwork and grades. Because everything at home was so unstable, I focused on being my own pillar and a cornerstone for many of my friends. I didn't discuss what was happening, though many of my teachers had an inkling. It was hard to miss the quiet kid coming in an hour or more early to school to find a dark corner to cry for a while.

Hotan was my vehicle to deliver a message to my friends and other teens and to let others learn from my mistakes. The name Hotan was originally inspired by a website on Japanese language that claimed it meant "origin, starting point," but that isn't accurate at all. In fact, it's more fitting to acknowledge Hotan is Biblical Greek for "when, inasmuch."

With this aim of delivering a message, I started to share a cautionary tale—one where it's okay to ask for help. Don't deal with the hard stuff alone and don't keep it hidden. Speak up and out. Know that you can plan ahead all you want, but life is unpredictable and at times, might feel as if its conspiring against you. It's normal. Life is a struggle. The lessons are there and so many more. Each one is illustrated numerous times in both realistic and fantasy-filled ways.

When high school ended, I had managed to write twenty-five thousand words. What you don't know was how many times I lost and had to rewrite the story. One time the computer died. Another time the floppy disk was destroyed. The worst was when my mother trashed it by ripping it and even setting a sketchbook on fire. I didn't give up. It may seem weird, but I started hiding parts of the story in the back of my math or animal science notebooks. I printed the current copy out, put it in a binder, and asked a friend to keep it at her house. This was the one thing no one could take from me: my ambition and desire to tell a story.

Life became a wild rollercoaster after I graduated. I was working several jobs and launching into college full time. The story was just collecting dust in a box I carried with me, but I was hellbent on never going back home. So much so that I lived out of my truck for a while. Years passed, and the story was forgotten for quite some time until I ran into some friends who I hadn't seen since high school.

"Did you ever finish that story about Hotan?"

The question rattled me. I had forgotten about the story, but somehow, it had made an impression on them. In fact, they wanted to know if it was done, if there was an end to Hotan's tale. So, I blew off the dust and started to figure out where I left off to finish the story. With no fear of someone destroying it, I finished the story with a little over fifty-thousand words.

I gave it to a few friends to read and enjoy, but life hit me, and the story was shelved. At least I managed to pull together how books two and three would flow. Ah, but a book can't write itself. I went to school for graphic design, but I was part of the ITT debacle and was one class shy of my degree. Then game programming and health issues made it hard to complete, and I resigned.

Things settled for a little while, but I found myself in the most insane six months of my life. The economy popped. Our new house of barely two years that was bought with equity was now far below value. Being in the construction industry left my husband and I laid off. I fell horribly ill, unable to keep water or food down, so the mother-in-law took me to the hospital.

"Good news, you're about a month along in your pregnancy!"

I paled. We had been trying for three years until we lost our jobs two weeks prior. Of course, it happened at the worst moment ever. Within a month, a freckle on the back of my left calf became a monstrous mole. I cried and pleaded to the doctors to biopsy. It was insane and took another month before one heard me out. My great grandmother had one in the same spot. I knew it was bad based on the look and the speed in which it grew.

"I'm so sorry, you were right. This is an atypical melanoma, and we need to remove it immediately."

I stared at the results. Four months pregnant with my first child, I couldn't believe how hard my life fell apart. I had twenty-four-hour morning sickness, and we were unemployed and unable to find steady work through 2009-2010 winter. Our mortgage lender was trying to speed up our foreclosure because we let them know we had no jobs and a stage three cancer diagnosis. I cried. Doctors gave no notice and would call the night before sometimes to tell me where to be for a morning appointment the next day. So many tears were shed. It all seemed unfair.

It was too much; just one of these life events would be enough to break a person.

In the end, they took out the back of my left calf. I had to be awake for it, and that was scary since I had never had a stitch or broken a bone. As for the foreclosure, I shut it down, very aware of the medical clause in my contract. I sent them the football stitching down my leg and the intimate reports from the surgery with "stage 3" and "pregnant" highlighted. Recovery was hell, puking and moving.

I sat alone in our new hovel. The house we thought we would never leave sold in a quick sale. My husband managed to land a job working long hours for half the pay. I looked at my books and the boxes I could never let go. They were part of my soul.

"Maybe I should do something with that novel from high school... leave something behind for our kid."

With one question, I found myself driven to learn more about what it would take to write at a professional level and publish my work. I had a story, a memorable story, but I needed to know what it would take to make it an actual novel. By the time I obtained the knowledge, I found myself crying once more. In order to fix it, bring it to standard, it would need one more rewrite. A flood of sour memories followed, but it was the best decision ever.

"It's part of life to struggle. Just makes those good days that much sweeter..."

Thus, my career as an author and the start of *Tattooed Angels Trilogy* was born!

Granted, the book underwent some changes. First of all, my love for Japanese culture had a whiplash. All my characters names were mostly Japanese inspired, which didn't support the concept that these were descendants, or technically members, of the Tribe of Levi or Levites as revealed in *Judgment*. For example,

Kyle was originally Kujoh. The other result was the working title had been "Sakugen," so I made changes to support the story and appeal to a wider range of readers. I was able to keep Hotan since there were links to Biblical Greek, and Hisota wasn't a Levite, and I had imagined him as Asian ethnicity.

I'll share some of the artwork I doodled during my high school and college eras. At this time, I was known as Valerie Cook. Only the completed sketches…

IMMORTALS LIST

1. Mind — Mr. Piedmont
2. Body — Abigail
3. Spirit — Metsy
4. Rebirth — Hotan
5. Earth — Cassandra and later, Annie
6. Fire — Kyle
7. Wind — Saphellia
8. Light — Lucius
9. Water — Callan
10. Metal — Lilly
11. Fear — Geliah and later, Hisota
12. Anger — Undiscovered
13. Lust — Jacob
14. Judgment — Talib
15. Insanity — Tina
16. Intelligence — Fae
17. Clarity — Undiscovered
18. Sight — Undiscovered
19. Touch — Undiscovered
20. Hearing — Undiscovered
21. Death — Iapetos

TATTOOED ANGELS TRILOGY PLAYLIST

Rebirth

1. Laterlus—TOOL
2. Save Ourselves—The Blackout
3. The Red—Chevelle
4. Parabola—TOOL
5. Brother—Stone Sour
6. 69 Tea—Seether
7. The Noose – Perfect Circle
8. So Cold—Breaking Benjamin
9. Broken—Seether (Original)

Judgment

1. Die Trying—Art of Dying
2. God Gave Us Land—Institute
3. Suicidal Dream – Silverchair
4. Hopeless—Breaking Benjamin
5. Heavenly—Skylar Blue

6. Something I Can Never Have—Flyleaf
7. Absolution—Pretty Reckless
8. Heart-Shaped Box—Nirvana
9. Black Hole Sun—Soundgarden
10. Hit the Floor—Thousand Foot Krutch
11. Anthem of the Angels—Breaking Benjamin
12. Familiar Taste of Poison—Halestorm
13. Forfeit—Chevelle
14. Shadow on the Sun—Audioslave
15. It's Over When It's Over (Destroy Myself)—Falling in Reverse
16. Fade Away—Breaking Benjamin
17. Panic Prone—Chevelle
18. Angels Fall—Breaking Benjamin
19. Shattered – The Letter Black
20. Snuff—Slipknot

Death

1. Black Honey—Thrice
2. Nowhere Kids—Smile Empty Soul
3. In Between—Linkin Park
4. Here's To The Heartache—Nothing More
5. Basement—Gemini Syndrome
6. Silence & Scars—Pop Evil
7. Bad Intentions—Digital Daggers
8. Swallow the Knife—Story of the Year
9. You're Not Alone—Lacey Sturm
10. Be Somebody—Thousand Foot Krutch
11. Careless Whisper—Seether
12. Honest—Thousand Foot Krutch
13. Wake Up—Thrice

14. Good Enough—Hoobastank
15. Duality—Slipknot
16. Love Me till It Hurts—Papa Roach
17. Back Against the Wall—Cage the Elephant
18. False Alarm—Smile Empty Soul
19. Dark On Me—Starset
20. Still Frames—Trapt
21. The Love We Had Before—Fireflight
22. Savior—Rise Against
23. O'Lord—Smile Empty Soul

ARTWORK

Sketch 1: Geliah and Hotan using his power. This is from the first encounter scene in the church in Rebirth.

Sketch 2 ABOVE: Hotan looking up. BELOW: Iapetos doodle on the back
of a business card. My little sister tagged it with an alien smiley.

Sketch 3 Jake and Annie.

Sketch 4 Shellie and Hotan

Sketch 5 Hotan

Sketch 6 Geliah and Guitar (Incomplete)

Sketch 7 From Left to Right: Hotan, Histota, and Kyle.

Sketch 8 Saphellia. At one point I thought I
would have her as a vigilante warrior or hero. I know,
weird right? In the end, she had a more significant
role as Talib's support.

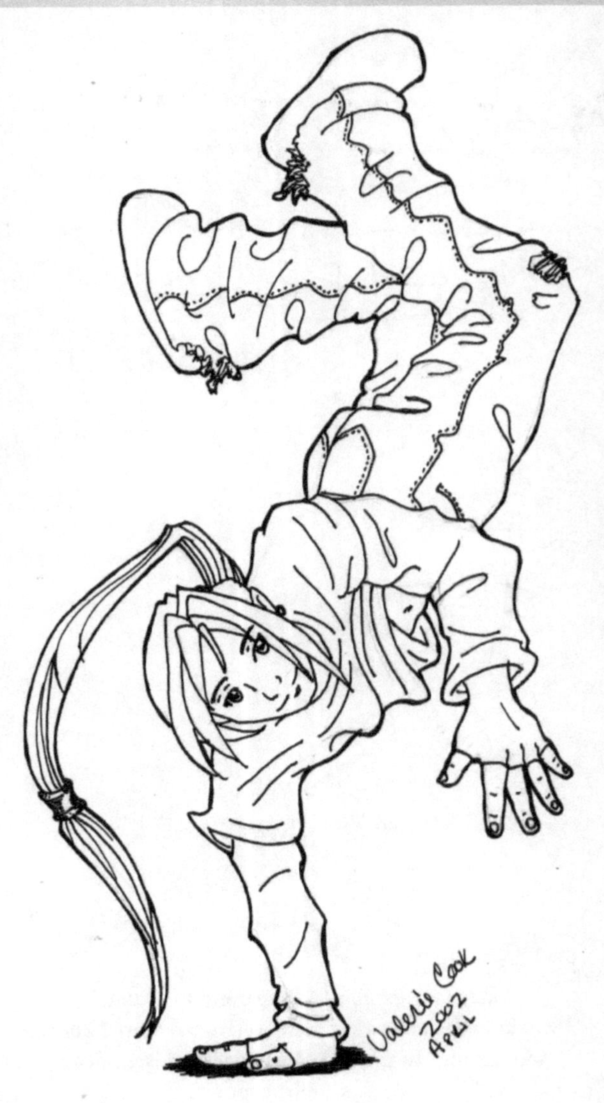

Sketch 9 Kyle

Sketch 10 When I sketched out Hotan's back tattoos,
I thought having two different wings would reflect
Life and Death. This one was to reflect Death.

Sketch 11 This wing was designed to reflect Life.
In the end, Rebirth is the result of overlapping
Life and Death as a way to symbolize Hotan's
power and the books' title.

Sketch 12 This is how I imagined
the crucifix in the church might look.

Sketch 13 Geliah battle mode.

Sketch 14 Shellie wishing you to Rock On!

Sketch 15 Hotan, Hisota, Kyle and Shellie. I couldn't decide whether she would have long or short hair, so all her sketches conflict!

Sketch 16 Iapetos. I originally thought I would give him a feathered wing and a bat wing, but in the end I figured the zombie equivalent for wings matched the element. There is a drawing somewhere of that version, way more detailed than this one, but after searching my house, I can't find it! NO!